TIMELESS

What Reviewers Say About
Rachel Spangler's Work

Does She Love You?

"Spangler has given us well developed characters that we can love and hate, sometimes at the same time."—*Lambda Literary Review*

Trails Merge

"Sparks fly and denial runs deep in this excellent second novel by Spangler. The author's love of the subject shines through as skiing, family values and romance fill the pages of this heartwarming story. The setting is stunning, making this reviewer nostalgic for her childhood days spent skiing the bunny hills of Wisconsin."—*Curve* magazine

Learning Curve

"Spangler's title, *Learning Curve*, refers to the growth both of these women make, as they deal with attraction and avoidance. They share a mutual lust, but can lust alone surpass their differences? The answer to that question is told with humor, adventure, and heat."—*Just About Write*

"[Spangler's] potential shines through, particularly her ability to tap into the angst that accompanies any attempt to alter the perceptions of others...Your homework assignment, read on."—*Curve*

The Long Way Home

"Rachel Spangler's third book, *The Long Way Home*, explores how we remake ourselves and the consequence of not being true to our real selves. In the case of Raine, her perceived notions of small-town life may have been tainted by being 17. The reality of what she finds when she returns as an adult surprises her and has her wondering if she'd been wrong about her home town, her parents, and her friends. Spangler's story will have you staying up very late as you near the end of the book."—*Lambda Literary Review*

LoveLife

"Rachel Spangler does a wonderful job creating characters that are not only realistic but also draw the reader into their worlds. The lives these women lead are so ordinary that they could be you or I, but it's the tale Spangler weaves between Elaine, Lisa, and Joey that is so beautifully written and extraordinary."—*CherryGrrl.com*

Visit us at www.boldstrokesbooks.com

By the Author

Learning Curve

Trails Merge

The Long Way Home

LoveLife

Spanish Heart

Does She Love You?

Timeless

TIMELESS

by
Rachel Spangler

2014

ISBN 13: 978-1-62639-050-8

This Trade Paperback Original Is Published By
Bold Strokes Books, Inc.
P.O. Box 249
Valley Falls, NY 12185

First Edition: April 2014

CREDITS

Editors: Lynda Sandoval and Shelley Thrasher
Production Design: Susan Ramundo
Cover Design By Sheri (graphicartist2020@hotmail.com)

Acknowledgments

When I initially conceived of the idea for this book, I thought it would be fun, a little tongue in cheek mixed with some campy fantasy. I still think there are places where that playfulness shines through, but as my main characters developed, they demanded more thought, depth, and emotional fortitude than I'd expected. Suddenly, a fun story about getting a do-over turned into an examination of what we owe ourselves and those who cross our paths. The issue of bullying is one that cannot be ignored when facing a high school setting, and unfortunately, it touches us all in some way. Those conflicts can shape a young existence, and the ways in which we make sense of them can have a defining effect on the people we become. While likely few of us have ever had to confront our past in the dramatic fashion these characters do, I firmly believe none of us can ever fully leave the past behind until we've learned the lessons those experiences are meant to teach us. It's that process of confronting, growing, and reinventing oneself that ultimately drives this book.

I'm deeply indebted to several very creative people who inspired me to push beyond the boundaries I previously set for my writing. My friend and neighbor, Sarah Gerkensmeyer, is a brilliant writer of magical realism who's taught me so much about finding the magic in the mundane. She's demonstrated wonderful courage in embracing the unknown, and her example permeated my decision-making process throughout this novel. In moments when I feared I might be straying too far from the genre I've come to consider home, I turned to friends and fellow romance writers Georgia Beers and Melissa Brayden. I probably would have caved several times without their reassurances, but my sexy self-esteem queen and my sparkly ninja princess expressed only excitement and genuine encouragement. I have my neighbor and man twin, Andrew Cullison, to thank (once again) for the title of this novel, even though I know he was really pulling for it to be spelled "Timelez." Finally, I firmly believe this was my smoothest writing/editing experience ever because Lynda Sandoval was involved from start to finish. She was enthusiastic, open, available, and easygoing.

Her ability to pinpoint and communicate what the story needed kept me confident, and her sense of humor held my insecurities at bay. Our front porch chats and comments in the margins kept me laughing even on the hard days. I cannot overemphasize how much her easygoing professionalism has improved my entire creative process.

As usual, Barb Dallinger and Toni Whitaker served as my sounding board, focus group, and first readers. Their feedback was especially important because they've been with me virtually from the beginning of my career. They eased the fear that I'd stretched too far outside my comfort zone. Much thanks to Shelley Thrasher, who once again served as my copy editor and literary laser beam. Sheri, as usual, captured so many of the emotions in this book with her stellar cover. The Bold Strokes team of proofreaders, production managers, Web designers, eBook formatters, and social media gurus do so much behind the scenes to make me look good, and I appreciate each one of them greatly.

Thank you to the readers. Every time I feel alone or lazy or consider cutting a corner, I think about your comments, e-mails, and encouragement. You've elevated my writing from a hobby to a true labor of love.

Saving the best for last, I have my family to thank for everything good in my life. Jackie is pure joy. His youthful idealism weighed heavily on my mind while writing this book. He forced me to consider the world he will someday inhabit and contemplate my own responsibility in making sure that world is worthy of him. Susie continues to be my inspiration in all matters of the heart. That combined with her knowledge of the challenges faced by student teachers and gay teachers in small towns contributed a great deal to the development of these characters. She's my best friend, my partner, my wife, my everything.

As I look back over my expansive list of people to thank, I'm reminded once again I am richly blessed not through merit, but through the abundant grace of God. Soli Deo Gloria.

Dedication

This book is for all the teachers who have ever given
a piece of themselves to help shape a life, especially Susie,
who continues to teach me so much about what truly matters.
Of course, it's still all her fault.

CHAPTER ONE

"Y ou've got to put yourself out there more, Stevie." Edmond's voice came through clearly on the speaker of my iPhone.

I lay on my bed and stared at the line where my high ceiling met the rising brick wall. Holding the phone against my cheek, I thought of how I'd describe the intersection of two such unique textures. Of course there was the aesthetic, the rich colors, the materials, the symmetry, but in this moment I felt more drawn to what the structure represented. The very building blocks of my loft symbolized stability, strength, and most of all, safety. They offered a symbolic balance to my current phone conversation with my publicist.

"Make yourself vulnerable, available, transparent. It's what writers do."

"Thanks for the explanation. All this time I thought writers wrote."

"Unpublished writers, maybe. But you're a successful novelist, and you want to be a produced playwright, which means you have to network."

"I'm not good at networking. It's all fake small talk and sweaty palms. I don't want to waste an evening being socially awkward with people I've never met and will probably never see again."

"It doesn't have to be strangers. I got a call from Rory St. James yesterday. She wanted your phone number."

I sat up at the mention of Rory's name. The small-town gay activist who'd confronted her demons head-on had been in the news a lot lately after remaking herself and finding love in the town she'd once fled. The same hometown I'd left in my rearview mirror. Everyone we'd grown up with was a bit in awe of Rory, myself included. I was also impressed she even knew I existed. "Why does she want to talk to me?"

"She's on some arts committee in Darlington." Edmond sounded like he found the idea amusing. "They want to give you an award."

That wasn't so bad, but it wasn't so great either. I probably should've been flattered but felt only a mix of relief and disappointment Rory had called on a formality. "Just have her mail the certificate to your office, will ya?"

"They want you to go there to accept it."

"Pass."

"What do you mean 'pass'? It's free publicity."

"It's fluff, I'm busy, I don't want to." I flopped back onto the bed, unwilling to give the idea of a return to Darlington another thought. "Whatever. Just pass. Okay?"

"Fine." Edmond acquiesced, but the flippancy of his tone made me suspect the topic wasn't fully closed.

"Have you had any bites on the play?" I asked, ready for a change of subject.

"Not yet, but you'll have another shot at the Theater of Youth fund-raiser next week. Especially if you agree to say a few words."

"Not going to happen." The tension in my neck ratcheted up a notch at the prospect of spending a night in a room full of politically charged actors and activists. "I'm not going to the actual dinner, but I'll send a check."

Edmond blew out an exasperated breath directly into the phone. "This is *your* charity of choice. *You're* the one who mentioned the event to me. You said you loved youth theater."

"I do. That's why I'll send a check, but I don't want to get into politics."

"Even politics you agree with? You won't lift your voice for something you claim to love?"

I threw off the covers and put my bare feet on the cool hardwood floor. I didn't have to defend myself to him. He worked for me, not the other way around. Not that I'd ever have the guts or the inclination to tell him that. Still, I wouldn't be pushed into a political minefield. I'd lived almost thirty years by staying above the fray and had no intention of slipping now.

"Stevie, these kids need this program, and they need people in a position of power to speak for them. You've got the time, the money, and the talent. What do you have to lose?"

"Why do you care? If youth theater matters so much to you, then why don't you give the speech or direct a play?" Why couldn't anything be easy? I just wanted to give money to a good cause without fighting with anyone.

"I'm not the one shopping a new play. I'm not the one selling books. You are, and you hired me to help."

"Right, I hired you so I could focus on my writing and you could handle all the publicity." Actually I'd hired him because he was the only publicist I'd ever heard of. And he only took my call because I went to school with Rory, but still I paid him a nice cut of my royalties so I wouldn't have to exert any energy on anything but the actual writing.

"You have to give me something to publicize first."

"I gave you the script for the play."

"Yes, you've got a great play, but so does half of Manhattan."

"Fine." I threw up my free hand in defeat. "If their plays are better than mine, I can live with that. I just want to be judged on my merits."

"You're adorable." Edmond laughed. "But you clearly don't understand how this business works. Without a solid hook you won't get judged at all. The big names won't even read the synopsis of an unknown."

"I'm not an unknown. I have three high-selling novels."

"They could be best-selling novels if you'd publicize them." Edmond's voice rose in volume and pitch as his frustration built. "And I could sell a best-selling author, but I can't sell someone who refuses to put herself out there."

I wandered across my apartment to my one big window. Ignoring the reflection of my black hair standing out at odd angles, I pressed my forehead to the cool glass and stared down into the gray streets of New York. I sighed, unwilling to be swept into an argument. I hated confrontation, and this one had already drained me enough for one day. "What do you want from me?"

"Something, anything personal to help me connect you to a producer. Give me an impassioned speech about theater education, or play up your small-town-girl-makes-it-big backstory. Hell, fuck a Rockette in the middle of Times Square to get your name in the tabloids. Do something I can spin."

Damn. He'd led me right back to the event in Darlington because he knew I'd never consider the other two options. Well, I was open to sleeping with a Rockette, but not the tabloids, and that's the part he cared about. "I don't want to go back to Darlington."

"Why not? Look what it did for Rory St. James's career. Connecting yourself to her right now would move you way up the social food chain, and I'm not just saying that because she's my client too," Edmond said with a hint of pride in his voice. "Go back to your hometown for one night, talk to people you already know, accept an award without a speech, and then come home."

"It's not simple." My resolve wavered but didn't crack. I had a bad feeling about this whole thing, though I couldn't articulate why.

"Sure it is. I get a human-interest story, and you get an award and your picture taken with a celebrity. Rory gets to mentor an up-and-coming artist. Everyone wins."

"She doesn't want to mentor me, and it doesn't matter because I'm not Rory St. James. I have no ax to grind. My writing isn't about Darlington. It's not even about being gay. My hometown means nothing to me. It's just a place I used to live."

"Then why are you afraid to go back there?"

"I'm not afraid." I was protesting, but I wasn't sure what I felt about Darlington. Maybe fear was part of it, but more than anything the idea exhausted me, much the same way this conversation did. I'd spent my youth trying to get by, trying to do just enough to stay solidly in the middle. I didn't want to stand out as exceptional, but I didn't want to be an outsider either. Maybe that's what bothered me about this award. I'd stand out. I'd be acknowledged and therefore exposed.

Still, at least I could leave after a day. Even if I did humiliate myself, I wouldn't have to live with the consequences there like I would if I messed up in New York. Plus in Darlington no one whose opinion actually mattered would be around to see if I fell flat. I could slip in and slip out, then leave all the publicity spin to Edmond. I did want to see my play produced, and while I hated taking a chance, this one seemed the least risky of my current options.

"Come on, Stevie. You'll be in and out, and I'll even drive down to hold your hand along the way."

I wasn't sure if his presence would make me feel better or worse, but at least with Edmond around I wouldn't have to worry about keeping up my end of the conversation since he rarely let anyone else get a word in. "Fine, I'll do it. For one day."

"Yes, of course, just one day. How bad can one day be?"

❖

"Hey, Stevie," someone called.

I scanned the crowd at St. Louis's Lambert Airport until I saw a sign that read GELLER. Cringing at the blatant display of attention, I forced myself not to grab the sign out of Rory's hands and toss it into the nearest trashcan. Instead I jammed my hands into the pockets of my olive-green cargo pants and said, "Hey, I don't know if you remember me, but—"

"Of course I remember you." Rory laughed easily. She was even more magnetic than she'd been in high school, and that was saying a lot. "Beth made the sign. She loves cutesy little things like that and I…well, I love her."

I couldn't help but smile at the silly grin on Rory's face. Who would've thought the mere mention of a plain Midwestern farmer's daughter could turn such a formidable warrior into mush. A hint of longing tapped at my own heart, but I shrugged it off and grabbed my bag. "Thanks for picking me up."

"No worries. Beth and I enjoyed the chance to spend a morning in the Central West End. She's in the car. We couldn't find a place to park." Rory nodded toward the luggage carousel. "Do you have any more bags?"

"No, just the one. I'm only here overnight."

Rory nodded sympathetically as we headed toward the parking lot. "Are you silently thanking God for that now?"

"What? No," I lied. I'd been counting the hours until my return flight would touch down at JFK tomorrow night. I'd actually started counting before I left as I lay awake trying to calculate how many hours of sleep I could get if I fell asleep right that instant. Of course I didn't fall asleep right then. With all the thoughts of my return to Darlington, the pressure to drum up good publicity, and the fear of a public appearance I didn't sleep at all, so as the sun began to peek above the crowded New York skyline, I shifted my countdown to reflect the number of hours until I'd be back in my own bed once more. Only thirty-four to go.

"It's okay. I was in your shoes not long ago, which is why I appreciate your coming back. It's important for the kids around here to see success stories like yours. It shows them there's life out there, you know?"

I didn't know, really. I'd never considered myself a success story, and certainly not a role model. Sure, I'd published a few books, but I wasn't what most people would call famous. I still had so much more to accomplish, which of course was the only reason I'd agreed to this trip in the first place.

As we stepped outside, a blue Prius pulled to a stop and Beth Deveroux got out. I might not have recognized her if I hadn't been expecting her. She'd grown out of her teenage awkwardness and into an hourglass frame. Her form-fitting blue jeans and a light-blue V-neck sweater made it a little clearer why Rory went all romantic at just the mention of her. I'd last seen her at her parents' funeral eleven years ago, and she looked like a new woman now. Not just older and happier, but also beautiful. "Hi, Stevie."

"Hi, Beth." I tried to stick out my hand, but Beth drew me into a hug. I couldn't remember the last time I'd been hugged. Not a real hug anyway. People in New York often did that shoulder-grab-and-lean-in sort of greeting, but Beth chose a full-on arm wrap and body press.

"Are you hungry?" Beth asked, stepping back.

"No, I'm good."

"Okay, let's get on the road then." Beth handed the keys to Rory with a sweet kiss, then said, "Stevie, why don't you ride up front? You've got longer legs than I do."

"Thanks." Normally I'd refuse so I could try to avoid making conversation, but after being on a plane for two hours, I did feel a little cramped. Or maybe the stress of my responsibilities and my past had started to weigh me down as we headed away from the city and toward the great expanse of farmland along I-55.

"When was the last time you came home?" Beth asked.

"About five years ago, for my parents' retirement party. I haven't had a reason to visit since they moved to Boca Raton. I don't have any other family in the area."

"Is there anyone you want to see while you're in Darlington?" Rory asked. "You're welcome to use one of our cars while you're here."

"I haven't kept in touch with anyone since graduation. You know how busy life gets."

"Sure." Rory only glanced from the road to search my expression with those trademark emerald eyes for a second. "Well, Edmond and Miles will get in around five o'clock tonight, and then we're all going out to dinner with Jody."

"Jody?"

"Jody Hadland, my co-chair for the arts committee. She teaches at the high school."

"Miss Hadland? The student teacher?" Memories flooded my mind and caused my heart to beat faster. We all have that first crush, the one that confirms those nagging suspicions about our own sexuality. For me, that crush was Miss Hadland.

"You had her when she was a student teacher? She never told me that," Rory said.

"She probably doesn't remember me."

"Oh no, she does. She said you were one of her most talented students. I just didn't know it was before she got hired full-time."

"She really called me one of her best students?" The compliment sent a flush of warmth to my cheeks. I'd had her for two classes my senior year, and while they'd been my favorites, I'd spent both of them huddled quietly in the back corner trying not to get called on or caught staring at her legs.

"Yeah. She's the one who suggested we have you back."

Under other circumstances I would've been disappointed Rory wasn't the driving force behind the award, but the fact that Miss Hadland remembered me enough to follow my career gave me a thrill I didn't care to examine too closely.

"She's made all the arrangements, which reminds me. I need to call my dean at the college tonight and make sure she remembers the assembly tomorrow."

Rory continued to ramble, but I allowed my mind to wander. The city faded into suburbs, then to farmland, but the insecurities I'd expected to suffocate me were sublimated by the pleasant memories of my first and only schoolgirl crush. Miss Hadland had given me a peek at the type of woman I'd later come to recognize as my type, the perfect mix of smart and beautiful I still found irresistible.

Rory knocked on the door of my bedroom at five o'clock sharp. I felt weird staying at her farmhouse on the edge of town. We'd never been friends in high school. She was older and infinitely cooler. I'd known Beth a little better, but while she was friendly with the whole town, we'd never actually been friends. Maybe I should've opted to stay in a hotel, but there wasn't really one in town, just a motel, and maybe even that term was too generous for the set of rooms for rent in a concrete building by the railroad tracks. Rory and Beth's home clearly offered the better option, even if the setup meant more social contact than I would've preferred.

"Hey, we need to get going soon, but I wanted to make sure you have everything you need."

Beth had left out two extra blankets, two extra pillows, three towels, two washcloths, and enough magazines to fill a dentist's waiting room. I held up one of the bottles of water I'd found on the bedside table. "I'm sure I could survive the zombie apocalypse in here."

Rory laughed, shaking a wisp of chestnut-colored hair from her forehead. "Beth is nothing if not a diligent hostess."

"She's great and so are you. Thanks for putting me up. I hope I'm not too much of a bother."

"Don't be silly. You've been here over two hours and we haven't even heard you yet. The cat has made more noise than you have."

I'd hidden in my room with the dual purpose of passing the time calmly and staying out of Rory and Beth's way, but maybe I'd been unintentionally rude. I should've napped. I tried, but everything felt too surreal, so I settled for some quiet time staring out the window at a vast, vacant cornfield. Should I have stayed downstairs and chatted with my hosts? I already feared my ability to make small talk during dinner tonight, and breakfast tomorrow, and at the awards assembly. I hadn't planned on downtime too.

"Are you nervous about tonight?" Rory asked casually, but I clearly read the concern in her expressive eyes. Her worry amplified my own.

"Um, no, I mean maybe a little, but I—"

"It's okay, you don't have to explain. My first week back in town I didn't leave my room once. I wouldn't even go to the grocery store until Beth dragged me there."

"Well, you don't have to worry. I'll go to dinner of my own free will. I've got nothing against Darlington. It's just fine by me. Not the place for me to live, but who am I to judge, right?"

"Good for you. It took me months to leave the past in the past and start to move forward," Rory said. "You're a much stronger woman than I."

"Not at all." If I'd been strong in the face of my publicist I wouldn't even be here now. "You had a lot more to overcome. I've never had a hard time letting go of the past because it never mattered in the first place. I guess I've just been lucky that way."

Rory's expression turned introspective, causing her dimples to fade.

"What?"

"Oh, I don't know. My past was certainly complicated, but even the bad parts helped make me who I am. Without facing those struggles I wouldn't have learned the things I learned about myself, about the people I love. I wouldn't trade any of it."

Damn, I admired her. We'd been raised in the same town, gone to the same schools, chosen similar career paths, and we were both gay. How had she turned out so strong, so reflective, so self-assured? Then again she'd always been that way. A born leader. I, on the other hand, had wallflower written all over my DNA. "We're really different people."

Rory slung one arm around my shoulder and said, "Maybe, but we've both ended up in the same place tonight, and who knows where we'll go from here."

❖

"Rory! Stevie!" Edmond burst into the restaurant, and his presence in Darlington accosted my senses like the stiff February wind blowing through the still-open door. Rory immediately jumped into his embrace while I took an involuntary step back. Reaching out with one arm, he caught me by the shoulder and pulled me into an awkward group hug. "Look at this, both my little Midwest lezzies together in the spot where it all began. I'm so proud."

He released me just far enough to hold me at arm's length, the bright paisley pattern of his shirt dizzying me into submission. "How are you holding up, cupcake?"

"I'm fine," I said, mortified, then in an attempt to preempt any more embarrassing questions added, "Everything's great."

"Damn right. This is a Kodak moment." He pulled a camera out of the pocket of his skinny jeans but gave me little time to wonder how he'd squeezed himself into pants that tight, much less added a camera before he handed it to an attractive man just stepping in from the cold. "Get a picture of us all together, babe?"

I had no time to protest before he'd rearranged himself between Rory and me so we all faced the camera. I summoned my photo smile automatically, and the flashbulb temporarily blinded me. Everything happened so fast. I barely had time to consider what this blur of activity would look like to the other restaurant patrons, but as Edmond turned his attention to Beth, simultaneously hugging her and complimenting her hair, I took the chance to glance around.

The Highlands was the nicest restaurant in Darlington, which was about like saying it was the biggest shrimp in a salad. The carpet, a small step above the indoor/outdoor variety, reminded me of a patio or putting green. The tablecloths shone a shade off from white under the fluorescent light, and the walls held paintings of woodsy scenes or placid lakes. The dinner crowd leaned toward the older side of fifty, and while some glanced our way, most of them seemed perfectly content to focus on the huge slabs of meat or piles of carbs on their plates. Best of all, I didn't see anyone who appeared to recognize me. The longer I lasted without having to chat with some casual acquaintance of my parents, the better.

"Apparently if I wait for my darling boyfriend to make introductions, I'll be standing here all night." The man who'd taken our picture extended his hand. "So, hi. I'm Miles."

Very handsome and only slightly less polished than Edmond, he wore a less garish blue oxford shirt and standard gray slacks, but both were fashionable and fit like they were made for him. "I'm Stevie."

"It's a pleasure to finally meet you. Edmond talks about you all the time."

I glanced over at Edmond in time to see Rory give him a playful shove and felt a stab of envy at their easy camaraderie. "I'm sorry. He's probably exasperated with me on a regular basis."

"Not at all. He admires you, and yes, sometimes he wishes you'd cooperate more, but only because he's so proud of you and wants to show you off."

I didn't know what to say, or if I should even try to say anything around the little catch of emotion in my throat. Miles had no reason to lie. Then again, maybe he simply loved Edmond and wanted to play the role of supportive business spouse. Still, I appreciated his attempt to include me, and his kind brown eyes soothed my insecurities. "Thank you."

A young hostess led us to a large table in the back corner of the restaurant. While still in the main dining room, the position shielded us a little from the other patrons, and I dared to hope I could pass the evening without drawing any attention to myself. I'd have to make plenty of small talk at the awards ceremony, but why deal with today what I could put off until tomorrow? At least at dinner I knew everyone and how they related to each other. I allowed myself to relax a little in my seat next to Miles and across from Beth while Rory and Edmond chatted easily about news from Chicago. Perhaps this evening out in Darlington could be like any other night out with a group of friends. After all, we were in the Midwest, where people weren't prone to scenes or drama. Though pettiness and gossip always flowed in the undercurrents of small towns, stoicism reigned here, and unlike in New York City, politeness generally overruled curiosity.

The waitress brought menus and water, conversations went on amicably around me, and I contented myself to wonder if the subtle highlights in Miles's hair were natural or if he had a truly gifted stylist.

Then, from across the room, a woman drew my attention. To the casual observer she would've merely been another patron entering a busy restaurant on a weeknight. There was nothing unusual about the way she smoothed her hair, so blond it was almost white, as she untangled the delicate strands from the scarf she slowly unwrapped from her neck. No one would likely note anything out of the ordinary in the way her long camel coat hung open down the front, revealing a green V-neck sweater and khaki dress slacks. And nothing stood out about the pink flush that tinged her pale skin either from the cold or excitement. No one else in the room even seemed to notice her arrival or the fact that I seemed to have captivated her attention in the same consuming way she had mine.

She appeared to realize she'd been caught staring the same moment I did, and we both looked away, then immediately back at one another before grinning sheepishly. As she threaded a path between tables and waitresses carrying trays laden with food, I rose to greet her. Stepping forward to initiate a social interaction for the first time all day, I extended my hand while she was still several steps away. "Hi, I'm not sure if you recognize me, but—"

"Stevie. Of course I recognize you. Even if your pictures weren't on the back of your books, I'd still know you anywhere. Welcome home."

I tried not to grimace. I didn't consider Darlington home, though I didn't think of New York that way either. The concept of home eluded me, but then again at the moment everything eluded me. Everything but the dazzling blue of her eyes.

My eyes are blue, but not at all like hers, not so engaging or so complicated a mix of shades and hues, and not with the pure lightness that shone through them. My writer's brain searched fruitlessly for a natural comparison—the Colorado sky? a sun-soaked sea? a robin's egg? They all fell short, and I was staring again.

"It's very nice to see you, Miss Hadland," I finally managed to say. Then I just couldn't help myself from asking, "It's still Miss Hadland, right?"

She smiled a sweet but knowing smile. "Only to my students. Please call me Jody."

"Classroom habits die hard."

"Really? It's been over ten years. Surely you don't still think of all your teachers as perpetually in a position of authority?"

"No, honestly I don't think of most of my teachers at all, much less as having authority in my life, but you never had any heavy authority to begin with. Student teachers rank below substitutes in the high-school food chain."

She raised her eyebrows. "I'm glad to know I left such a strong impression."

"No, I didn't mean that." It was hard to make myself clear with my foot in my mouth and my head full of clouds. "I meant to say I'll always think of you as a teacher because you were such a good one."

Jody's smile grew from one of politeness to genuine pleasure. "Nice recovery."

"I mean it. Your theater class my senior year is still my favorite of all the classes I've ever taken, even in college."

"Really? Why have I never seen you on a stage then?"

"Oh, me? Never." I hoped my nausea didn't show. "Exposing myself on paper is nerve-racking enough. I could never lay myself bare in front of an audience. But I pulled heavily from your teachings while writing my play."

"You've written a play?"

"I have…I mean it's still unproduced. It's not much really, just a first attempt."

"Damn it, Stevie, stop doing that," Edmond called loudly from the other end of the table. Both Jody and I turned toward him. I'd forgotten he was there, which is exceedingly hard to do with Edmond.

"Her play is amazing. It's very Wendy Wasserstein mixed with…I don't know…some other smart, independent woman. And even if it wasn't, we're trying to sell the rights, Stevie, so telling people it's 'not much' isn't helpful."

"Right. I'm not good at publicity," I said, embarrassed both to be caught entranced by Jody and to be called out publicly. "This is Edmond, by the way, my booking agent, publicist, and the all-around boss of me."

"It's a pleasure to meet you, Jody," Edmond said graciously. "Now sit down and tell me lots of embarrassing high-school stories about Stevie so I have something to blackmail her with the next time she won't listen to me."

Jody looked at me expectantly, clearly deferring her decision to my wishes. I wanted her to sit by me more than I'd wanted anything in a long time, but I wouldn't overrule the loudest person at the table. Suddenly I wasn't grateful to him for keeping the conversation going. I wanted him to stay out of it altogether, but I couldn't say that. I couldn't just stand there either. Everyone stared at me now. "Yeah, go ahead. I'm sure you two have a lot in common. You should get to know each other."

Jody's smile faded back into one of courtesy, and I watched in disappointment as she acquiesced and took the seat next to him. It was for the best. They probably did have a lot in common, and he'd have no trouble holding up his end of the conversation.

As I returned to my place and tried to steady my buzzing nerves, I caught a look of understanding, perhaps tinged with amusement, pass between Beth and Rory. Had I been too obvious in my favorable appraisal of Jody? I wasn't surprised my admiration showed through. I'd meant everything I'd said about her influences on my work. She'd introduced me to theater, helped foster a love of literature, and taught me the true power of language. She deserved praise, but she didn't deserve to be ogled by a grown woman as if I were a cross between a love-struck schoolboy and a salivating animal. So much for going unnoticed. Of all the ways I'd considered embarrassing myself, revealing a crush on a former teacher hadn't been one of them.

I was leaving in less than thirty hours and couldn't imagine returning to Darlington in the foreseeable future, but for some reason that fact seemed less comforting than it had in the past. At least my embarrassment would be short-lived, but I also felt a subtle pang of regret that I likely wouldn't get another chance to talk with Jody.

❖

Dinner passed easily enough. Edmond and Rory took turns holding court from their end of the table while Beth and Miles made cheerful conversation at ours, occasionally stopping to ask my opinion or explain an inside joke. They never left me out, but I had plenty of time to steal little glances at Jody. I couldn't say she hadn't aged in the last decade, but the signs of time were minimal. If I didn't know she had a few years on me, I would've placed her in her mid-twenties. Something about her face…maybe the slight upturn at the end of her slender nose, or the sparkle in her eyes, or the way her grin hinted at something mischievous just often enough to catch me off guard. But whatever the cause, she carried an air of perpetual youth.

I pulled my gaze away to see Beth eyeing me sympathetically. Could everyone in the room tell I hadn't been on a date in three months?

"We'd better call it a night," Miles said, pushing back from the table. We've got some work to do at the house if we're going to get it on the market this spring."

"You have a house here?" I asked, eager for a diversion.

"Yes, I worked at the college until about two months ago, when I transferred to the admissions office at DePaul University." He smiled sweetly. "I wanted to be closer to Edmond."

"We miss him terribly," Beth said. "And we hold Edmond personally responsible for cutting our gay and lesbian group by one fifth."

"It's not my fault you had only five gays in the village," Edmond teased her. "Surely you could recruit some more."

The table went quiet, and Jody seemed suddenly interested in folding her napkin until Edmond realized even though he was among friends, Darlington wasn't the best place to publicly joke about recruitment, especially with teachers at the table. Despite the fact that Rory and Beth had clearly been granted some level of acceptance, wariness and a level of caution permeated my senses here. That awareness of my surroundings had been born from years of watching, testing, and observing what types of behaviors were rewarded, which were tolerated, and which were met with rebuke, silent or otherwise. Those lessons had guided me through my youth and stayed with me always. Rory, on the other hand, seemed quicker to move on as she rose and extended her arm to Edmond, saying, "Ladies, shall we adjourn?"

"We shall," Edmond answered cheerfully and, looping his arm through hers, headed toward the parking lot.

We all said good-bye to Edmond, who hugged me again, and to Miles, who thankfully did not, but as we turned to go, Jody lingered.

"So, I guess I'll see you tomorrow?" I asked, wishing I'd come up with something more impressive or charming or at least a question I didn't already know the answer to.

"Yes, of course. I look forward to it, but I won't be free before the assembly. I have a class until ten o'clock, and after that we won't have much time to do anything but lead you to the stage."

I didn't know what bothered me more, the thought of the stage or the reminder I wouldn't get another chance to talk with her. *Say something, anything.* My brain begged my mouth to keep the conversation going, but I managed only to say, "It's okay, I understand."

Jody nodded. "So you have everything you need for tomorrow?"

"Yes." I started to back away. Who was I kidding, wishing for more time with her? I'd likely make a fool of myself, and on the off chance I didn't, what would it matter? I'd be around for only twenty-six more hours. "I'm sure I'll be fine, thanks."

I took another step back and bumped into Beth. She steadied me with a gentle hand on my shoulder before saying, "I'm sure you're tired, but it might be better for you two to run by the high school tonight. You know, to go over the itinerary and walk through the setup for the assembly."

"Honey," Rory interjected. "They're both professionals. I'm sure they don't need a dry run on something this straightforward."

"I didn't mean to imply they couldn't handle it," Beth said, her tone understanding but her gaze purposefully angling from Rory back to me. "But not everyone loves to just jump up on the stage. Having all the information ahead of time might put their minds at ease."

"Well, I don't want to keep Stevie out too late, but it might not be a bad idea to check things out tonight. If we do need to make any changes, tomorrow will be too late," Jody said tentatively, her smile shy but hopeful as she turned to address me directly. "That is, if Stevie doesn't mind."

"No, it's fine with me." I might have been tired, but I wouldn't be able to sleep if I lost another chance to talk to Jody.

"Good," Beth said. "It's best to be prepared."

Rory wrapped her arm around Beth's waist and kissed her quickly on the temple. "That's my little librarian for you. Why don't we just follow you to the school, Jody?"

"We don't need to go." Beth subtly steered Rory toward their car. "I'm sure Jody can handle things."

"We're Stevie's ride," Rory said.

"Jody can drop her off when they are done. Can't you, Jody?"

"Sure." Jody's voice carried a hint of the awareness that warmed my cheeks even in the cold February evening. Beth had arranged for us to be alone together. Why didn't it surprise me that the darling of Darlington liked to play matchmaker? I didn't know if I should trip her or hug her, so instead I shrugged my acceptance.

Jody unlocked the front door to the high school and flipped on the lights. The main hallway flashed into view, causing the memories to surge so strong and swift I took a step back. Fluorescent glow ricocheted off every surface, from the tile floor to the gleaming red lockers and out through the double panes of glass lining the front office. I took a deep breath to steady myself, only to be accosted by the smell of institutional cleaning supplies and the lingering scent of cafeteria food. The combination reminded me of a hospital, but without the acrid tinge of antiseptic. This smell hung heavier in the air, and not nearly as sharp, like years of closed doors and body heat had worn off all the edges.

Jody led me through the main corridor. I trailed behind, firmly holding a mental lock on sentimentality and nostalgia. I stayed close to the wall, close enough to run my hand along the lone red stripe about halfway up. Had someone decided, in a last-second attempt to break the monotony of white, that this minor accent of the school color would make the place seem more cheerful? It didn't. Red ink rarely symbolized good things, especially in a high school.

Jody stopped and glanced over her shoulder, her blue eyes questioning but her smile hopeful. "How's it feel to be back?"

"Good," I lied. I didn't feel anything. I wouldn't let myself.

"Really? You look like you're about to throw up."

"Do I? I'm sorry. I didn't mean to—"

"Relax, it's fine." She reached out as if she intended to touch me but then thought better of it. "It'd be weird to come back after so long. You're allowed to be a little freaked-out."

"Am I?" I sighed. "I don't know what I'm supposed to feel. I don't have fond memories of this place. High school wasn't the proverbial best time of my life, but I don't have the animosity Rory did. I don't carry any anger. High school was just something I had to do, like paying my light bill or, I don't know, flossing."

Jody threw back her head and laughed, a beautiful sound rolling out in an octave higher than the tone she spoke in and fading into a silent bounce of her shoulders. "I've been here over a decade, and I've never heard anyone equate their experience to a four-year teeth cleaning."

"I'm sorry. I didn't mean to denigrate your life's work. Sometimes words just come out before I think them through, which is why I generally try to keep my mouth shut."

"Don't be sorry. You're funny, and right about the flossing analogy. School isn't fun all the time. It can be tedious, but it should never be painful. And ultimately, diligence in your studies keeps important parts of yourself from rotting away. You've always had a way with words."

"Really? I feel like my tongue is stuck to the roof of my mouth most of the time."

"You never spoke excessively, but when you did, or more noticeably when you wrote, you had an economy of language and precision of vocabulary far beyond your age. You've refined those skills throughout your career, but I saw the seed of that talent even when you were in my class."

Pride pressed at my chest as I let the compliment sink in. I didn't know what to say, but maybe I didn't have to say anything, since Jody had obviously seen something to like in me, tongue-tied and all.

She opened the gym door and lifted a series of switches. Each one triggered a heavy metallic thump from the old rafters and a gentle buzz of electricity as the overhead lights slowly stirred to life.

The space seemed hollow and darkly cavernous in the early stages of illumination. Once again the smell hit first. It had the same base of cleaning products, but instead of food, the overarching scent here was sweat and scuffed rubber. The memories pushed at the back of my mind harder this time, the far-off echoes of shoes squeaking as they shuffled across the floor and the clamor of a ball hitting the backboard or bouncing off a rim. I felt rustling of fabric, the press of bodies settling into metal folding chairs, the strain of a band—without the members who now wore mortarboards—striking up "Pomp and Circumstance."

"So what's the plan for tomorrow?" I asked, slamming those sensory doors to the past.

"Well, like I said, I've got a class right before the assembly, so Rory will bring you to the school. You guys can wait in the locker room if you want to avoid the crowd." I must have grimaced because Jody stopped. "What's wrong?"

"Probably nothing." I blushed. "But can you maybe find some more appropriate place to put two out lesbians than a high-school-girls' locker room?"

Jody stared at me wide-eyed for a second before letting her laughter flow freely again. "Right. Maybe the balcony would be more comfortable."

"I think so. Go on."

"When I get out of class, I'll come meet you, and we'll go to the stage." She indicated a worn-out blue platform in the middle of the gym with several chairs and a podium. "You'll sit with me and Rory and the dean of Bramble College. I'll say a few words about your time as a student, and Rory will talk about your current work. Then we'll call you up to give you the award."

"That's very nice of you," I said. "Thank you for thinking of me."

Jody eyes sparkled with amusement. "You don't have to give an acceptance speech now, or at all really."

"Oh, no, I didn't intend to. It just occurred to me that I never thanked you, for the award, or keeping up with my writing, or even remembering me. It's all very unexpected."

"Really?" Jody seemed genuinely confused.

"Sure. I mean how many students have you had in the last decade?"

"Hundreds."

"Why should I stand out? I wasn't vocal or athletic or particularly involved. I wasn't even in the top ten percent of my class academically. And I haven't been around since then. I'm not one of those people who come to reunions or homecoming."

"And why's that?"

"I don't have any glory days to relive."

"But why?" Jody was pushing me. "You're smart and successful. You've made a name for yourself. And from what limited time I had you as a student, I could tell both your mind and your sense of humor were sharp, but you keep everything to yourself, then and now."

I sat down in the first row of the bleachers. "I don't expect you to understand. You probably flew through high school."

"Why do you say that?"

"You're beautiful and blonde and smart and outgoing and funny…"

Her face turned red, causing me to realize I'd just showered her in compliments.

Did she think I was coming on to her?

Was I?

"Is that how you saw me? How you see me?"

I could lie. I could rein in the embarrassing emotional response I'd let slip out, but instead I surprised even myself by plunging on. "Of course. I admired you so much as a student teacher. You were only a few years older than most of the class, but you had it all together. You struck me as one of those people who always knew the right thing to do."

"Oh, Stevie." She sighed and sat down beside me. "Part of me is relieved to hear I fooled everyone, but it's not fair to let you believe a lie. Student teaching was a horrible time for me. I was wracked with doubt about every decision I made. The pressure got so bad I almost quit."

"What? Why?"

"I didn't know what I was doing in the classroom. Mr. Owens offered no help. I felt constantly judged by the students and the other teachers, and all the time I battled panic-attack-inducing memories of my own high-school experiences."

This news shocked me. If I couldn't see the anguish in her eyes, I would've accused her of acting. "I thought people became teachers because they loved school and didn't want to leave."

"The opposite was true for me. I loved the course work. I loved to read and the school musicals and plays, but those were my escape, my refuge. The hallways terrified me. The cliques and backbiting made me sick. Literally—I got an ulcer at sixteen. I wallowed at the bottom of the social food chain."

"But why? You're smart and funny and attractive."

Her eyes watered with emotion. "You're the only one who saw me that way. I'm short and scrawny, a book nerd and a theater geek. I never wore the trendy clothes, and I never swooned over the boys."

Things fell into place. "Did people know you were gay?"

"Most of them just knew I was different, and they threw a lot of names and slurs my way. Some of them happened to fit, but in the late nineties, Oquendo, Illinois wasn't a hotbed of gay culture, so homosexuality wasn't on most people's radar. I didn't even know for sure I was gay until I went to college."

"But you did know during student teaching, and you understood what high schools were like. You understood how bad they could be. Why choose such a hard career path? And why choose Darlington?"

"I grew up not far from here. I know what these kids' lives are like. The name-calling, the bullying, the backstabbing almost crushed me, and no one even noticed. The teachers were too busy to care, or even worse, they played along. It was every person for herself.

Having to face the torment alone was the worst part." Her shoulders sagged under the invisible weight of those memories. I could almost see a cloud of desperation settle over us until she sat up and lifted her chin. "I swore if I became a teacher I'd do better for my students. I could offer them a little shelter. I wasn't naïve enough to think I could make a small-town high school celebrate differences, but even if I couldn't stop the rising tide of hate, I could weather the storm with them. I could let them know they didn't have to struggle alone."

I got a chill. This was the stuff legendary teachers were made of. How many lives had she saved? But at what personal cost?

"You probably think I'm crazy."

"No. You're amazing, inspiring. Maybe if I'd had four years with you as a teacher I'd be a completely different person today. You've sacrificed so much for your students. I just wonder what kind of toll all that work has taken on you."

She brushed off my concern. "I haven't given up much, and what I have, they've given back tenfold."

"What about the toll the closet takes on your identity and your personal life?"

She rolled her head from side to side slowly, as if trying to release some pent-up tension as she considered the question. I got the urge to massage her shoulders, to run my thumbs down the soft skin along the graceful curve of her neck. Instead I clasped my hands together tightly in my lap.

"I'm out to my parents, my brother, Rory and Beth. I don't deny anything when asked outright, and people who are sensitive to these things, people who are looking and know what to look for can always tell."

I'd realized from the first time I'd seen her that we shared the undeniable connection neither of us would've dared speak but both clearly understood. Could the unspoken sustain someone forever? "Don't you want to come out on a wider scale? Don't get me wrong, I'm no flag waver, but I enjoy the freedom of being able to write without censorship. Or date openly, even if it doesn't happen often."

"I won't say it's not hard at times, but not because of my own desires. It's all the small-mindedness I encounter in my students, and more frequently my colleagues, that hurts most. When people make a fag joke or say 'that's so gay,' I'd like to say, 'You don't know what you're talking about. I'm gay and I've made a good life here.'" She shrugged again, pushing on with less passion and more reason. "But if I were out I'd be seen as pushing a personal agenda rather than standing up against bigotry. I'm in a better position right now by staying closeted."

"I admire you, really, but I couldn't do it. I paid my dues to get out and live my own life. It's hard enough to have strangers judge my work. The thought of putting my whole life out there for scrutiny all the time would paralyze me." I shivered. "I might never leave my bed in the morning."

"Some days I feel that way. For all my talk about making sure students know they aren't alone, my own life can get pretty solitary."

"Do you date?" I asked, torn between wishing the best for her and not wanting to think about some lucky woman who got to hold her at the end of a long day.

"Not often." She looked around the gym. "Even if I did have a chance to meet women, this is a lot to compete with. The strain of my job often crushes possibilities before they have a chance to blossom."

"It must be hard to feel romantic while looking over your shoulder."

"I still live in Oquendo, which gives me a half hour to unwind at the end of the day and keeps students from just driving by my house to see when I'm home." The resignation hung heavy in her voice and slowed her words. "But I'm here several nights a week working on the school play or conferencing with parents. Even when I go to St. Louis to get away, I'm always running into a former student or someone from town. Some times are better than others, but you're right. I can never fully relax."

I hated to think of her tense all the time, constantly worried about how she might misstep. Then again, I was no stranger to the consequences of social pressure. Maybe we carried similar baggage, just for different reasons.

"You know," Jody said softly as she stared across the gym. "My biggest worry isn't that I'll never meet the right person. It's that I won't be able to recognize her through all the smoke and mirrors I've built up around myself."

I didn't know what to say. Jody's confession caused a deep ache to settle in my chest. I wanted to comfort her, to tell her everything would be all right, to say she was amazing and doing the right thing, and when the time came, all the walls she'd constructed would fall. But how could I alleviate her fears when I shared them? I liked to think if the right woman came along I'd be able to risk anything for her, but the walls I'd erected had never faced a serious test, and they'd been built on a much less noble foundation than Jody's.

"I'm sorry." Jody stood. "I didn't mean to keep you out so late, and I certainly didn't mean to dump all my insecurities on you. I've been a terrible host and an all-around conversation killer."

"No, please don't say that." I rushed to assure her. "This is honestly the best night I've had in a long time."

"Wow, you don't get out much, do you?"

I laughed. "No, I really don't, but that's beside the point. I've enjoyed talking to you. I wish we had more time."

"Honestly?"

"Yes." I could hardly believe I'd not only said that, but meant it. I had twenty-four hours left until I landed back in New York, and that thought still comforted me, but I wished Jody wouldn't be a thousand miles away.

"Thank you, but I'd better get you back to Beth and Rory's before they start to worry."

I checked my watch. Ten o'clock. Where had the time gone? Beth and Rory would no doubt wonder what we'd been doing, but I suspected hope would be their dominant emotion rather than worry.

Back in Jody's car, I watched the few lights left on along Main Street fade behind us. The stars were much clearer here than in the city, so I stared at them even though I really wanted to stare at Jody. "Do you ever think about leaving? I mean I know the kids need you, but there are a lot of kids in need in a lot of places."

"I don't rule anything out. I don't know if I want to teach in Darlington forever, but if I decided to leave, it wouldn't be because I got tired or gave up." She pulled into the long gravel driveway of Beth and Rory's farmhouse, then killed the engine. "I won't run from anything, but some days I do wonder what it would feel like to run toward something or someone."

The words caught in my throat, the emotion behind them so raw and achingly beautiful. I should've kissed her. She was so close and so beautiful there in the starlight. I should have leaned in and taken her soft, pink lips with my own. I should have run my fingers along the smooth skin of her cheek and through her light strands of hair until I cupped the back of her head, holding her loosely but passionately against me.

What I should *not* have done is thank her for the ride and tell her I'd see her tomorrow, then fumble my way out of the seat belt and make an awkward retreat to the house. Yet that's exactly what I did.

At least I'd given myself plenty to obsess about while I lay awake all night.

CHAPTER TWO

The sun rose early Friday morning, probably no earlier than usual, but it certainly felt that way. The thin curtain of my guestroom paired with the vast, open plains outside allowed the early morning rays unimpeded access to my eyelids. I'd gotten more sleep than I had the night before, which was only a couple hours, and there was no chance I'd get any more.

Normally I slept so soundly even the hounds of hell couldn't stir me before ten a.m., but once I awoke, I stayed that way. I spent a solid half hour attempting to trick myself into believing I wasn't actually awake, then another trying to find something interesting to read in the copy of *Midwest Living* Beth had left on the bedside table for me. I pulled out my iPhone and checked my mail, only to find nothing worth responding to. I even read some news headlines before flopping back onto the bed and staring at the ceiling.

Immediately my mind returned to Jody and the time we'd spent together the night before, which was exactly what I'd tried to avoid. I didn't want to think of her eyes and how the magnitude of their blueness defied comparison. I didn't want to marvel at her passionate approach to teaching or wonder what it would feel like to have her passion directed at me. I certainly didn't want to obsess over the fear that I'd missed a chance to kiss her or worry I'd probably never get another one. What did I mean, probably? I definitely wouldn't. In ten hours I'd be on my way back to New York, and happily so. Jody was special, both as a teacher and as a woman, but eight million people lived in New York City. Odds were that plenty of special women lived there too.

I looked at the clock again. How was it possible for it to still only be seven o'clock? The sun had been up for four hours. This might be the start of a never-ending day.

After showering, dressing, and spending about three times as long as usual taming my frizzy mane of dark hair into something resembling a unified attempt at wavy, I finally went downstairs.

My hosts sat at the dining room table, chatting quietly over coffee, so lost in each other they didn't hear me approach. They were stunning together. Rory cut an imposing figure, lean and fit with her firm jaw and intense gaze, while Beth exuded femininity, with soft curves and a graceful manner. They anchored one another, offering balance both in their aesthetic and their personalities. I'd never been one to buy into "the other half" mentality of relationships, but these two offered compelling evidence of the theory's validity.

"Morning," I said, hoping my exhaustion didn't show.

"Good morning," Rory said cheerfully. "You're up early."

"How'd you sleep?" Beth asked.

"Fine. I think I'm just still on New York time."

"Yeah, jet lag hurts, and you won't be here long enough to adjust to this time zone."

"It's not a problem." Or least I hoped it wouldn't be.

"I couldn't decide what to make for breakfast, so I waited for your input. Eggs and bacon? Pancakes and sausage? French toast with all the trimmings?"

"You don't have to go to any trouble for me," I said, my stomach roiling at the thought of putting food into it this early. "I usually just drink coffee."

Beth frowned slightly. "Are you sure? It's no trouble at all."

"Really, but go ahead and make whatever you want for yourselves."

"I can just grab something on campus," Beth said.

"I ate some fruit and yogurt before my run this morning," Rory added.

"You've already gone for a run?" I liked her a little less.

"I know. The thought would've horrified me two years ago, but with Beth's cooking I had to do something or I'd weigh four hundred pounds."

"She's too hard on herself." Beth raked a hand through Rory's hair and tousled the chestnut mop on her way to the kitchen. "She's in perfect shape. She's still got the muscles of a seventeen-year-old."

I believed it. Rory had always been athletic, and while she'd gained a little weight since high school, it appeared to be mostly muscle. I doubted anything she ate could make her less appealing. I, on the other hand, ate healthier with each passing year, took yoga classes, and always chose the stairs over the elevator but could do little to stop the accumulating pounds or the gravitational pull directing them all to my midsection. Six months shy of my thirtieth birthday, I was far from sagging into the cement, but I worked harder than ever to keep both my belt and my bra from suffering under the added strain of my slowly expanding body. Of course, sitting in a chair writing all day didn't help, but who had the time or energy to jog every morning? Aside, obviously, from Rory.

"So how's your brother?" I asked Rory, hoping she'd run with the topic.

"He's getting married in June," she said with a grin.

"Really?" Davey had been a year behind me in high school and always seemed like a nice-enough guy, though a lot quieter than Rory.

"Yup, to Nikki Belliard. She graduated with you, right?"

"Wow, yeah. We were in a lot of classes together senior year. She was always nice to me." Actually Nikki was probably the closest thing I had to a friend during that time. "We rode the bench together in basketball."

"That's surprising. She's a pretty good softball player."

"She's plenty athletic, but she didn't have the competitive drive to mix it up in the paint."

"Makes sense. She's an elementary teacher now," Rory said. "What about you? What's your excuse for warming the pine? Lack of skills or motivation?"

"Both," I said emphatically. "I've never cared for sports much."

"Why'd you play?"

"Seemed like the thing to do at the time." I shrugged. "I did a lot of things because it seemed easier than saying no. I went along to get along."

"Did you date guys?"

"No. Thankfully I didn't get asked much." That fact probably should have bothered me more, but even in high school, I only felt relief. "Most guys wanted a girl who was into them, and I never gave off those signals."

"Did you know you were gay the whole time?"

"I had more of a gradual realization, but it started early in high school. I wasn't traumatized, because at least I'd found a name for the difference growing between my classmates and me. Besides, what's one more thing to get through in the grand scheme of things?"

Rory grinned. "You don't get ruffled easily, do you?"

"No, I guess I don't. I mean, I knew people would be jerks about me being gay, but people are jerks for a lot of reasons. I'd dreamed of New York since I was about ten. I had a plan, and I worked toward it. That was enough for me."

"I wonder how life would be different if we all thought that way."

"'We all' who?"

"All the gay people in every small-town school across the country."

I shrugged. "I don't know. I never saw myself as part of the masses."

"We never do at that age, but just look at the numbers. The Kinsey report says we're ten percent of the population basically across the board. So, in a town the size of Darlington, we should have about five hundred gay or lesbian residents."

I waved off the figure. "I doubt the majority of gay people stay here, so the statistic would hardly hold up."

"I agree. Among the adults it's likely much lower, but high-school kids don't have any choice in where they live. Their location is as much of a luck of the draw as their sexual orientation."

I pondered this idea in grand introverted fashion, quietly mulling over the concept while Rory plowed on. "How many students did you have in your graduating class?"

"Maybe ninety."

"Say one hundred, since neither of us is a math person."

I nodded.

"Out of one hundred students, that should mean ten people were gay, and you've got four classes' worth of students, so you should have forty gay or lesbian students at Darlington High School at any given moment. Right?"

"I suppose, in a purely hypothetical sense." ·

"Fine. Say half of them are outliers—maybe they don't know they're gay yet or maybe farmers produce a below-average number of gay offspring, even though there's no evidence of that." Rory began to pace, reminding me of a lion. Her movements, while scattered, seemed to build in purpose as she pursued her argument. I half expected her to pounce on the table. "Even on the conservative end, that still means twenty gay and lesbian students there at all times."

"I suppose that's not an unreasonable assumption."

"So why isn't anyone else reaching that conclusion?" she asked, opening her hands palms up like a magician who'd performed some feat of magic. "Why is no one saying these kids are here and we have to do more for them?"

I remembered Jody's face hardened with resolve last night as she spoke about her determination to be there for those students, but I also remembered the toll that kind of dedication took on every part of her life. I did care about those kids. I ached for them even, but I was also relieved to no longer be one of them.

❖

Classes were in session when Rory and I arrived at the school, so we had the hallway to ourselves. She strolled along confidently, ever the returning star, while I shuffled in her wake. Maybe some things would never change. I wasn't afraid of high school itself or anything it represented. I wasn't a student anymore, and while I said a silent prayer of thanks for that, I had bigger issues to worry about.

In half an hour I'd be on a platform in front of more than four hundred people. Large assemblies were not my idea of a good time even under the best circumstances, but the idea of such an event being called in my honor made my empty stomach tighten. Compound my nerves with a serious lack of sleep or food, and I could barely bring myself to put one foot in front of the other.

"Hey, did you know Drew Phillips is the principal now?" Rory asked.

"The basketball coach? Really?" His name didn't bring back pleasant memories. No wonder Rory and Jody were worried about the gay kids in school. "Who thought promoting him was a good idea?"

"The good ole boys always gotta have one of their own in power to uphold the status quo."

"I suppose. Darlington has never trusted outsiders."

"I'm not an outsider. You're not an outsider. Lots of people from around here aren't dicks. Or for that matter don't even have dicks. When was the last time this place had a woman in charge?"

"Not when I went here. Probably not in my lifetime."

"Not in anyone's lifetime. This place is a harem. One man at the top, a bunch of women underneath."

Poor Jody. She didn't stand a chance of changing the power structure, but she'd keep trying for her kids.

Rory stopped in front of a large trophy case and pointed to a gold softball engraved with the words CONFERENCE CHAMPIONS. "Hey, we helped win this trophy."

"You helped win that trophy," I said without a hint of regret. "I carried bats off the field."

"Every team member is important, even the bat girl. And let's be honest, bat girl sounds pretty sexy."

I laughed harder than the joke warranted. Maybe I just needed something to break my tension, or perhaps I was getting a little loopy.

She moved down another couple of cases, inspecting each item as she went. I just focused on breathing normally. I didn't have frequent panic attacks, but only because I held them in check by sheer force of will. They simply drew more attention than I wanted. I kept telling myself this event was almost over. One hour onstage and I'd be free. I'd already packed my suitcase and stowed it in the car. Maybe I could ask Rory to take me to St. Louis early. I could fly standby or sit in the airport like all the other anonymous travelers. Just one hour of being front and center, and then I could fade back into the crowd.

"Here's your class picture."

I tried to focus on the eight-by-ten photograph of all my classmates on the first day of senior year. The faces were a blur in my memory now, but Rory began to point out people immediately, as if playing some small-town version of Where's Waldo?

"There's Nikki," she said, pointing to the first row. "And there's you."

"My hair stuck out enough to signal incoming aircraft."

Rory laughed.

"I should have cut it all off, but that wasn't the style then. Not that blimp hair was stylish either."

"Shorter hair would've made you look butcher."

I shrugged. Of course that had factored into my decision.

Rory squinted and leaned closer. "Which five do you think are gay?"

Not this again. "Well, me."

She gave me a little shove. "Okay, there's one."

"What about him?" She pointed to a blond young man in the top row.

"I doubt it. He died in Afghanistan a year after graduation."

"Damn," she muttered. "Who would've thought that war would go on for so long? Did your class lose any others?"

"Not to the war, but Kelsey Patel committed suicide two months before graduation."

"What?" She stepped back and stared at me, her hunter-green eyes wide and wounded, before she turned back to the picture. "Which one?"

I scanned the faces until I found the tan-skinned girl with the big brown eyes. "There."

Rory studied her solemnly. "Why don't I remember her?"

"Her parents ran one of the gas stations and liquor stores for a while. They moved here my sophomore year, I think. You'd already left for Chicago when she died."

"What was she like?"

"I honestly don't remember much." I searched my memory for anything other than hearing she'd overdosed on pills one night. The family kept the funeral private, and the teachers seemed eager to brush the incident under the rug. Still, shouldn't I remember more than her death? "We had only a few classes together. She was the only Indian-American I'd ever met. The only vegetarian too. She struck me as odd but probably ahead of her time, and certainly ahead of Darlington."

"Was she gay?"

"I don't know. People called her a lezzie and a dyke, but she was smart and I think kind of politically minded. She probably would've come out if she were gay. Kids only made fun of her because they didn't know what to do with her."

"People don't understand that antigay bullying is a vicious social tool used to keep a wide range of outsiders in check." The fire ignited in Rory's eyes. She was commanding, even informally. She'd be a true force onstage. "The stigma burns everyone it touches and keeps even the straightest of kids from expressing a hint of difference."

"I wonder why more people can't see that."

"I try to draw those connections. So many of us do." The frustration hung thick in her voice. "But we keep failing these kids."

My chest constricted in the face of her pain. "You don't fail them, Rory. You do what you can, and you're good at it."

"We're not good enough, not as a society, not even as individuals."

A twinge of defensiveness pricked my skin. "The work you do probably saves more lives than you know. These kids are blessed to have you back here and to have teachers like Jody to advocate for them, but we can't all be those people. We aren't all warriors or symbols of triumph. I can't imagine choosing the life you have."

"I guess that's where we really differ. I've never seen the work I do as a choice. It's not personality or ability. I get tired of being a big gay symbol sometimes too. All the travel, all the speaking to reluctant audiences and arguing with small-minded bigots. I don't fight for me anymore." Her voice caught slightly as she pointed to Kelsey's picture. "I do it for kids like her."

I stared at Kelsey, then at Rory. She was right about one thing. These kids deserved someone like her, and someone like Jody—people with clear visions and a holy purpose to drive them. What they didn't need was someone who got sick at the thought of being in the same gym with them or someone who counted down the hours until she could leave town. They didn't need someone who holed up in a loft and wrote books in an attempt to avoid even basic social interactions, someone who didn't have the courage or composure to give a simple acceptance speech, much less an impassioned oration on their behalf. Yes, they needed symbols and advocates and leaders, but I was none of those things.

❖

Jody found us waiting in the balcony area of the bleachers while students began to flow in below us. She moved confidently and chatted easily, appearing as calm and graceful as ever, and I once again found it hard to believe she'd ever doubted her place in a school. She'd be the hero in some kid's story someday. She probably already had been.

"Hi, you two," she said, her eyes bright. "Ready to get this show on the road?"

"You know it," Rory said with a little bounce. "And I just saw my boss come in too. You want me to flag her down for us?"

"Please, and ask her if she can stay around for some photos with the scholarship recipients after the assembly."

"Sure." Rory patted me on the back as she strode off, leaving Jody and me alone again.

"How you feeling?" she asked, her expression turning serious.

"I'll be okay."

"Really?"

I shook my head. "I don't know. I'm pretty nervous."

"Do you get nervous before all your public experiences?"

"I try not to do too many of them, and when I do it's generally with book clubs or panels at conferences. This is my high school."

"What difference does that make?"

"I spent four years here trying not to be noticed, and now I'll be center stage. It feels like a bit of a farce to me."

"Stevie." She touched my hand quickly, gently, but enough to establish a more solid connection between us. "You belong here. You earned your way onto that stage whether you asked for it or not. Your success has meaning beyond what you can imagine. All you have to do is accept that."

I closed my eyes and focused on her voice, her words, her touch. Some of the tension in my shoulders eased. She provided such a calming presence, an anchor and a warm blanket all rolled into one. I marveled at her ability to soothe me even in these emotionally chaotic circumstances. For a fleeting moment I wondered what it would be like to see more of her, to know her outside of Darlington.

"What are you thinking about Stevie?"

"I wish we had a chance to spend more time together away from the school, and the media circus, and the pressure to be anything for anyone else."

Her smile grew so big it crinkled the edges of her eyes. "Few things would make me happier than for you to visit again."

My chest constricted. I hadn't meant here. I couldn't come back to Darlington. I wouldn't. Less than twenty-four hours in town had exhausted me. I couldn't eat or sleep, and the weight of responsibility to some unseen gay children was enough to crush me. I wished no ill will on any of them, but I had to get out.

"Hey, there you are," Edmond called. "It's picture time."

I exhaled forcefully, subconsciously searching for an exit, but Jody gave my shoulder a gentle squeeze. "Come on, it won't be so bad."

I tried to believe her, but my nerves frayed a little more with each flashbulb that went off in my face. First another picture with Edmond and Rory, then just Edmond, then just Rory. When a student photographer jumped into the game, along with a reporter from the local paper, the white light caused spots in my vision. I plastered on a fake smile and tried to turn my head in the appropriate direction every time someone shouted, "Stevie," or worse, "Miss Geller." Hands reached in to rearrange us, adding Jody and the dean of the college, whom I'd yet to be introduced to. Then someone said, "Let's get Mr. Phillips in some of these."

A man squeezed next to me as close as possible without letting our bodies touch in any way.

"Hey, Drew," Rory said under her breath. "How's it hanging?"

"Rory, I want you out of my school as soon as the assembly is over." He delivered the line through gritted teeth.

Rory snickered. "I love how much it pains you that I'm a distinguished alum."

"Look this way," someone called, and we all turned.

"Did you even say hello to your guest, Drew?" Rory kept needling him. "You know the one we called this assembly for? The one getting a *big* award?"

"*Ms.* Geller." He sneered in my direction.

What a jerk. I never did anything to him. Or did my mere existence annoy him? Another flash went off, and my airway constricted a bit more. This whole ordeal was hard enough without getting pulled into their pissing contest. I didn't need his tension piled on top of my own. I didn't need any of this pressure.

I began surreptitiously searching for somewhere to hide. If I could just find a corner to myself, I could take a couple of deep breaths and pull myself together, but students filled the bleachers and milled around in the doorway. Some of them were even bustling around near the stage. Dear God, how many kids went to this school? It seemed like so many more than four hundred. And then there were the teachers. Some I'd had, some I didn't know. Would I be expected to talk to them? Would they remember me? Would I remember anything they'd taught me? My hands began to shake. I took a few steps back, then a few steps more. Rory and Edmond were laughing about something between them, and Jody chatted casually with a student. Drew remained steadfast in his attempt to ignore me. I took a few more steps back without eliciting any notice from anyone.

This was my chance. Two steps from the door, I turned slowly, angling my body toward the exit when an arm on my shoulder almost caused me to jump out of my skin.

"Don't even think about it," Edmond said through an overly enthusiastic smile.

"I can't do this." I pleaded, completely unconcerned with the irrationality of the request. "You have to get me out of this."

"Too late. You're on."

Something was wrong. Very wrong.

Jody and Rory stood together at the podium taking turns speaking about me. They talked about me as a person, as a student, as a writer, or at least I thought that's what they were talking about, but I could barely hear anything. I strained to make out their words, but I couldn't concentrate over the dull roar in my ears. The white noise of my brain sounded like the ocean. Not a real ocean, mind you, but the fake ocean you hear when you put a large seashell up to your ear.

Occasionally I heard them say my name, the sound like sirens calling me, a distant echo carrying their song over the waves.

I blinked, I shook my head, I even stuck my finger in my ear to try to clear it. I must have looked absurd, but I didn't care. As much as I didn't want to make a scene, I worried I was having a stroke. That didn't make any sense, but none of this made sense. Could this be an allergic reaction? An acute panic attack?

I turned from Rory to Jody—so strong, so proud, so kind, and standing so close—but the edges of their features grew soft and faded as my vision narrowed. I summoned every faculty I had at my disposal, grasping at any sensory cues. I no longer thought of my survival in terms of hours, but minutes. How long had they been talking? It felt like an eternity before they turned to me, smiling expectantly.

A thought pushed weakly on the quicksand filling my brain. They wanted me to come to the podium. My panic had given way to numbness, but it had the same effect. Could I possibly die of stage fright? That would make headlines for Edmond, but hopefully not the kind of publicity he wanted. At least if I keeled over I wouldn't have to deal with him pressuring me anymore.

No. I wouldn't give in or give up. As nerve-racking as this assembly was to endure, it would be exponentially worse to collapse in front of four hundred students and Jody. I didn't care if I was dying. I would not be a spectacle for my hometown. I would not draw any more attention to myself. Two small steps to the podium, two handshakes, and two steps back to my seat. Up and down. I could do this.

Bracing my hands on my knees, I tried to push myself to a standing position, but it was no use—not the impulse, not the mechanics. Everything failed me. I managed to propel myself upright, but my knees wouldn't lock.

I wobbled, awash with embarrassment, but even my self-consciousness was short-lived. The gymnasium spun like a demonic carnival ride, causing all the colors to blur together. The podium shifted and pitched forward, reminding me of a subway train coming to an unexpected stop. My body was shutting down.

I locked eyes with Jody, wordlessly begging for help, pleading for her to understand. Then I crumpled. Going down in slow motion did nothing to alleviate the feeling of helplessness but gave me time to see horror register on the faces around me. Jody's lips parted in shock. Rory reached out to catch me, so chivalrous. Such a Rory thing to do. I would've rolled my eyes if I'd had any control of my muscles, but I didn't. I didn't have control of anything. Somehow it felt like I hadn't had control of anything for a very long time.

A splitting pain crashed though the back of my head, and suddenly the colors were clear—brilliantly, excruciatingly clear. Blinding white followed by an angry red. Then mercifully everything went black.

CHAPTER THREE

I came to slowly, the sounds around me fading in much the same way they'd faded out, only in reverse. Nothingness turned to a dull roar and then to whispered murmurs. I couldn't hear any of the words, but they were probably about me. A wave of bile surged into my throat. Was I sick from hitting my head, or was it a symptom of my embarrassment? It didn't matter. No way could I salvage this event or anyone's opinion of me. I just wanted to get out alive and right now.

I tried to open my eyes, but the bright fluorescent lights of the gym were too much to handle and only magnified the pounding in my head. I was clearly on my back, but the floor beneath me didn't feel like a carpeted podium. It felt like the shellacked wood flooring of the gym. The smell of scuffed rubber filled my nostrils. Had I fallen off the riser, or had someone moved me? Either way, I was freezing. I shivered and rubbed my bare arms.

Bare arms? I'd been wearing long sleeves. Had they removed my shirt? And my pants? I registered the cold floor on the back of my calves too. Headache be damned, I couldn't lie here half-naked. I tried to sit up, but my body felt so absurdly heavy.

"Stay still," someone said. I didn't recognize the voice. "Stevie? Stevie, can you hear me?"

I nodded.

"You need to lie still. You hit your head pretty hard, kiddo."

Kiddo?

I tried to squint through the light again, and this time I made out a few shadows hovering above me.

"Can't we move her?" That voice belonged to Jody, and I felt mildly comforted to hear she didn't sound angry or embarrassed, just concerned. "Should I call her mom?"

My mom?

"Stevie, can you open your eyes?" the other voice asked.

I managed to open them a little more, but my vision was still hazy.

"Good girl," she said, then added more quietly, "her pupils aren't dilated."

"Concussion?" Jody asked.

"Maybe."

"Does anything hurt, Stevie?"

"My head." The words sounded weak and rough, but at least I could speak again.

"I bet. You came down hard. What about your neck?"

I moved my head slowly from side to size. "Neck's fine."

"Excellent news."

"What's your name?"

"Stevie Geller."

"Good. Do you know where you are?"

"Darlington High School."

"Yes. Do you know what happened?"

"I passed out."

The woman didn't respond right away. "What's the date, Stevie?"

"February 28, 2013."

I got no affirmative feedback. Did I get it wrong? Why? I knew the assembly was on the twenty-eighth. I'd been dreading the date for a month.

"Did she say 2013?" Jody asked, fear creeping into her voice.

"Yes," I answered.

"We'd better call her parents."

"My parents live in Boca Raton."

Another silence, and this time I strained to see their facial expressions. Worry lines creased Jody's forehead, but something else seemed different too. Her hair fell past her shoulders, and she'd pulled it back into a ponytail. I turned to the other woman. She looked familiar, but I couldn't remember why.

"Let's get her to the locker room first."

"Can you sit up now, Stevie?"

I groaned my way into a sitting position and stared at my legs. I wore white athletic shorts and sneakers. What the hell? That wasn't a fashion choice I would've made, even with a gun to my head. Who'd changed my clothes?

"Do you need a hand?" Another vaguely familiar voice asked, this one deeper, rougher, maybe Mr. Phillips? That would explain the lack of concern.

"Jody can help me. You guys go on without us."

Jody and the other woman looped an arm under each of mine and lifted me to a standing position. The crowd clapped. How embarrassing. Had the students watched the whole ordeal? I refused to look at them, instead focusing on my mysterious new tennis shoes as the women half-walked, half-carried me to the locker room.

I heard someone shout, "Shake it off, Stevie." I wanted to roll my eyes at that completely unhelpful piece of advice, but my brain hurt too much to properly process sarcasm.

The locker room was cooler and darker than the gym, allowing me to see better as they helped me onto a trainer's table. The trainer? The school nurse, that's who the other voice belonged to. "You're Mrs. Snow, right?"

She nodded. "Things coming back to you now?"

"A little. Sorry I didn't remember you at first," I said, lying back. "It's been ten years."

Mrs. Snow and Jody exchanged a look I couldn't decipher.

"What is it?"

"Nothing. Just relax and talk to Miss Hadland. I'm going to go call your mom."

"My mom lives in Florida now," I repeated irritably.

"Okay, well, humor me and let me call the hospital, all right?"

"Fine." I closed my eyes.

"Don't let her fall asleep, Jody."

"Stevie." Jody squeezed my hand. "You heard her. You have to stay awake."

"Okay," I mumbled, already drifting off.

"Stevie, come on. Stay with me."

"I'm sorry," I said.

"It's okay. You're going to be fine."

"No, I mean I'm sorry for everything." Another wave of embarrassment rolled over me, triggering a bout of nausea. "I didn't mean to ruin your assembly."

"What assembly?"

"The awards assembly. I shouldn't have come back here. I just, my career, you know?"

"You're not making any sense, Stevie." She sounded unduly confused. "You don't have anything to apologize for."

"I do. I made a fool of myself and wrecked all your hard work. I sent the wrong message to the students, and I know Drew Phillips won't let you forget that."

"Shh. I don't know what you're talking about. Mr. Phillips isn't mad at either of us."

"Oh, come on. The guy's mad at the whole world. He doesn't care how hard you work for those kids. If he found out you were gay, he'd make your life hell."

Jody gasped, and I heard her chair scrape across the concrete floor. Opening my eyes, I gritted my teeth against the dizziness to focus on the shock on her face. Her eyes were wide and moved erratically from me to our surroundings. Her body language seemed totally discordant with the conversation. Actually, there was more to her appearance. She looked terrified of me. And young. Inexplicably young. "Jody?"

"Hurt or not, you need to call me Miss Hadland."

"Why?"

"Because I'm still your teacher."

"What?"

Something about the way she scanned me up and down caused me to reexamine my attire...my uniform. A basketball uniform? "What happened to me?"

"You got hit in the head with a basketball."

"No, I didn't."

"Yes, you did. It knocked you out. I was in the front row of the audience. I saw the whole thing," she said vehemently. Then lowering her voice, she asked, "How did you know I'm gay?"

"You told me."

"I didn't."

"Yes, you did. You said you had a horrible high-school existence and became a teacher to make sure no other kid ever had to go through that alone, but you have to stay in the closet to do it."

She opened and closed her mouth as if silently gasping for air. "I've never told anyone that."

"Well then, how do I know, Jody? How do I know you're gay?"

She glanced frantically over her shoulder. "Please stop saying that, and stop calling me Jody."

I began to hyperventilate again as my eyes moved from her panic-stricken face to her long hair, to my clothes. What was happening?

"Stevie, I got ahold of your mom. She's working tonight, but she's going to send your dad over to drive you to the hospital."

"My mom? Working? My dad?" My voice trembled even as it rose until a horrible question pushed past the fear. "What year is it?"

Mrs. Snow turned from my terror to Jody's expression of disbelief before finally saying, "It's 2002."

The number ricocheted through my screaming brain even as the darkness consumed me again.

❖

I recognized the sounds of the night nursing shift and the smell of antiseptic, along with the IV running down my arm before I even opened my eyes. Those factors alone might have unsettled most people, but I'd grown up in this place. Hospitals meant safety to me. I remembered lying on the floor behind the nurses' station with my coloring books, or hiding from my older brother under the chairs in the waiting room. Mostly, though, the hospital reminded me of my parents.

I lay on the gurney, breathing deeply until I gathered enough strength to open my eyes. A monitor beeped beside me, and I turned my head to see the screen. With little more than a glance, I registered my steady pulse, my sufficient oxygen levels, and my slightly elevated blood pressure. The pain in my head had also subsided significantly, likely due to the IV, which as best I could tell was currently only delivering some hydrating fluids but had likely started off with a strong dose of acetaminophen.

I closed my eyes again, resting my head on one of the slightly elevated beds I'd often napped on as a child. Everything would be okay now. The doctors would get to the bottom of whatever occurred and have me on a plane to New York soon. In the meantime, I could finally get some much-needed sleep. I relaxed into the paper-covered pillow and dozed off again, until somewhere in the lovely space between sleep and awareness I heard my parents talking.

The sound of my mother's voice both soothed and afflicted me. Like most people, I associated my mother with comfort and safety. Even as an adult who'd lived alone for years, I still wished to have her closer every time I got sick. However, having her close now meant she wasn't in Florida, but in fact still worked in Darlington.

The next logical leap came unwanted and unbidden to my mind.

I could no longer ignore the possibility. I was a senior in high school.

"We've run a series of tests, but aside from a nasty contusion at the back of her head," my mother said from the other side of a partition dividing the hospital room, "she doesn't seem to have anything medically wrong with her."

"So she has amnesia?" my father asked.

"It's not like the movies. Amnesia doesn't generally manifest after such commonplace events like falling over. Short-term memory loss can be associated with a severe concussion, but as far as we can tell there's no substantial swelling of her brain."

"Is she really displaying memory loss?" Mrs. Snow asked. Her presence in the room and in the conversation surprised me. Who else was here? Jody? Somehow I doubted that. She probably hated me now. At the very least she had to think me a loose cannon with the power to end her career before it even began. I had to make her understand I'd never do anything to hurt her.

No, damn it. I couldn't be worried about scoring points with a beautiful woman. I had much bigger problems, like how I'd lost eleven years of my life.

"Yeah," my dad added. "She didn't forget anything. She's added a decade to her life, right down to the details about her career as an award-winning author."

"It doesn't make sense. Not from a traditionally medical standpoint."

"What do you mean traditionally?" My dad always managed to keep up with medical conversations at the outset since he spent so much time around doctors and nurses, but eventually he always asked the question that made it clear he worked in the administrative side of the hospital.

"I mean the brain is a funny organ, one we may never fully understand. And Stevie's always had a vivid imagination."

"She's never fabricated anything like this before. She's never lied or even yelled at anyone." I could sense the undercurrent of fear in his voice.

"No, she's not acting out. Her terror when she got here was very real. Even if I wasn't her mother, I could've clearly seen how genuinely confused she was. But as a doctor, I suspected the disorientation stemmed from intracranial pressure, and I've seen no evidence of that, not even on a minor scale."

"I don't want to overstep my bounds here," Mrs. Snow said tentatively. "I'm just a school nurse, but could the blunt trauma have triggered some sort of mental break?"

I fisted my hands into the sheets of my bed and bit my lip to keep from screaming out in my own defense. I wasn't crazy. I wasn't making anything up, and Jody's reaction proved the events of the last decade weren't the product of my overactive imagination. She said herself she'd never told anyone the things I repeated to her in the locker room.

"We have to consider a mental disorder as valid a possibility as anything," my mother said, sounding resigned and sad.

"Mallory," my father said, "my daughter is not a nut job."

"She's my daughter too," she snapped, before taking a deep breath. "And I hope very much this condition is temporary, but in the meantime, I won't let the stigma of mental illness stand in the way of seeking adequate medical treatment."

Adequate medical treatment? What did that mean? A mental institution? Surely they wouldn't do that.

My father sighed. "Do you want me to call for a transport to St. Louis?

"Let's wait until she wakes up again and see if there's any improvement."

No, no, no! This couldn't be happening. I hadn't had a mental break. Had I? Even if I had, sending me to a mental ward where I'd be poked and prodded and scrutinized every second of every day would not make me better. Extra scrutiny had gotten me into this mess in the first place. I'd snapped and passed out because of all the attention. And even if I went to a psych hospital, what could I tell them? The truth? Was there any possible way to convince someone I'd come from the future? No. The more I talked, the deeper they'd pull me into the system, and who could blame them? Time travel didn't exist.

God, maybe I should be locked up.

There had to be some other explanation, and I had to find it fast. Once I got placed under the care of a psychiatrist, I'd never get away. This was my last chance to try to work things out on my own. Yet…how could I convince them I wasn't crazy when I wasn't entirely sure of my sanity? I'd faked and fumbled my way through a lot of situations in my life, but never anything of this magnitude. Then again, I'd never had so much at stake. Could I really play along with a do-over of my senior year in high school? A multitude of fears flooded my senses, the bitter taste stinging my mouth and clogging my throat. But before I had a chance to pick them apart, one of the monitors beside my bed began to beep loudly.

The curtain dividing the room was pulled back swiftly, revealing the concerned faces of my parents.

"Stevie," my mom said with forced calmness, "it's okay. I'm right here."

"Mom." The word left my lips as I reached for her instinctively.

She pulled me into a hug, and I rested my head on her shoulder, soaking up the feel of her starched white lab coat against my cheek. I inhaled her scent. The subtle jasmine of her perfume undercut heavier doses of latex and Dial soap, a byproduct of obsessively fighting the spread of germs. "It's okay, honey. I've got you."

Her presence, her words soothed me, but they also reminded me why I needed to stay with her. If I had to be transported into the past, at least it should be to a place I knew, a place I could feel safe. Familiarity was the only remaining strand between complete darkness and me. I intended to cling to it with every ounce of strength I had left.

My mom pulled away slowly and studied my eyes, either judging the size of my pupils or searching for something only a mother could see. "You look a lot better. How do you feel?"

"Okay, I think." I answered tentatively, fearing the questions I knew would come next. Looking past her, I added, "I'm sorry for making trouble, Mrs. Snow."

"It's all right." She smiled over-politely. "Do you remember what happened?"

Here's where I had to begin spinning my web. I thought of everything I'd ever read about storytelling, especially how to build credibility as a narrator. "I was at a basketball game. I think something hit me. I don't know. I woke up on the floor. You were there, along with Jo—um, Miss Hadland."

My father smiled brightly, but my mother eyes narrowed skeptically. "Do you know what the date is?"

"February." I then paused long enough to see the corners of my dad's mouth quirk upward. "February 28th."

"And do you remember the day of the week?"

"Friday," I answered, then grimaced at their frowns. "Or is that just wishful thinking?"

My dad gave a strangled chuckle. "Can't blame her trying to move a day closer to the weekend."

"What year is it?" my mother, never one to pull punches, asked.

I closed my eyes and took a deep breath, summoning all my remaining fortitude. "It's my senior year of high school, 2002."

"There you go. Improvement," my dad said triumphantly. "That's what we needed to see, right? He turned to Mrs. Snow, who nodded, relief evident in her features.

Only Mom remained doubtful. She stared at me, hard. No matter what else might've changed over time, she was still a human lie detector. I'd never been able to get anything by her as a child, and I rarely even tried. I fought the urge to squirm under her scrutiny. The only thing that kept me from faltering was the deep-seated knowledge that I wasn't a child anymore, despite what the calendar said. I'd finely honed my skills as an award-winning fiction writer and a budding playwright, and this was the most important role I'd ever craft.

"Fine." She sat back. "I don't see any harm in keeping her overnight."

Everyone in the room visibly relaxed. Her proclamation fell short of the "all clear" I'd hoped for, but I'd received a reprieve and some much-needed time to refine my plan.

My mom stood up and squeezed my hand. "Why don't you try to sleep? We'll run more tests tomorrow."

I nodded.

"I'll be in my office if you need anything, okay?" Dad said, seeming like he didn't want to leave but knew he should.

"Thanks," I said, then added, "I'm glad you're here."

He kissed the top of my head. "I wouldn't be anywhere else."

He followed my mom out of the room, and I lay back thinking about all the other places he could be. I thought of where we all should be right now and how that contrasted with where we were. Tomorrow I'd concern myself with ways to deal with the disparity between those realities, but if I had any hope of facing the challenges ahead, tonight I needed to sleep.

❖

With the exception of shift change, it's always hard to tell the time of day in a hospital. In a room without windows, noon often feels similar to midnight, and given my current dilemma, I was particularly sensitive to time deprivation. Each time I woke up throughout the night, I immediately reached for my iPhone, only to be hit with a wave of disorienting sadness that it hadn't been invented yet. I stared at the stark-white ceiling. What other resources did I have at my disposal? I had to find a way back to the future—or what should be present day. But since I'd yet to decide what'd actually happened, the dilemma overwhelmed me so fully I feared another relapse into panic.

I had to focus on staying out of the mental ward. As soon as my mother believed I'd had enough time to rest, her questions would get tougher and more detailed. While some amount of memory loss seemed acceptable after a concussion, I needed to remember the big-picture items from my senior year. I wished again for a wireless connection to Google this day in history. I had to find another way to orient myself to the current time.

A nurse peeked around the curtain quietly. "You're awake."

"Yeah, kind of. I've been dozing."

"Do you want me to get your mom? She's in her on-call room."

"No, don't bother her. She probably needs some rest too."

The nurse patted my hand, no doubt thinking me a very caring daughter. "How's your pain?"

"Manageable. My headache's almost gone."

She checked the contents of my IV bag and referenced a chart near my monitor. "You're still on the pain meds."

"Oh, well, my vision is better too."

"That's encouraging," she said. "But don't overdo it. You don't need to be reading or watching TV yet."

Reading and TV. What great ideas, if not for the part where she said I shouldn't use them. "Okay, I guess I should probably get some more rest then."

She patted my arm. "I'll check back in an hour with your next dose of meds. I'm sure your mom will be in then too."

An hour. I had one hour to get my act together. I considered turning on the TV but worried the noise would attract too much attention. Prohibitions on reading be damned. I needed to find a newspaper.

I slid off the gurney and tested my balance. Aside from being brutally cold on my bare feet, the floor remained solid, and I slowly came to trust it wouldn't roll or pitch beneath me like it had at the assembly. Actually, I felt steadier than I expected overall. Even my head didn't hurt much. Honestly, most mornings felt at least this rough before I had my coffee. They must have given me the good meds.

Moving a few steps in either direction as far as my IV would allow me to go without drawing attention to myself, I searched for a magazine. I spotted an old *Highlights* on the chair next to the bed, but that wouldn't help much. I checked behind the curtain and found a small trashcan. Praying the janitor hadn't been overzealous last night, I tiptoed over and rifled through the top layer looking for anything with a date on it. Just under some sterile gauze packaging I found a

Darlington newspaper. They came out only once a week, which meant this one was probably a few days old, but it would have to do.

I scooted back over to the bed and climbed in as quietly as I could. The front-page story was about a local nursing home's big fund-raiser, a spaghetti dinner. The event had been Olympics themed. The Olympics. They apparently had just ended in Salt Lake City. Good to know. I searched my memory for more detail. I could only think of funding scandals and Mitt Romney, but were these things I knew from high school or from his yet-to-happen presidential run? I had no memory of watching the games.

I kept flipping and found a piece about a recent anthrax scare in St. Louis that turned out to be nothing. Anthrax. Should I be scared of chemical weapons? Did I hate the Dixie Chicks? September eleventh would still be fresh in everyone's mind. Should I be worried? *Yeah, try me. I'm a New Yorker.* Except I wasn't yet. I'd only been there once, just a few months ago when we'd visited NYU and Columbia. I remembered the visit vividly and added it to my mental list of conversation topics.

Another story was about someone from Darlington serving in Afghanistan. He said he could be there for up to a year but doubted the war would last that long. I said a silent prayer for him and for the many more to come who couldn't begin to imagine what they were in for.

I flipped one more page to the obituaries and probably would've skimmed past them if not for last name Deveroux in bold letters over the picture of a middle-aged couple. I didn't need to read the story for my eyes to fill with tears.

Beth's parents had died instantly when a drunk driver crossed the centerline and hit them head-on. I had attended the visitation with my parents, apparently just last weekend, and waited in line over an hour to pay our respects. Poor Beth. She'd just lost her parents. She must be devastated.

She couldn't imagine the woman she'd become. She didn't have Rory by her side. Did she have anyone? Could I help in some way? I might be able to give her a hug. She seemed to like those. But what would I say? The things I knew about her would only throw her into more chaos, and my sudden interest in her life after years of casual interactions would likely only draw attention to both of us. Besides, I hoped I wasn't stuck in the past, or this nightmare, or whatever I was experiencing for much longer.

"She was awake earlier but resting calmly," the nurse said from just outside the door.

"Any change in her vitals?" my mother asked.

I quickly stuffed the newspaper under the children's magazine, lay back, and closed my eyes.

"Everything's normal. Nothing to suggest she's not completely healthy."

"No," my mother said, "nothing outwardly anyway."

"Mallory," my father warned her, "don't assume the worst."

"I'm a doctor and a mother. That's never a good combination in a hospital."

"Admitting it is the first step to recovery."

I heard the curtain slide back and hoped my theater class with Jody had given me enough to do an adequate job of acting the part of someone just roused from sleep. "Hi, Mom and Dad."

"Good morning. How you feeling?" my mom asked, her hand going immediately to my forehead.

"I'm a lot better."

"Good to hear," Dad said. "You gave us quite a scare last night."

I didn't know how to respond. Should I try to explain my behavior, or should I feign innocence? Seeing as I had no explanation, I chose option B. "I'm sorry. I don't remember a lot about last night."

My mother frowned. Clearly I'd given the wrong answer. "Do you remember why you're here?"

At least I knew the answer to this one. "I got hit with a basketball, and it knocked me out."

"Do you remember how you got here?"

"No." Honesty was probably the best policy on that one. "I know Mrs. Snow helped me. She was still here when I woke up."

That got a nod of approval. "Do you remember anything you told her at the high school?"

"No." I answered perhaps too quickly. Then I pretended to mull it over. "I don't remember anything from the school."

"You don't remember talking to Miss Hadland?"

Shit, what has she told them? Surely she wouldn't have outed herself. "Not really. I remember her asking me questions, like my name. Was that at the hospital or school?"

"The school." My mom wasn't giving me much in the way of context clues, probably on purpose.

I couldn't help but ask. "I don't remember her at the hospital though. Was she here?"

"She came with you, but Mrs. Snow sent her home before you woke up," my dad explained, but my mom gave him a look clearly indicating he'd interfered with her investigation. They did the whole good cop, bad cop thing well.

"Do you know who the president is?"

I grimaced. "Unfortunately, George W. Bush."

My father snorted, but my mother stayed focused. "What's your favorite class this semester?"

I smiled. This answer was the same one I'd given Jody two nights ago, or ten years from now. "Theater with Miss Hadland."

"I thought Mr. Owens taught theater," Dad said.

"Miss Hadland's the student teacher right now for both his classes. She's infinitely superior."

Mom smiled. "You haven't forgotten your vocabulary."

"Where are you planning to go to college?" Dad asked, sounding like he just couldn't stand to be left out of the game of twenty questions.

"NYU."

"Really?" they both asked.

Shit, had I not decided yet? Too late now, and what difference did it make in the long run? "I'm pretty sure that's where I want to go. If it's okay with you."

"Of course it is," Mom said, breaking out of doctor mode to hug me.

Dad wrapped his arms around both of us. "We're proud of you, Stevie."

He did sound proud, but he sounded sad too. He likely knew what I hadn't understood the first time we'd had this conversation. This spring would mark the last time we'd live within eight hundred miles of each other. We'd visit and talk on the phone, but from here on out my life would be my own, distinct from theirs.

Did their knowledge of those facts explain the freedom they gave me during my senior year? Of course they'd trusted me, but perhaps they were also preparing me to live on my own. That free rein would be helpful as I tried to figure out why I'd returned to this moment, but it also made me a little regretful of my attempt to leave the past behind since I'd be leaving them a second time.

❖

My afternoon passed slowly between bouts of boredom and waves of sheer panic. On the surface everything seemed mundane, familiar, even comfortable at times. If I was still in high school, getting knocked out in front of my friends would have embarrassed me, but otherwise I wouldn't have had much to say about the aftermath of my injury. However, I wasn't supposed to be in high school, so even the most normal of interactions sent me spinning to the brink of a panic attack. Only the continuing threat of a mental hospital kept my complete breakdown at bay.

I slept when I could, simply because it was my only uncomplicated option. When I slept, I didn't think. I didn't even dream. Part of me still believed this whole ordeal was a dream. It felt like the kind of thing my mind would do to torture my nights. I'd always had the most vivid imagination, which served me well as a writer but often made for restless nights. The prospect of this all being an elaborate nightmare seemed like the most logical possibility, and I drifted off to sleep many times expecting to awaken back in my own bed, or at least on the stage in the gym. Each time I opened my eyes, I suffered a nauseating sort of mental whiplash from being jerked back eleven years into my past.

I also seriously considered that I might actually be in a coma. Perhaps I did have a stroke at the awards assembly. I had no idea how comas worked since most of my references came from movies or soap operas, but didn't some people report vivid dreams when they came to? Maybe I just needed rest or a medical procedure, and I'd wake up in this very hospital but back in the right year. If I wasn't having a run-of-the-mill bad dream, I favored the coma theory the best. Of course that meant I'd suffered a stroke, probably a pretty bad one if

I'd slipped into a coma. I might have complications when I came to. But at least this prospect was logical and one I would awaken from. I *would* wake up, right? Didn't some people stay in comas forever? Or just die as a result? Clearly, the option had some flaws.

The final explanation, the one I feared most, the one I guarded against at all times, was the possibility I'd actually suffered a mental break. What if my mother had been right in her initial assessment and I'd completely fabricated a future for myself, one I hadn't lived, one I might never live? My first reason for rejecting this theory was the sheer level of detail in my memories. Then again, didn't most crazy people believe the truth of their claims? Wasn't that what made them crazy? If I'd simply created an elaborately detailed life in my mind but knew it to be false, I'd just be, well, probably a writer.

Was I susceptible to this particular brand of insanity because of my artistic side? Fiction writers weren't exactly known for their grip on reality. Maybe I should embrace a psychological evaluation instead of hiding from one.

I might've given up completely and checked myself into the psych ward if not for the memory of Jody's face when I nearly outed her. If I were only eighteen, I would've known her for little more than a month and would've never had a one-on-one conversation with her. I would've never thought to call her Jody, and even if I'd guessed her sexual orientation, I wouldn't have any details about her life in years past or her fears about the future. Furthermore, her reaction had made it clear I hadn't just stumbled onto some random teacher's insecurity. No, Jody held the key to my sanity, or what was left of it anyway, and if by some aberration of the laws of time and nature I wasn't experiencing a nightmare or medical breakdown, Jody might be the only thing grounding me to a future I'd already lived.

❖

Saturday dawned much the same way as the day before, with a nurse coming to check on me. They now let me sleep for longer periods of time. They'd also removed my IV and started feeding me normal food again. I suspected if my mother wasn't working this weekend, they would've sent me home by now. Home? Could I just go back into my old room and sleep in my old bed? I didn't seem to have much choice in the matter. At least the room might jog my memories about this stage in my life. My mother had stopped her quiz-style questions, but I knew other details were missing and feared them popping up to blow my cover.

As if on cue, I was drawn from my reflections by a knock at my already-open door. Jody stepped timidly into the room, her eyes filled with concern.

"Hi," I said.

"Hi. Want some company?"

"Sure." I sat up and tried to run my hands through my bed head, but it was no use. My hair was too unruly to be tamed without the serums and relaxers I wouldn't have access to for years.

"How you feeling?"

"Better," I said, then hedged my bets. "A few things are a little hazy, but I'm slowly getting back to my old self, you know?"

"I don't really."

"Oh?"

"I've only known you about a month," she said softly. "I'm sorry, but when you went down the other night, I didn't even know your last name."

I shifted nervously. "Bet you'll remember it now."

She sighed. "Yes, I'm sure I will."

"Nothing like a dramatic concussion to get the teacher's attention."

"Stevie," she said, then stopped, rubbed her eyes, and tried again. "You know I'm not here about the concussion, right?"

"Do I?" Of course I did. Her beautiful eyes were dark and sunken. She clearly hadn't slept, and she perched so precariously close to the edge of the chair I feared she might topple off. I fought hard against my instinct to soothe her. How could I explain something I didn't understand, something I'd told my parents I didn't remember?

"Do you honestly not recall the conversation we had in the locker room?"

"I'm sorry. I remember you being there. I remember…I was scared and confused. I'm sorry if I said something…rude?"

Her eyes narrowed suspiciously. "Have you and I ever seen each other outside of school?"

"I don't think so."

"We've never talked about, I don't know, anything?"

I exhaled. I wanted to help her so much my head throbbed, but how could I? I didn't want to lie. I didn't want to make her feel as crazy as I did. What could I possibly tell her to ease her fears without giving myself away? "I don't know what to say, Jod—Miss Hadland."

Her eyes widened. "What did you call me?"

"Miss Hadland," I answered quickly.

"No, you started to call me 'Jody.'"

"I didn't mean to. You can trust me about that, and anything else I might have said while concussed," I said slowly, trying to convey my sincerity with every word. "It's over now. It won't happen again."

"Thank you." She blinked away a tear. "But there's more, isn't there? You're not telling me something. Something you know, somehow."

"I don't. I just…I don't really know what you mean."

"I'm not sure either, but you can talk to me. I need you to talk to me." She sighed. "I'm sorry if I scared you the other night, but we can't help each other if we don't open up to each other."

Open up? You have no idea what you're asking. She wanted me to tell her about herself, or at least what I knew about her. She believed she'd put herself at risk by coming here, but she couldn't understand how every minute spent talking to me risked exposing something bigger and more complicated than her sexual orientation. Even under the best of circumstances, I wasn't a risk taker. Now, in the face of her anguish, I was an outright coward. How could I make her see I couldn't give her what she needed, but that had nothing to do with her?

"I feel badly, but I don't remember what I said to scare everyone."

She rolled her head from side to side, trying to relax her neck. "All right. Maybe it was me, or maybe it was nothing. I could be crazy for all I know."

My heart ached with the knowledge that I was likely the crazy one and with the disappointment that I'd let her bear any responsibility for my issues. Thankfully, we were interrupted before I caved and aired my own insecurities in a misguided attempt to rescue her.

"Hello, Miss Hadland," my mom said from the doorway. Dad stood behind her wearing new set of clothes. They'd both obviously gotten some rest last night.

"Hello, Doctor and Mr. Geller." Jody stood to shake their hands.

"It's nice of you to come visit Stevie on your Saturday morning."

"She gave us quite the scare the other day. I don't want to keep her up too long, but I wanted to check on her."

"That's dedication," Dad said. "No wonder you're Stevie's favorite teacher."

Jody blushed and glanced back at me. "I find that hard to believe. I've only had Stevie in class for a month."

"No, it's true. We asked her yesterday, and she said you were 'infinitely superior' to her other teachers."

"Dad." My embarrassment registered so clearly in my tone even I had no problem believing I was a teenager.

"What a nice ego boost for a student teacher who's only been on the job for a few weeks. I wouldn't have thought I'd been around long enough to make an impression on Stevie at all," Jody said, then regarded me closely once more. "Stevie has a lot more going on under her quiet surface than I previously realized."

"We're very proud of her," Dad said, missing the private message behind her words. "Did you know she's planning to go to NYU in the fall?"

"Impressive choice."

"Do you think they'll challenge her a little more than Darlington High School?" my mother asked.

"Possibly, but I'll keep a close eye on her this semester and make sure she has what she needs to succeed. There'll be no time for senioritis with the future she's got planned."

My dad laughed. "Did you hear that, Stevester? There'll be no getting away from this one. She's going to ride you hard."

I coughed and stared down at my lap, trying to avoid the inappropriate thoughts flashing through my mind.

"I'd better get going," Jody said, her smile likely appearing genuine to my parents, but I detected her emotional strain just beyond the façade. "I don't want to wear out the patient."

"I'll show you out," Dad offered.

"Good-bye, Miss Hadland," I said.

"Feel better, Stevie."

I watched her go, craning my neck a little to follow her petite form down the hallway. When she was out of sight, I noticed my mother watching me intently.

"How you feeling?" she asked.

"Much better," I said honestly. Even seeing Jody upset was better than not seeing her at all.

"You certainly have a lot more color to your complexion this morning," she said. "Is there anything else you want to tell me?"

God, would the questions never end? I wouldn't come out to her until I went away to college. Her reaction came back to me in vivid detail now, sending a chill up my spine. It's not that she didn't take it well. On the contrary, she'd said she'd known for years and quipped, "A mother always knows, but you have to let your children find out some things for themselves."

I shook off the echo of the future and wondered what else she already knew but refused to say.

❖

I went home with my mother when her shift ended. While the hospital was familiar, its cleanliness and uniformity saved me from the sensory recall that overwhelmed me when I entered my old room. The place was a mess. Aside from the clean sheets my dad had probably put on the bed, the space looked lived in. It felt surreal to see my touches freshly applied to a room I hadn't occupied for ages. Books lay scattered and stacked everywhere—some I remembered, some I didn't. An ancient laptop sat on a desk, and I recalled how proud I'd been to receive the computer. At the time it had seemed almost magical compared to the bulky desktop in the family room.

A pile of clothes lay on the floor in the corner. Had I really liked turquoise that much? I opened my closet and examined a horrifying array of peasant tops and shockingly low-rise jeans. Surely I owned some looser-fitting pants?

One step at a time. I spied a tracksuit tossed over my desk chair. The white pants also had turquoise accents, but fashion wasn't my top priority now. After several nights in a hospital gown, anything offered a step up in both comfort and visual appeal. I slipped out of the pair of scrubs my mom had lent me before leaving the hospital. They were too big, and well, *my mom's*—an awkward combination in any decade. I held up the pants of the tracksuit only to notice the impossibly small waist and rolled my eyes. I'd never fit into them. They had to be a size six. I found the tag. Nope, a size four. I actually laughed aloud. No effing way had I ever worn a size four.

I turned to the large mirror over my dresser and started to pinch the fat around my middle, only to stop with my pinching finger empty over a freakishly flat stomach. "My God, I'm skinny."

I stared at the reflection of my teenage body, lean and fit and a size four. A size four? I'd always hated my appearance in high school. I'd considered myself chunky. I never thought I looked like the girls in the magazines, but damn, I was close. I patted the spot where my paunch would develop in the coming years and laughed again.

"Hello, abs," I said to the mirror. "Of all the things I'll lose, I think I'll miss you most. And boobs, I hate to break it to you, but you're never going to get any bigger. You will, however, get lower."

I stared at myself long and hard, wondering what kind of teenage hell had made me disdain this reflection every morning of my youth. Would I look back on my thirty-year-old body with the same sense of wonder when I was forty-five?

My hair shot out in a crazy mess, of course, but it seemed hard to complain when the hair came with the body of an eighteen-year-old. The thought shook me out of my amusement. I was admiring a teenager's body. My own, but still—was it wrong for a grown woman to be so pleased about an eighteen-year-old's flat stomach and high breasts? *Awkward.* I pulled on the track pants and chose a faded T-shirt from the floor.

Wandering around the room, I tried to jog my memory. I picked up books and pictures, trying to remember their significance. Did they have any significance, or were they merely snapshots of a fleeting moment in my life? Of course I knew what mattered in the long run, but how could I tell what held importance for me at eighteen? I sat on the bed and sifted through remnants of my life for an hour but still felt no closer to understanding why I was here. Or what I should do about it.

My room was in our full, finished basement, and I'd also inherited the adjacent rec room and bathroom all to myself when my older brother left for college. Honestly, the space probably had a few more square feet than my current apartment but certainly lacked the view. Still, I appreciated the privacy as I went through my old things. Mom checked on me once. She touched my forehead, even though both of us were certain I didn't have a fever. She probably just wanted to make a physical connection. An hour later, Dad brought down some fried rice and a purple Gatorade, two of my favorites. Aside from the ever-present fear that they'd ask me a question I couldn't answer, I kind of enjoyed having them take care of me again.

There were worse places to be stuck than my parents' house. I could have landed in an utter nightmare or some truly awful place to spend a coma.

Oh. My. Gawd!

I couldn't believe I'd actually complimented my choice of places to have a coma. This couldn't be happening. I shouldn't be here. I certainly couldn't stay here. My senior year had been just fine, but it was finished and needed to stay that way. Now on my third night in my past, worry clawed at my chest. Nothing made sense, and I'd come no closer to finding any answers than I had been in the locker room.

What if I got stranded here?

What if I'd never actually been anywhere else?

It had been so much easier to argue away those possibilities with Jody in front of me. Now, alone in a basement bedroom that hadn't been mine for years, self-doubt and helplessness rolled in around me like an oppressive fog. Either the world had gone crazy or I had, and there didn't appear to be anything I could do. Giving in to the darkness I could no longer hold at bay, I closed my door and cried myself to sleep.

CHAPTER FOUR

My crying jag from the night before must have worn me out, or maybe it was the mental strain of questioning my sanity, but either way I slept until almost noon the next day. Disappointment threatened to consume me before I'd even fully awakened, as once again I suffered through the disorientation of opening my eyes to a past I wasn't eager to repeat. I used what little fortitude I had left to hold my desperation in check. I showered, then rifled through my dresser drawers for something that didn't make me look like an aquamarine cross between Britney Spears and Laura Ingalls Wilder before settling on sweat pants and the only hoodie I appeared to own. I fought off another wave of frustration. Who only owns one hoodie?

A knock on the door interrupted my fashion commentary. "Stevie, you've got company," Mom said.

Company? Jody? My spirits rose at the prospect of seeing her again, but they plummeted when I opened my bedroom door to a teenage girl holding a backpack.

"Hey, Stevie. How you feeling?" the girl asked.

"Good. Much better," I said, trying to act normal while I searched her hazel eyes and pale complexion for some clue as to her identity. My mom stood behind her, and I didn't want to hint at my confusion for fear she'd whisk me back to the hospital.

"Lucky you have such a hard head." She laughed, flipping a switch in my mind.

"Yeah, thanks for coming by, Nikki." *Nikki Belliard.* Nikki, who would marry Rory's little brother. Nikki, who'd become an elementary teacher. Nikki, who didn't know any of that but was still nice enough to check on me.

"Do you want to come in?" I asked.

"Duh." She handed me her backpack on her way past me.

I glanced at my mom, who nodded her approval before turning to go. "Just don't get too wound up. You're supposed to be resting."

Nikki flopped onto my bed. "You're welcome for bringing your stuff home."

My stuff? I looked at the bag. So this was mine, not hers. Good to know. I fought the urge to dump its contents on the bed and rummage through them for clues the way an animal rifles through trash in search of food. "Yeah, thanks."

"So, do you have amnesia or something?" Nikki asked.

"What? No. Why would you say that?"

"Chill out, I'm just teasing, 'cause you got hit on the head, remember?"

"Oh, yeah," I said casually. Did everyone expect me to have forgotten something? My mom told my dad short-term memory loss was common with a concussion, and now Nikki implied the same. How much could I use that excuse without sounding too many alarms? I decided to test the waters. "I actually don't remember the basketball game at all."

"Really? Wow." Nikki propped up on her elbow, and I scooted farther from the bed under the guise of searching for something in my desk. I guess in high school it was common enough to lie around with a friend, but in the intervening years I'd learned straight girls in my bed never led to anything good.

"I just, I forget things until someone reminds me. Then it all comes rushing back. The info isn't gone. It's just not up front where I need it."

Nikki's expression turned serious. "Did you tell your mom?"

"Yeah," I lied. "She said short-term memory loss is normal, but I don't want to worry her with the details. I'm fine really. I was just wondering if maybe you could help me with a few things for school tomorrow."

"Sure." She sat up all the way, eager to be of aid. Memories of her filled my mind. She was one of the good ones, a joiner of student council, sports, yearbook committee. She'd know everything. I needed to keep her close without frightening her to the point that she'd tell my mom how much help I needed.

"I know I'm taking theater and AP English with Miss Hadland." I opened my backpack and spread the books out in front of me. The first one was a Spanish book. Right, four years of Spanish. *Whole lot of good that did me.* "And I've got Spanish with Señora Wallace."

"Yup, I'm glad she's back from maternity leave. The sub drove me crazy."

"Yes!" I said, perhaps overly excited to remember another piece of minutia. "She had a little girl."

Nikki nodded, unimpressed.

I pulled a trigonometry book from the backpack. "Then trig with Mr. Glass, who also teaches keyboarding, right?"

"Right."

Then I was out of books. I did a quick count; something had to be missing. "What classes do we have together?"

"Spanish, trig, gym, and study hall."

Gym and study hall, those were the last two. Whew, I had a full schedule. Now I needed to put it in order. I said a silent prayer that went something like *please let me wake up before school tomorrow, please, please, please if there is a God or a doctor out there who can help me, please, please, please save me from high school.* But while I'd always suspected God existed, I'd seen little evidence she worked on call, so I decided to hedge my bets by taking a little chance. "Okay, I remember all my classes and teachers, and I remember I have English first, then Spanish, and theater is last, but I forgot the rest of the order.

"After Spanish is trig, then study hall," she said slowly, all amusement replaced by concern. "Then I think you have keyboarding, but I'm not in that class."

"And gym comes before I go to theater," I said, filling in the blank. "See, I told you I could remember once someone jump-starts me."

"Will you forget again before tomorrow?"

I hope not. I should probably write the schedule down just in case. "No. Once it's back, it's back to stay."

"Good." She stood up. "'Cause class was no fun without you on Friday, and I had to sit all by myself at our lockers in the morning."

Our lockers? They were right next to each other. She handed me another puzzle piece to snap into place.

"See you tomorrow?"

"Probably." I tried not to sound too terrified.

She hugged me good-bye, and I awkwardly put one arm around to pat her back. I wasn't much on hugging practical strangers good-bye, but then again, it wasn't often a stranger also happened to be my best friend.

Monday morning hadn't yet dawned when my mom knocked on my door. I used the darkness of my room to hide my fear and disappointment at waking up in my parents' home yet again. I hated the sickening feeling that accompanied the realization but hoped I wouldn't be around long enough to grow used to it.

"How you feeling?" Mom asked, taking a seat on the side of my bed.

"I'm fine." I grumbled, tired of the question and the lie I always told in response.

"Ready to go back to school?"

"Already?"

"It's been four days, but if you're not feeling well enough, you should tell me now."

I traced the seams of my bedspread with my index finger while I considered my choices. I didn't want to go to school. The thought of walking into those crowded hallways or sitting exposed to the world in a little desk while trying to remember knowledge I'd never used almost froze me in panic. However, if I wanted to stay home, I'd face more questions, ones I might not have the answers to. Would I blow my cover? Would my mom run more tests? Would she seek a psychiatric evaluation just to be cautious? I couldn't risk it. At least at school I could fade into the crowd. At home, I'd be on my own.

I gritted my teeth and tried to compose myself the best I could, given the circumstances and ungodly hour. "I guess I should go to school."

"All right then, but I want you to promise you'll call me if you get overwhelmed or start to experience any concussion symptoms, okay?"

"Sure, Mom." I hoped I wouldn't have to, but I rated the prospect of being overwhelmed at some point in the day to be pretty high. In fact, I was quickly approaching it now.

An hour later, I stood in front of the double doors I'd entered with Jody just last week. And to think I'd found the experience surreal then.

I took a deep breath and started an internal pep talk I hoped to keep running all day. *Keep your head low, get in, get through, get out. You did this once. You can do it again.*

I entered the long, locker-lined hallway with my eyes on the floor a few feet in front of me, refusing to make eye contact with anyone. The corridor wasn't too crowded since I'd gotten there a little early in the hopes of finding more clues in my locker. Now if only I could find it. I had some vague memory of it being on the first floor, so I headed there first. The thing about lockers, though, is they all look exactly alike on the outside, so unless I remembered the number, I was out of luck. I reached the end of the hallway and turned back around, still focused on my feet.

The start of my second pass through the hallway came to an abrupt halt when my shoulder collided with someone else's, sending us both stumbling back a few feet. "Sorry," I muttered.

"Sure you are." Something about the voice caught my attention. Something familiar, but not because I recognized the speaker so much as I recognized the emotion behind it. The low tone held a palpable resignation, as if the person had reconciled herself to some sort of torment while simultaneously resenting the lot she'd drawn. I'd come to recognize the characteristic in New York among broken artists and stockbrokers alike. I'd even felt the stirrings of that depression in myself over the past couple days. But I'd never expected to hear such darkness in someone so young. Curiosity overcame fear. I broke my rule against making eye contact and stared into the haunting brown eyes of Kelsey Patel.

I jumped back and gasped. By now I probably should've been used to the shocks that accompanied losing eleven years of my life, but nothing could have prepared me to meet the very living gaze of a dead girl. Apparently, being gawked at was nothing new for Kelsey, who shook her head. "What's your problem?"

"I, um…I just—" *I see dead people?* "Concussion."

"What?"

"I have a concussion. I got hit in the head, and then when you, I mean when I bumped into you—"

"Oh," her expression softened, and she pushed a strand of straight, dark hair out of her face. "Did it hurt?"

"No, I just…I don't know. I got disoriented."

"Maybe you shouldn't be here." She didn't have even the hint of an accent, suggesting she wasn't a first-generation American, but her darker complexion made her stand out against the pasty white winter tones of the rest of the school.

"You have no idea how much I shouldn't be here right now," I said before I could check myself.

"Then go home."

I choked up. Home. Where was that? When was that? And more importantly, would I ever get back there? "I'm fine, thanks."

Kelsey shrugged, her defenses falling back into place. "Whatever."

She walked on, but I stood rooted to the floor at my end of the hallway. Why had I thought I could survive this day? I'd always been able to slide by unnoticed, but I had too many variables now. Tears welled up in my eyes. I'd barely held myself together when the worst thing I had to face was trigonometry, but throwing long-dead teenagers into the mix pushed me over the edge. I'd made a valiant effort but couldn't do it. I'd lost my motivation. My heart rate slowed, and my limbs grew unbearably lethargic. I'd given up and started shutting down. I needed to check myself back into the hospital. I was about to lie down when the office door opened and Jody stepped into the hallway.

So beautiful, so young, so vibrant, she had her fair hair pulled back in a ponytail, giving me a clear view of her intoxicating smile and the hint of a sparkle in her blue eyes. She wore a navy skirt with white piping. I'm sure she thought the ensemble made her appear older, but in reality it appeared she'd raided her mom's closet. Someday she'd learn students respected her for what she did in the classroom and not because she wore pantyhose to cover her deliciously muscled calves. Someday she'd find her voice and her power, but in the meantime she was stunning in her search. Why hadn't I kissed her when I'd had the chance?

She turned abruptly, as if sensing me watching her, and all the exuberance faded from her smile. Her expression remained polite but grew increasingly distant the closer she got to me.

"Walk with me?" she asked, her teacher voice clearly negating the question mark on the end of her sentence.

What could I do? Even if she wasn't an authority figure, I would've readily agreed to follow her anywhere.

She headed quickly into the stairwell and then slowed. "How are you feeling?"

"Fine, physically. I guess I'm mostly back to normal."

"What about emotionally?"

Of course she'd pick up on that. I smiled in spite of the turmoil spinning inside me. "I don't know. A little overwrought, I suppose."

"How can I help you, Stevie?"

"You have bigger issues to worry about right now."

She stopped and finally met my eyes. "What issues would those be?"

Shit, why did I keep doing this? I only wanted to help, to let her off the hook. I didn't mean to imply I had some sort of inside knowledge. "You're a student teacher. You've got lesson plans to write, people to impress, and papers to research. That can't be easy, especially under the microscopic gaze of Drew Phillips."

"First of all, you're very empathetic to think about my workload and academic responsibilities. Not many high-school seniors ever give a thought to what student teachers do."

"Well, I've been thinking about college a lot lately."

She nodded skeptically. "Second, *Mr.* Phillips is the gym teacher. I don't know what he has to do with anything."

I hung my head. I needed to shut up. "Right. I'm sorry. Maybe I'm not back to my old self yet."

"Stevie, if you don't talk to me, I can't help you."

Trust me. Even if I did talk, you couldn't help me. I had to give her something else to focus on. "I do need my assignments for your classes on Friday. Maybe you could help me with those."

She stared at me for a long, heavy minute before sighing. "Why don't you come in during your study hall, and I'll go over the lessons with you."

"Sounds great." Like a fool I smiled and nodded when I should've run. She was the one person at school who was really onto me. I should stay as far away from her as possible, not set up extra time in her presence, but I couldn't stop myself.

The door to the stairs opened below us, and I glanced down to see Nikki. "Hey, I gotta go, okay?"

Jody nodded. "All right."

I made my escape before I could do or say anything else. Nikki saw me coming and laughed. "Did you forget what floor your locker is on?"

"Something like that," I said, giving one last look over my shoulder at Jody, who stood on the landing watching me go. My chest ached at the sight of her. She was too smart and too intuitive to be put off for long. Sooner or later we'd have to have a serious conversation about the connections we shared, and somehow that prospect wasn't nearly as unpleasant as it should've been.

The morning went surprisingly well. I sat in the back of the class during English, and Jody, ever the professional, didn't once hint that anything was going on between us other than a teacher/student relationship. And we were about to start reading Tim O'Brien's *The Things They Carried,* which was totally in my literary wheelhouse. Aside from the occasional stab of attraction toward the teacher, I felt like I had the class under control.

Spanish got off to a solid start because Nikki directed me to my assigned seat without me even having to ask. Señora Wallace told me I could take all the time I needed to catch up on my work. I wondered how long it would take to relearn Spanish. Of course in New York I'd picked up a few words, but I doubted any of the things my Puerto

Rican neighbors shouted at each other would ever show up on a high-school test. Trigonometry was even less eventful, with Mr. Glass working through problems on the board. I could've been there or not, and he would've never known the difference.

By the time I got to keyboarding, I'd begun to think I could actually pull this off. Nikki wasn't in the class with me, but thanks to my career choice, I had better than average computer and typing skills. Plus, if Mr. Glass's class-engagement policy was anything like it had just been in trig, I didn't have to worry about drawing attention to myself. I took a chance on not having assigned seats and chose a computer in the back of the room. I was so engrossed in trying to remember the ins and outs of Windows after being a Mac user for years, I didn't notice Kelsey attempt to take the seat next to me until she landed on the floor.

I stared down at her sitting in a splay of legs and notebooks. She took a few deep breaths and gathered her things quietly.

"What happened?" I asked. "Did you miss the chair?"

She glared at me. "Yeah, it must have jumped right out from under me."

I extended my hand, and she looked at it like I might hit her. When she realized I only meant to help her up, she glanced over her shoulder quickly. I followed her line of sight to three guys snickering in the opposite corner. All the pieces made sense. They'd kicked the chair out from under her just as she began to sit down, but instead of going off on them she was protecting me by not involving me in the situation.

She stood on her own and stacked her books neatly beside her without another word.

I pulled her chair closer. "Are you okay?"

"Fine," she said through clenched teeth.

She wasn't fine, clearly. Even if I didn't know how this part of my dream ended, I could see she'd already neared her breaking point. Why did I have so few memories of her? Had I blocked them or just been too absorbed in my own survival skills to pay attention to the trials of anyone else?

I turned back to the guys. Two of them had moved on, but the third one stared me down. His broad shoulders and muscled chest alone dwarfed Kelsey's whole body. He had dark facial hair and the sneer that suggested he might have failed a grade somewhere along the way. Michael Redly. My memory had blocked the name until now. A football star with rugged good looks and an alpha-male mentality, he served as a living stereotype of a first-rate jock and top-notch asshole.

I turned away to hide the burn of shame under my skin. I didn't want to shy away from a bully, but damned if I wasn't a little afraid of him. He had the power to make anyone's high-school existence hell, and I couldn't handle one more complication now. Making myself a target could expose me to all sorts of problems that went well beyond my social status.

Thankfully, Mr. Glass entered the room and started class, which is to say he gave us our assignment. We had to type a 500-word piece he projected onto the whiteboard, then copy and paste it into three different documents. Why? I don't know, but high school had never been the place to search for logic.

I opened a new document and began to type. I kept my eyes on the projection page while my fingers flew across the keyboard. The entire exercise would take ten minutes max. I wondered what we'd do after our warm-up. I snuck a peek at the clock as I neared the end of my assignment, only to notice Kelsey staring at me in wide-eyed, open-mouthed disbelief. She'd typed about three lines. The girl sitting to the side of me had finished about the same amount. I surreptitiously scanned the monitors around the room. No one else had more than a full paragraph while I moved onto my second page.

I immediately slowed down, but Kelsey had clearly seen my typing speed and the accompanying results. I took my sweet time proofreading the page but still finished before anyone else, so I clicked the keystrokes to copy and paste my work into new documents.

"How did you do that?" Kelsey whispered.

"What?"

"How did you just make the text appear without using your mouse?"

"I just hit control C to copy and control V to paste."

She tried, but nothing happened, causing her to glare at me incredulously.

"Sorry. You have to "select all" first. Do control A."

She repeated the process with the added step and actually smiled when it worked. "How did you learn to do that?"

"I don't know. I just picked it up somewhere along the way. It's no big deal. You could just use your mouse to do the same thing."

"Not when they unplug your mouse."

"What?"

She held up her computer mouse, and sure enough the cord dangled freely from the end that should've been connected to the computer tower.

"Just plug it back in."

"I have to crawl under the desk and reach behind the towers to find the right outlet."

I heard the unspoken fear. She'd be on the floor, out of sight of the teacher, and completely vulnerable to anyone around her. The keystrokes weren't just a matter of convenience. They offered safety.

I pursed my lips, trying to stem the temper I'd learned to express more readily in adulthood. I couldn't blow up in the middle of class, but I could still help her. "There's a bunch of shortcuts. Give me a piece of paper, and I'll write them out for you."

She pulled a sheet out of her spiral notebook, still looking a little leery. "Can you also write down how you learned to type that fast?"

I laughed nervously. "Lots of practice."

"In the last four days?" Kelsey asked. "'Cause you were slower than me last week."

"Really?" I shrugged. "Just been spacing out, I guess."

I lowered my head and set to work without waiting for a response. I'd made it almost to lunch before doing something stupid, and hopefully I could dodge this too. It seemed rude to think, but no one paid attention to Kelsey anyway. I needed to be more careful in the future about being too proficient in my studies though. I couldn't suddenly make a bid for valedictorian. I almost groaned when I realized I'd just considered my long-term prospects for survival. A few good hours did not contentment make. This dream had to end sometime, didn't it? Dare I hope for sometime soon? Just because I could keep up the charade didn't mean I wanted to.

I wandered into the hallway after the lunch bell. Thankfully we had open campus, and I could get away for a bit. I was headed for the front door when Nikki stopped me. "Where you going?"

"Um, out?"

"Did you bring your car?"

"No. Mom didn't think I should drive yet."

"Right, so where you going?"

"I was going to walk."

She shook her head like I'd lost my mind, and clearly this was not an unfair assumption.

"Or I could stay in," I offered weakly.

"Or you could go with me." She finally laughed. "You need a Happy Meal."

I cringed. I hadn't eaten at a McDonalds since I'd read *Fast Food Nation* in college. Which of course meant not yet. Maybe I could spring for something a little nicer. I felt my back pocket, finding it empty. Where was my wallet? Or didn't I carry one yet?

"What's the matter?" Nikki asked.

"I don't have my lunch money."

She smiled sweetly and threw her arm around my shoulder. "I'll cover you."

I wanted to run and hide, but I couldn't do this alone. I needed all the help I could get, and Nikki was offering me a lot, so I resigned myself to accepting her support as graciously as possible. "Thanks. I owe you one."

❖

Jody had her back to me as she bent over her desk to make a note on some papers. I rested my shoulder on the doorjamb to her classroom and let myself watch her. She hummed softly and swayed gently to the music in her head. She'd shed her suit coat, revealing a white oxford. The accompanying navy skirt hugged her hips in a way that made my breath catch painfully in my chest. She didn't seem so young anymore, and frankly, neither did I. Maybe the uptick in my libido came with the other youthful changes in my body, but even the most hormonally charged teenager wouldn't have been capable of imagining the scenarios that flashed through my mind. All hot-for-teacher fetishes aside, nothing good would ever come from my current line of thought.

I cleared my throat, startling Jody so badly she jumped, then landed, clutching her chest and laughing. "Stevie, I swear if you scare me one more time I'm going to give you a detention."

"I'm sorry." I laughed for the first time in days. "You told me to come in during my study hall."

"Right, I remember." She perched on the edge of her desk. "I just got lost in thought."

"Penny for them?"

"My thoughts?"

"Sure." I took a seat at the student desk closest to her. "Lay 'em on me."

She arched an eyebrow. "I think that might be an inappropriate request."

"Only if the thoughts are inappropriate."

"Stevie, look, you're a great kid, young woman, person." She sighed. "But you're a student, and you can't talk to me like a peer."

I wanted to scream, "*I am your peer.*" Instead I hung my head and said, "I didn't mean to be disrespectful."

"It's not that, but I'm trying to establish myself as a teacher. I'm trying to find my voice, and it's not easy."

"I'm sure it's not. You're only a few years older than I am, and you look younger than that. It's probably hard to make people take you seriously. But I do, and I'm sorry if my comments made you feel otherwise."

She opened her mouth like she wanted to say more but held back, so I pushed on tentatively. "You're a good teacher. You're going to be a great teacher someday. The students here need you, but I know that will take a toll on you personally."

"My personal life isn't the issue here," she said with conviction, but I noticed the tremble in her hands.

"No, of course not. I didn't mean to pry. I just thought if you were working on something—a lesson plan, a pedagogical statement, issues of classroom management, whatever—I could be a sounding board." I was floundering. The more I tried to be supportive, the more it sounded like a cheap come-on. I needed to shut up, but I couldn't. "You know, as a student. You help me see the lessons from your point of view. I help you see them from mine.

"You're very intuitive, aren't you?" she asked, seeming wary but not outright dismissive of my offer.

"I don't know."

"I pulled your file on Friday."

The sudden change in topics threw me. "Really? Why?"

She sat down beside me and toyed with a strand of hair that had fallen from her ponytail. "You can say you don't remember Thursday night, and maybe you don't, but you said things to me no seventeen-year-old should know."

"I'm eighteen." I didn't know why I felt the need to make that statement now. Perhaps I thought the extra year might lend me some credibility, but more likely I wanted her to know I was of legal age to make my own decisions.

"Still, your comments didn't make sense to me, so I went through your records to try to find some answers."

"And?" I'd kind of like some answers myself.

"You've got impressive transcripts. Great grades, high test scores, plenty of extracurricular activities. I'm not surprised you got into NYU."

"Why do I feel like there's bad news coming? Did you find I'm an elite operative for some underground literati organization?"

She shook her head, but the corner of her mouth twitched up, betraying amusement despite her serious tone. "No, there's nothing there to indicate you're anything other than an average high-school senior."

I exhaled a breath heavy with relief. "Well, that's good."

"Is it?" Her brow furrowed. "You seem like so much more than average to me. You're smart, and you notice things other teenagers don't. You're also maddeningly disarming."

My stomach did a little flip-flop move right up into my throat. She found me disarming?

"What I can't figure out is why no one else ever saw any of this in you."

"Saw? Past tense?" Had the heat gone up in the whole room or just under my collar? "Does that mean you have me pegged now?"

"See what I mean?" She held out her hand in my direction as if I'd just demonstrated a valuable piece of evidence. "You catch things. You make connections to larger conclusions. Why aren't you a student leader? Why aren't you at the top of your class? Why don't you even talk during class discussions?"

"I think you're digging for something that's not there. I don't extrapolate any great life lessons. I don't want to be a symbol or some voice crying out in the wilderness." I backpedaled quickly. This isn't where I'd wanted this conversation to go. *I'm not you. I'm not Rory.* "I'm solidly average."

"You're not. Average students don't say 'extrapolate' or talk about pedagogical statements or describe themselves in terms of ancient Biblical allusions."

I stood up, pushing away from the desk and trying not to pace. Of course I wasn't the average teenager, but what did she want me to say? That I was some sort of child genius? A literary savant? I didn't want to lie to her, but I couldn't tell the truth, either. Frustration twisted the muscles in my back. Even on my best days I didn't handle conflict well, and right now I was drowning in it. My defenses rose. "Why are you determined to label me as above average?"

She stepped closer, pushing just into my personal space and sending my blood pulsing through my ears. "Why are you so invested in believing the status quo is good enough?"

"It was good enough the first time, so forgive me if I want to stick with what worked until I figure out how to get out of here without going insane." I covered my mouth, then flopped back into the chair and put my head down on the desk. I couldn't pull the words back in, no matter how much I wished them away.

I sat perfectly still, part of me relieved to have it out there. Now maybe she could just call the hospital to come get me. At least then I wouldn't have to go to gym class.

"Stevie," she said softly, and crouched down so her face was next to mine. "Look at me."

I lifted my head and met those compassionate blue eyes, so soothing no matter the circumstances.

"You're not insane. And you're going to make it just fine. You're going to graduate in a few months. You're headed to NYU, and you'll thrive there. You and I both know that."

"Yeah," I said, my throat raw with emotion.

"I understand wanting to stick with what has worked for you in years past. Trust me, I know all about the urge to blend into the crowd. I don't fault you for that. I probably would've done the same if I could have."

I heard the pain in her voice. Even if I hadn't known her story, I wouldn't have doubted her sincerity.

"But unless we're willing to take some risks, to challenge the perceptions of ourselves, we're doomed to keep repeating our mistakes, to keep selling out and settling for good-enough when we could make a real difference."

Why the hell did everyone want to change me these days? First Edmond, then Rory, now Jody. I liked my life just fine. Well, except for the whole coma-nightmare scenario I was currently facing. Then again, I wouldn't be having this dream if people had left well-enough alone. "I appreciate what you're trying to do here. I really do, but I'm not one of your charity cases. I don't need you to unlock my hidden potential."

Her frown and sagging shoulders caused my chest to constrict so tight it nearly broke my heart. I didn't want to sound harsh, and I got an extra shot of guilt for using her reason for teaching against her, but the last thing I needed was extra scrutiny. Why did the one person I most wanted to be around pose the greatest risk?

"Fine," she said, returning to her polite professional façade. "I guess I misread the situation."

Of course she had. How could she not? Who looks at a high-school student and assumes she's a twenty-nine-year-old fiction writer in a time-travel nightmare? I wished this conversation could end differently, but I'd yet to find a way to make sense of anything, much less change it. Perhaps the best thing I could do for both of us was stick to the roles we knew. "Do you have those assignments I missed?"

She eyed me expectantly for a few seconds more before she acquiesced and became the teacher I'd asked her to be. I watched as she detached herself emotionally and physically distanced herself by returning to the other side of the desk. She shuffled paperwork, then began to recite an abbreviated version of last Friday's English-lit lesson plan. I missed her immediately, and I had only myself to blame, but this was just the way things had to be for us right now.

❖

I arrived in gym class with the golden ticket in my pocket. My mother, the doctor, had written a note excusing me from all exercise for up to ten days and anything that might risk physical contact for the rest of the month. There'd be no locker-room changes or awkward showers with real teenagers. I also wouldn't have to face basketball practice since they were in the last two weeks of the season. In fact, gym would've been a breeze if not for the prospect of facing Drew Phillips.

I could barely stomach the man for a photo op in present day with Rory by my side. I had no idea how I'd face him one-on-one when he clearly held all the power. I didn't have to wonder long since he spotted me the moment I entered the gym. "Geller, front and center."

What was this, the marines? He certainly had the haircut for it, but even marines didn't wear their pants as high as he did.

"Yes, sir?"

"Glad to see you came to."

"Thank you, sir." *I think.*

"And what did we learn from this experience?"

I snorted. I couldn't help it. "I'm sorry?"

"What did you learn from your embarrassing incident last week?"

Well, let's see. I learned a concussion can induce time travel. I learned you, sir, will get more powerful, but you'll never stop being a douche. I learned Jody is a better teacher in her first week than you are after a decade on the job. I'd actually learned a lot of things, but I doubted he wanted to hear any of them.

"I've got a concussion," I said, falling back on the now-comforting excuse and producing the note from Doctor Mom. "I don't remember anything from Thursday night."

He scowled as he read the letter, but even he was too afraid of a lawsuit to go against a medical excuse. "Go ahead and sit this one out, but I want you to think about what got you in this mess in the first place, so maybe next time you'll pay attention to the task at hand instead of daydreaming during a game."

So that was the lesson? I hadn't been paying enough attention to a high-school basketball game? I literally bit my tongue to keep from laughing. My daydreams would become the building block for a successful literary career, and basketball would become something I honestly forgot I even did. *Quite the life lesson there, Drew.*

I held my smirk in check as I headed for the bleachers, tossing a casual, "Yes, sir" over my shoulder as I went.

I watched disinterestedly as my female classmates did aerobics to a video Drew pressed "play" on, then spent the rest of his time observing the boys' weight training. What a stupid, sexist double standard. He probably didn't want his girls to bulk up because he was so doughy. I'd dated a couple of women who could have snapped him in half, even as stubby as he was.

Where was this venom coming from? Sure, the guy was a jerk, but what did I care? He hadn't annoyed me nearly as much the first time around. I couldn't get bent out of shape about every redneck in this place. Maybe I'd picked up on some of Rory's animosity, or perhaps I resented the power he'd someday lord over Jody. Then again maybe the whole mind-numbingly boring sexism before me was just the last in a long line of injustices burning my brain at the moment. Either way, I needed to settle down. I had one more class to get through after this one, and intro to theater with Jody would test me a lot more than Drew Phillips's stupidity.

❖

"Stevie?"

"Yes?"

"Your monologue?"

"Yes?"

People giggled, and I realized I'd been caught daydreaming. Who knew high school made for such a long day? We were halfway through theater class, and I'd yet to engage the material in any way. Jody had done a lesson on monologues, which was interesting eleven years ago. But given my ensuing studies in theater and my own attempts at playwriting, I no longer found the topic so enthralling. My mind wandered from the material to the teacher. She was clearly exhausted, emotionally and probably physically too. I understood she loved the work and the students, but I also knew the doubts were eating her alive. She was in the act of choosing a lonely path, one that would give her moments of fulfillment, no doubt, but would also lead to regret and uncertainty years down the road.

"Stevie," she said patiently, "did you choose a monologue?"

"Maybe the basketball knocked it out of her head," Deelia Pats said, then smiled like she thought herself clever.

"There are extenuating circumstances," Jody said.

"No, it's fine." I was thankful this assignment would be easy enough since I'd done plenty of monologues throughout college.

"I'll do Zubaida Ula's monologue from *The Laramie Project*."

"*The Laramie Project*?" Deelia wrinkled her nose in distaste. "Isn't that a fag movie?"

"Deelia," Jody snapped, the harshness of her tone immediately getting everyone's attention. "I won't allow discriminatory language in this classroom."

"What? Fag's not a cuss word."

"It's worse, a violent word, a weapon word, an attack on an entire subset of people, and if I hear it again I'll send you to the principal."

Deelia folded her arms across her chest and pursed her lips but didn't push any further. She'd probably never been sent to the principal in her life. She was the class priss, always perfectly dressed and perfectly situated atop the social hierarchy.

"Kelsey, what did you choose?" Jody asked, doing a fine job of acting unperturbed, but I could see her chest rise and fall a little faster than usual. I wished I could squeeze her hand the way she had mine before the assembly.

"Hamlet's 'To Be or Not To Be' soliloquy," Kelsey answered, looking at me suspiciously.

I turned away to see Deelia staring at me with the same intensity, only less confused and more malicious. Great. Who knew fulfilling a silly assignment would get me stuck in multiple sets of crosshairs? I slouched lower in my seat and prayed for the final bell to ring soon.

I jumped out of my chair the second class ended, but before I could get to the door Kelsey stepped in front of me. "Where did you get your monologue?"

"What?"

"*The Laramie Project* just debuted at Sundance. I read an article about it last week. There's no way you could've seen the movie yet."

Shit, another damn timeline fail. "I saw the play first, before they made the movie."

Kelsey wasn't buying it. The other students filed out of the classroom, leaving only Jody at her desk. She shifted through papers but had to be listening. "When did you see the play? I'm pretty sure it didn't come anywhere near here."

"New York," I answered quickly, pulling the only ace in my pocket. "I went to New York last fall to visit some schools. We saw it then."

Except we hadn't. We'd seen *The Lion King*. My parents wouldn't have thought to see *The Laramie Project* then, and quite frankly neither would I since I didn't know Moises Kaufman existed until I got to NYU. But Kelsey and Jody didn't know that.

"Okay, but where did you get the actual script of the monologue to read for class?"

Dear Lord, take me now. When were the questions going to end? Was she actively trying to trip me up? And in front of Jody? Why the hell couldn't any of this be easy? "I Googled it."

Another furrowed brow from Kelsey indicated I'd once again slipped up.

"What's Googled it?"

Holy shit, was this the dark ages? Surely Google existed. Had the term not reached Darlington? "I found it online."

"I didn't think of that," Kelsey said. "I don't have a computer at home."

I regretted my reaction immediately. Maybe she hadn't intentionally grilled me. Maybe she was genuinely interested. I forgot about the digital divide in high school. Personal computers might not be uncommon, but they weren't in every home. And even fewer of my classmates had reliable Internet access. "Maybe you could use the one in the library sometime," I offered weakly.

"Maybe," Kelsey said, then turned to go.

I probably should've said more, maybe offered to let her use my computer, but we weren't friends, and she was clearly suspicious of me already, so I kept my mouth shut and headed toward my locker.

I wanted to get out of there. My dad would be waiting, so I could make a quick getaway. But I worried about forgetting something, and given the circumstances I wouldn't be surprised if I'd forgotten a lot of things. I stared at my locker, running through my classes and trying to remember which books I'd need for homework.

A few doors down, Michael and Deelia were making out against her locker, but he obviously wasn't getting the participation level he wanted because he asked, "What's the matter with you?"

"Miss Hadland chewed me out for saying 'fag.'"

"What?"

"Stevie's reading from a play about faggots." They both looked at me, and I wanted to crawl into my locker. "And Miss Hadland went off about how we can't call them that, or she'd send me to the principal."

"What the hell else are you supposed to call them? Butt pirates? Cocksuckers?"

She laughed and I cringed.

"Hadland's probably a dyke." Michael almost spit the word. "If she sends you to the principal, tell him she hit on you."

My stomach clenched, and my head throbbed again. That was enough. Homework be damned, I had to get out of there. Slamming my locker a little harder than I'd meant to, I jogged down the hallway and out the front door. I couldn't stand one more minute in this place.

I managed to remain conversational with my parents, who had a multitude of questions about my first day back. But between having to wake up at the ass crack of dawn and the exhaustion-inducing events of my day, I was ready for sleep by six o'clock. I could've easily slept for twelve hours if not for my homework, so after helping clear the table like a good child, I headed to the basement to start my second shift.

I fired up the ancient laptop, and since I still used the same five passwords, I logged in easily. First I needed to Google *The Laramie Project* to see if I could actually get my monologue for theater class. Well, I didn't need it since I had it memorized, but Kelsey's questions had shaken me. I tried to keep my eyes open as I clicked on the Internet icon, and I almost jumped out of my seat at the sound of dial-up tones immediately followed by my dad yelling, "Stevie, I'm on the phone!"

Dial-up Internet and shared phone lines, two more items to add to the list of things I didn't miss about my teenage years. I prayed again for this experience to be a dream. It had to be, didn't it? I couldn't have imagined something as wonderful as high-speed Internet and smartphones.

I opened my Spanish book and tried to make sense of our reading. It only took a few minutes to realize that wasn't going to happen. Had I forgotten everything or never really learned it in the first place? I probably didn't expect to ever use it. Why did I assume anyone worth knowing, anyone worth listening to would speak English? I resolved to make an effort to communicate with my neighbors when I got home.

I would get home, wouldn't I? How long had I been gone? Almost a week? Would someone check on my apartment? I had friends. I wasn't a total loner. Someone from my writing group or the youth theater program would miss me eventually, but they wouldn't kick down the door right away. Would they contact Edmond? My parents? Maybe Beth had already called someone. She seemed like the type of person who thought of those things. Poor Beth...her parents had just died. She had enough to deal with. She didn't need to take care of me right now.

No, damn it, this wasn't right now, this was *the past*. Right now, Beth was great. So was Rory. So were we all.

Or at least I would be great as soon as I woke up. Wouldn't I?

My dad called down to let me know he was off the phone, and I tried to connect again, bracing myself for the gurgle and beep of the modem. The thing sounded like it was in the throes of death cycling through the tones once, then twice without connecting. Darlington,

Illinois was never at the forefront of new technologies. I might have to wait awhile. Maybe I should go shower.

No, I could work on my trig homework. I laughed aloud. I couldn't do trigonometry without the Internet. A shower was my only option, but when I came back to find the modem still struggling, it took all my strength not to throw the ancient relic across the room.

Screw it. I'd just type out the monologue myself and lie about finding it online. Now if only I could work Microsoft Word. Why were none of the buttons where they should be? I suddenly realized I was running Windows Millennium Edition as my operating system.

"No," I mumbled. "Geek, out." Forget the monologue. Forget trig. Forget my whole awful day. I crawled into bed without even turning off the lights. Hopefully I'd wake up tomorrow, but even if I didn't, no nightmare could be worse than the one I'd lived today.

CHAPTER FIVE

S tevie, what's your take on the chapter?" Jody asked, even though I hadn't raised my hand or made eye contact or given any other indication I wanted to engage in class discussion. "What do you see as the overarching lesson here?"

I exhaled loudly to let my exasperation be known. I didn't care if I came across as some teenage stereotype. I didn't want to be here, even if we were studying one of my favorite books. "The author is taking the ideas of bravery and courage and turning them on their heads."

"How so?" Jody pressed, her smile doing only a little to settle my annoyance.

"The main character decides to do something that society thinks is brave, in this case, go to war, but he only does so because he's a coward. If he had the courage of his convictions, he would've gone to Canada, but he goes to fight for things he doesn't believe in because he fears the opinions of others." I readied my air quotes to say, "He does the 'brave' thing out of fear."

Someone coughed in an overly fake way to cover a call of, "Bullshit."

Surprise, surprise. Brad, one of Michael's cronies, had clearly been the culprit. Jody gave him her best teacher stare, to which he only replied, "Sorry, I had something in my throat."

"Excuse me," Deelia said, raising her hand but not waiting to be called on before she spoke. "Did you just call soldiers cowards?"

"Not all soldiers." I defended my position halfheartedly. "Just the one in this book."

"He goes to war. He fights for your freedom."

"Well, we can debate whose freedom was at stake in Vietnam, but even giving you that point doesn't change the fact he acted for ignoble reasons."

"Miss Hadland, is 'ignoble' even a word?" one of the other students asked.

"Yes, and Stevie used it correctly."

Deelia pressed her. "So you think our soldiers are cowards too?"

"I said nothing of the sort, and neither did Stevie. Care to share your interpretation of the text, Deelia?" Jody fended off the attack nimbly enough, though a hint of pink rose in her pale cheeks.

"Well, he's afraid at first, but he ultimately fights for his country. He does the right thing. He's a hero."

"Stevie?" Jody prodded.

"The right thing in any given situation is subjective and generally socially constructed to reaffirm those who sit atop the hierarchies."

"I don't even know what you're talking about," Deelia said, her voice drenched in disdain.

Clearly. Her IQ might actually fall in the single-digit range, which was why I didn't generally engage people like her. I couldn't change someone's mind if we didn't speak the same language. Too bad she didn't have the same rule.

"This whole discussion offends me. I think you are both," she paused for dramatic effect, looking pointedly at me and then Jody, "anti-American."

I held in my laugh. That rhetoric had grown old for me long ago, but I imagined it stung for Jody in this post 9/11 political climate. Her cheeks colored, but she gave no other outward indication of her fear about what an accusation like that could do to her career. She didn't have tenure or even a permanent appointment to teach. Why had she chosen this book? Why had she called on me? I wanted to feel bad for her, but she'd brought this on herself, and from what I saw in present day, she'd continue to do so. If she wanted to put herself through this torture every day for the rest of her life, then so be it, but I didn't appreciate her dragging me into the fray with her.

❖

Spanish didn't go much better, as I almost certainly failed the pop quiz Señora Wallace gave. I might've been more bothered by my poor academic performance if I weren't still clinging to the hope of awakening from this dream. Did it really matter if I passed Spanish while in a nightmare? I needed to survive. I needed to keep my mind from falling into a darker place, but I didn't need to impress anyone along the way. That mentality held me over until I got to trigonometry and found my seat blocked by the lip-locked Deelia and Michael. Did they ever come up for air?

I waited patiently as long as I could stand before sighing heavily. I may have also mumbled something about them getting a room. My fuse continued to grow progressively shorter as this nightmare wore on. Thankfully they separated, though Deelia had to get a little dig in about me being jealous. I tried to let the comment pass, but once again she didn't know when to let something go.

"You really could be pretty, Stevie," she said. "Don't you think she could be pretty, Michael?"

Michael, for all his issues, obviously recognized that for the trap it was and replied with a noncommittal shrug.

"If you did something different with your hair and acted a little nicer to the boys, I'm sure you could get a boyfriend too."

Even if I'd wanted to reply politely to the backhanded compliment I wouldn't have known how.

"I could give you a makeover," Deelia offered, sounding rather insincere.

"No, thanks."

Michael's snort sounded remarkably like a warthog's. "Maybe she doesn't want a boyfriend. Maybe she wants a girlfriend."

Their friends all snickered, and my face flamed. I wanted to say so many things. I wanted to tell him I did want a girlfriend and in the coming years I'd have more than my fair share. I also wanted to say that if all men behaved like him, who could blame me for wanting a woman. Mostly, though, I wanted to say he probably only joked about gay people because of his insecurities about his own sexuality. Instead I held my tongue. I wouldn't let a Neanderthal pull me any deeper into his cave. I'd come out in my own time and on my own terms.

I slouched through another lecture on cosines and tangents, which I actually understood about a third of. I had only one more class to get through until lunch, and then I might seriously consider cutting the rest of the day. Hopefully Mr. Glass would be equally oblivious in keyboarding. If today was anything like yesterday, I could complete the assignment early and have time to collect my thoughts in peace.

Those hopes were dashed the minute Kelsey turned on her computer monitor beside me. Someone had already opened a document, and the words typed there were enough to make even my hardened New Yorker side see red. In a bold font read the words, **Kelsey Patel is a pussy eater who needs to sit on a cock**.

My stomach contracted like I'd been kicked. All the air fled my lungs, and my eyes watered. Kelsey swallowed a few times, then began to delete the message.

"No," I whispered harshly. "You have to show Mr. Glass."

She shook her head and wiped the words completely from her screen.

"Kelsey, that's sexual harassment."

"Not in Darlington. That's boys being boys."

"Bullshit." My voice sounded low and raspy even to my own ears.

"Trust me. I've been down that road." She didn't sound angry. Just tired. "Even if one of the teachers wanted to help, I can't prove it was him. They'd question him, then let him go, and he'd come down twice as hard on me."

"Twice as hard as that?"

She didn't answer, but the sadness in her deep-brown eyes spoke of things I couldn't even conceive of.

"What are you going to do?" I asked.

"Nothing."

"I can't just let that slide."

"Stay out of it," she whispered, fear evident in her voice for the first time. "Don't even look at him wrong, or you'll only make things worse for both of us."

I wanted to argue. I wanted to scream. I wanted to file a lawsuit or call his mother. I could go to Jody, but Kelsey was right. There was no justice for the Michael Redlys of the world. None I'd seen, anyway. Bullies in high school grew into bullies as adults. They became teachers like Drew Phillips, or dirty cops, or crooked politicians, and I couldn't do a damn thing to stop them.

Especially in a dream.

I forced the bile in my stomach to stay there and set to work on my assignment. Hitting the computer keys harder than necessary, I once again finished well ahead of the rest of class, but instead of pretending to proofread, I took a risk and got on the school's stronger Ethernet connection to look up information on comas. The exercise was probably futile, since I couldn't access anything in a dream that wasn't already in my brain to begin with, but I had to do something.

I threw out random search terms, from "coma," to "coma-induced dreams," all the way to "alternate realities." I learned plenty of technical terms, but nothing seemed to fit my situation. As a last-ditch effort, I searched for "mental breakdown." The results were not affirming. Hospitalization could be long-term and didn't sound fun. Then again, high school was turning out to be considerably worse than I remembered, and that was saying a lot. Hopelessness weighed down my limbs and stiffened my joints. How much longer could I go on like this?

I left the computer lab with no intention of returning after lunch. I'd never cut school as a teenager, but I knew other people got away with it. Except I bet they had cars. I slammed my locker, and the loud clang of metal on metal would've been more satisfying if Kelsey hadn't been standing on the other side of the door.

"What?" I asked a little harshly.

"Are you from the future?"

My blood ran cold, the ice in my veins fortifying my defenses. "Are you insane?"

"Maybe." The accusation didn't seem to bother Kelsey. "But you don't act like you used to."

"I have a concussion."

"Right, you said that, but then you search for comas and alternative realities."

I should've known she'd notice. What a stupid risk. "That was for a science project."

"I'm in all the senior science classes. You aren't taking any of them."

"It's a personal project," I said weakly.

"You're also doing a monologue that's not online. You type way faster than you did a week ago." Her voice rose as her argument gained steam. "You act like you've already done all the assignments before."

"All right, just shut up." Other people were starting to notice us.

"It's okay if you're from the future. I won't ask you to tell me anything, but I'm interested in time travel."

"There's no such thing as time travel."

"We don't know that. It hasn't been disproved. I think you're a great candidate."

"I am not."

"Okay, but you're gay though, right?"

I clutched her shirt and shook her so hard her back landed with a hollow metallic thud against a row of lockers. The flash of terror in her eyes must have mirrored my own when I realized what I'd done. I let go immediately, and we both stared at each other open-mouthed and breathless. The hallway fell completely silent, and everyone turned to stare. Finally, Michael started to laugh a deep, loud, frat-boy belly laugh. "Geller put the little freak in her place."

Other students joined in, and I noticed a mix of surprise and approval on their faces. I turned back to Kelsey. "I'm so sorry."

"Sure you are." She turned to go, then added, "I thought you were different."

"I am." I was pleading.

She rubbed the back of her head. "Doesn't look like it any more."

I needed to run. I needed to get out of there. I needed to go to the hospital, or the loony bin, but I couldn't leave her like this. Dream— or coma—aside, I couldn't leave things on a bad note with a girl who wouldn't survive the next few months.

I stepped in front of her. "We need to talk."

"So talk."

"Not here." I looked around. "Meet me in the library in ten minutes. Please?"

"Fine." She shrugged, her eyes hidden behind her hair. "It's not like I have other plans."

I stepped out of her way and watched her go. I had to catch my breath and calm down.

Nikki approached cautiously. "Hey, are you okay?"

"Yeah," I lied.

"Someone said you punched Kelsey Patel."

Great, the story was already spinning out of control. "No, I just knocked into her and she hit the locker. It was an accident."

"Really? That's all?"

No, that wasn't even half of it, but what else could I say? "I'm going to stay in for lunch."

"Did you forget your money again?"

"I just need to get some work done for this afternoon. You don't mind, do you?"

"Do whatever you need to, but let me know if you need help."

"Thanks." I wondered why we hadn't stayed in touch. She'd been a good friend to me, and I'd never returned the favor. Maybe I could go about righting that soon, but now I had to find a way to explain to Kelsey things I didn't even understand.

The library was as silent as libraries usually are. Kelsey had taken a seat at a table in the back. With everyone else out to lunch, I didn't have to worry about being heard, but I didn't know where to start. How could I even begin to explain the meltdown I'd just had?

Kelsey looked up at me expectantly, clearly not about to let me off the hook.

"I'm sorry." I voiced my most prevailing thought, and also the easiest one to articulate. "I didn't mean to snap. I'm under a lot of pressure, and you scared me, but that's no excuse for violence."

She shrugged. "I've had worse."

"I know, and that's all the more reason for me to be gentler. You asked some questions I wasn't prepared to answer."

"I wasn't judging you, you know? I support full equality for gays and lesbians."

"Really?" Had Rory and Michael both seen something I missed?

"I know what you're thinking, what everyone says about me. But I'm not gay."

I slid into the seat beside her. "Then why don't you defend yourself against the rumors?"

"I don't think there's anything wrong with being gay, so I don't get particularly offended by people suggesting I am. And besides, what good would it do? If I let them get a rise out of me, they'd only scream louder."

She was so depressingly enlightened. It didn't seem fair for her to take the abuse that should've logically been directed at me. At least I could speak on the issue of sexual orientation with authority and conviction. I owed her that much. "I am gay. Every slur is a punch in the gut, so I think you of all people can understand why I don't want the rest of our class to know I'm a lesbian."

She nodded. "It's your choice. I never intended to out you. I just thought you might need someone to talk to."

Tears stung my eyes. How could this kid who was constantly under fire be so selfless as to worry about the burdens I carried? "Thanks, but honestly I made peace with my sexuality years ago. I've got bigger issues right now."

"'Cause you're from the future?"

"Kelsey," I said through clenched teeth, then forced myself to take a deep breath. "You have to understand how certifiably crazy you sound."

"People thought Galileo and Plato were crazy too, but that didn't keep them from being right," she said matter-of-factly.

I stared at her, disbelieving. I'd never met a teenager with such certainty about her views and what they meant for her. Surely if she could see her own place in the context of great minds, she understood the uphill battle ahead of her. Maybe her resignation stemmed not from temporary trials of youth, but from her understanding of what lay ahead.

"Time travel, from what we know, is a physical improbability but not a proven impossibility." She continued to logically discuss absurdities. "I'm really into science *and* science fiction. I don't think they're as far apart as others do."

I had friends who wrote science fiction. I didn't read their work because it wasn't my thing, but some of them were among the smartest, most educated writers I knew. Some of them bordered on tortured genius. "Fine. Say time travel was possible. How would it happen?"

"I don't know if anyone can say for sure, but two major categories of thought exist. The first is that time is something we could learn to manipulate or bend to our wills. To do this you'd build a machine or harness some sort of power. Do you have a Tardis?"

"No."

"A flux capacitor?"

I rolled my eyes. "This is ridiculous. Those things are from movies. They're fiction, make-believe."

"Don't you think fiction is the best way to teach the hardest lessons in life?"

"Of course I do. That's why I'm a writer."

"You're a writer? What do you write?"

"Novels and plays, literary fiction mostly, with a hint of romance and…" I realized I'd just given away too much.

She grinned with a sense of accomplishment. "Admitting it's the first step."

"I admit something's off. I have memories of the future, or a life I don't seem to have lived yet."

"But you're not a Time Lord?"

"No." I replied emphatically.

"Did you come into contact with anything like radioactive ooze? Or, I don't know, a wizard?"

I needed to get out of there or just pull this conversation back into the real world, whatever that was. "I just…I passed out at an awards assembly in the gym and I…I…" I still wasn't totally sure why I went down. There might have been a lot of contributing factors, but none offered a complete explanation.

"You lost consciousness and woke up in a different time."

"I don't think I woke up. I think I'm dreaming. I think you're a dream."

She reached over and pinched me so hard I yelped and pulled my arm away.

"Nope, not likely a dream. You're too aware, and you feel pain."

"I could feel pain in a coma."

"Possibly, though a coma dream would likely function much the same way as a normal dream. They serve the same restorative purposes. Though maybe a coma dream would last longer due to the length of sleep."

"This has been a long dream, and more exhausting than restorative."

"Can you read numbers?"

"Yes?"

"See colors? Write? Move freely? Have all your normal bodily functions?"

"Yes."

"Can you do anything now you couldn't do in normal life—like fly, or play the piano, or jump from place to place without explanation?"

"No."

"Doesn't sound like a dream," she said resolutely.

I put my forehead down on the cool surface of the table, thankful for something tactile amid my swirling emotions and abstract fears. "Time travel isn't real."

"Why does the idea bother you so badly? You of all people should understand just because something isn't common or easy doesn't mean it can't be right or real."

My head hurt. "Are you suggesting that because I'm gay I should be more comfortable with losing eleven years of my life?"

"Well, if you've just jumped back, those years aren't lost. They're still there."

"But I'm not a Time Lord!" My voice rose in frustration. "I don't know how to get back."

Kelsey continued, clearly excited by the possibilities that distressed me. "I think you fall into the second category of time travel, the archetypal or mythical kind."

"What do you mean?"

"An archetype is like a universal story or symbol."

"I know the definition of an archetype. I'm a writer, remember?"

"Yeah, but it's not just fiction. Philosophy, religion, psychology, and even some branches of science and medicine recognize the value of an archetypal pattern."

Clearly my extra decade of experience couldn't compete with her understanding of science and culture. "But what does any of that have to do with me ending up back in high school?"

"I don't know enough to be sure. No one really does, but it seems like you're on a quest of some sort. How to put this delicately?" She rubbed her forehead. "I think you probably fucked up."

"What?"

"You didn't get put back in someone else's life or another part of history." She continued laying out her argument calmly even as my blood pressure rose exponentially. "You got sent back to a specific moment in your life. You're getting a do-over. The universe, or a spirit guide, or maybe your own psyche is offering you another chance at something, which probably means you missed an opportunity or did something wrong or chose the wrong path."

"I have a great life. I've got everything going for me." Well, maybe not everything, but most things. "I'm, at the very least, on the right path."

She held up her hands. "I'm just saying what it looks like to me, and honestly, what do you have to lose by considering the possibility?"

The idea of time travel seemed insane, but so did everything else in this scenario. "I just want my life back."

"Well, if this really is a prolonged dream, then finding some satisfactory resolution might help end it. The same is true for a quest. If you figure out how to right the wrong, you'll end the ordeal. Whatever definition you choose, dealing with it is the quickest way to return to your future life."

"And what if there's nothing to go back to? What if I've had a mental break?" My voice shook as I finally admitted my worst fears. "What if everything I loved was a lie, and everything I hate is the truth?"

Kelsey's expression once again grew dark and serious. "Sometimes insanity is a survival skill. If you're really crazy, do whatever you have to do to hold onto that, because when it's gone, you've got nothing left to live for."

Her words chilled me. I had to say something. If there was even the slightest chance I'd time traveled, I had to tell her what happened to her own life, but how did you tell someone they'd kill themselves in a month's time?

The bell rang, startling us both.

"We'd better go," Kelsey said casually. "I've got a science lab."

"You've got a science lab? Seriously? You tell me I'm on a time-travel quest and then leave?

"That's really all I can do until you figure out why you're here. Do that, and then maybe we could talk after school."

If only it were that simple. People dedicated their entire lives to figuring out the meaning of life and still failed. How the hell was I supposed to do it before school let out?

❖

I sleepwalked through the rest of the day. Thankfully I didn't have any more work to do since we were just practicing our monologues in theater class. Some students paired up, while others recited their work to the walls. I remained in my seat, pretending to read quietly, and occasionally allowed myself to steal sidelong glances at Jody.

We hadn't spoken since I'd forced some distance between us yesterday afternoon, and I missed her. Perfunctory comments in class didn't offer me the comfort I'd come to associate with her. It seemed funny to think about her in those terms since, until last week, I hadn't seen her in years. But she had such a calming effect on me in so many times of recent turmoil I'd come to feel closer to her than we actually were. I wished I could've talked to her about my conversation with Kelsey. She always seemed to know what I needed, even if I couldn't give the same to her.

She weaved her way around the classroom, talking to various students in various stages of memorizing and practicing their pieces for class. She engaged each one—or tried to. Several of the students were disinterested and a few even seemed hostile. Deelia acted like Jody had cooties when she leaned closer to examine something in the script. I remembered Michael's comment about accusing Jody of sexual harassment, and my palms began to sweat. My urge to protect Jody overrode my own troubled thoughts, and I raised my hand to get her attention.

She smiled broadly, sending a tingle up my arms as she headed my way. "Stevie, I thought maybe you weren't speaking to me after this morning."

I searched my jumble of memories. Oh, yeah, the conversation she forced me into that left us both branded as anti-American. Funny how long ago that seemed now. While I wasn't ready to concede the possibility of time travel yet, I had to admit my sense of time was certainly warped. "It's okay. You didn't know what you were getting into."

She arched one of her elegant eyebrows. "Didn't I?"

Had she purposefully thrown me under the bus?

"You'll be in New York in six months. It's time for you to find your voice."

"What makes you think I haven't found it already, and I'm judicious about where and how to best use it?"

"Who gets to decide what's best? Best for you? Best for the people around you? Best for your community?"

"You want me to be Rory."

"Rory?" She angled her head to the side as if considering the name. "I don't know anyone named Rory."

I rolled my eyes. "You will. She'll bowl you over. She'll be the hero this town doesn't even know it needs, but I'm not her."

She clearly didn't understand, but she tried to stay with me even as I bordered on fortune-telling. "I'm not asking you to be a hero. I'm asking you to just be you."

"Really? Just be myself?" I had to hold my tongue from calling her a hypocrite. I didn't need a "be myself" lecture from the woman who'd never come out of the closet, who'd given up on a personal life to please others, who'd send suitors running before they got a chance to see beneath her teacher persona. I stared into her blue eyes, seeing clearly her passion and her poise, but also her fear and her exhaustion.

Everyone else, everything else blurred around us. I saw only her. "I know you're tired."

She took a sharp intake of breath, but I continued quietly. "You don't have to be that person with me. You don't have to use the façade or the polished veneer. I see you. I hear you."

"Stevie…" She looked like she might run or cry.

"I'm fine. Take a minute to breathe. Don't let me be one more burden on your back."

She glanced around self-consciously. "Please stay after class."

I shook my head sadly. She couldn't see outside the job. She couldn't see her life, her *self*, as a whole person. "Yes, ma'am."

I remained in my desk while all the other students filed out of class. Kelsey stopped to wait for me at the door, but I nodded toward Jody, who'd taken a seat at her own desk and barely moved since our conversation.

Once everyone was gone, Jody finally made eye contact. "Do you want to explain yourself, Stevie?"

Not really. "I don't know what there is to explain. I'm sorry if I said something you found rude."

"It's not that you're rude. It's the opposite. Most students seem barely aware I'm alive. Others actively work to undermine me. But you…" She closed her eyes and exhaled slowly through barely parted lips. "You don't talk to me like a teacher. You don't even talk to me like you talk to your friends. I've watched you interact with your classmates, and there's nothing there."

I tried to push my hands through my hair, only to have them stick in a tangle of too-long curls, another reminder of my helplessness in this situation. "You want me to find my voice. You try to push me into saying things I want to keep to myself, and when I give in to you, when I succumb to the impossible task you ask of me, all I get is reprimanded?"

"I asked for you to address the text," she said weakly.

"No, you didn't. You asked for me to find my voice, for myself, for the people around me, for my community. You didn't say *you* got to decide when I should and shouldn't use it."

"Why me?"

"What?"

"Why me, Stevie?" Her impossibly blue eyes glistened with tears. "You have things to say on the books, on the plays, on your peers, and yet you unleash all your insights on me. Why?"

Because you unravel me. Because you affect me in ways no book ever has. Because you override my fear and compel me to speak truth through my pain and confusion.

I couldn't say any of that, not without freaking her out more, not without revealing too much of myself. And she wasn't asking for the truth anyway. She wanted comfort, logic, and all the things that currently eluded me. I rose from the desk and backed toward the door. I had to end this before one of us said or did something we couldn't undo. "I'm sorry. I didn't mean to upset you."

She threw up her hands. "Is that your way of ending this conversation without giving me the answers I'm searching for?"

I gave a mirthless laugh. "Pretty much. I'll see you tomorrow."

"Fine." She reverted back into her comfortable teacher skin. "Be ready to discuss the text in depth."

Kelsey was waiting by my locker, but the hallway was otherwise empty. Most students didn't stick around long after the last bell rang, and who could blame them?

"Did you figure out what you have to do to get out of here?" Kelsey asked hopefully.

"No." I tossed some books into my locker. "I had other things on my mind last period."

"I noticed," she said, her mouth forming an expression that fell just shy of a smile. "You've got a thing for Miss Hadland, huh?"

I closed the locker and rested my head up against it. "I should've kissed her when I had the chance."

Kelsey's eyebrows shot up, and I realized I'd said that out loud.

"Shit, sorry. I gotta get out of here."

"Wait, I thought we needed to talk."

I probably did need to talk, but not here. "Do you want to come to my house?"

"What?" She looked surprisingly happy but guarded. I marveled at the way she could project such conflicting emotions.

"You don't have to. I just need to get out of here."

"Yeah, sure." She actually smiled. Something childlike and innocent about the expression warmed me slightly after the chill I'd received from Jody.

She grew even more animated as we settled into my room. She looked at my laptop wide-eyed. "Is that a new Dell?"

"Well, it's new by 2002 standards, but it feels frustratingly old to me."

"Why?"

"It takes forever to open and may or may not connect to *dial-up* Internet."

"I read about how Ethernet is a big thing in cities. Is that the wave of the future?"

"No, wireless is. I now have the Internet on my cell phone. It fits into my pocket. I can push a button to ask a question and it'll show me the answer."

"Any question?" Her already-big eyes rounded like I'd told her Santa Claus existed.

"Pretty much."

"So is everyone a genius? Do they walk around asking their phones about quadratic equations?"

I laughed, a rolling laugh. "No, we mostly use them to post pictures of cats and argue with strangers about things they see on Fox News."

Her shoulders sagged and her expression turned almost painfully disappointed. "Maybe you shouldn't tell me too much about the future."

"Why not? I thought you wanted to help me get back."

"You can tell me about your future, but it might be dangerous for me to know too much more. I wouldn't want to change anything."

A sharp pain lanced through my chest. "Maybe we need to change a few things."

"You can't know that. If I'm going to help you, I need you to promise you won't tell me anything about my life."

"What if I can't promise that? What if I shout out something right now about your future?"

She thought for a minute while I held my breath painfully in my chest. "If you told me something bad happens to me, I'd be honor-bound to make sure that came to fruition. If you told me I'd die in a fiery crash tomorrow, I'd still have to get in the car. It would become like my destiny."

No, no, that wouldn't work at all.

What an impossible position to put me in. I needed to tell her what happened to her, but I didn't want to give her more inspiration to take those pills. How could I help her if she'd only insist on going through with the horrible fate I needed to save her from? "Do you really believe in destiny?"

"I don't know for sure." She sat down on my desk chair and laced her fingers together in a thoughtful pose. "But if you time-traveled to alter your life, that's a pretty strong argument that right and wrong paths exist for each of us."

I thought about how reasonable her argument sounded, and yet it wasn't reasonable or logical. "But if I've got to change my path, who's to say the people around me shouldn't change theirs too? By your own logic we can make the wrong choices."

"How about this?" She pinched the bridge of her nose as if thinking so hard gave her a headache. "Let's use you as the test case and me as the control group. You're the one who's time-traveled, or dreaming, or crazy. Let's see if we can alter your reality, and if you're successful maybe we'll talk about altering mine."

"What if I like jump back to my future before we get a chance to discuss yours?"

She shrugged. "Then we aren't meant to address mine."

"Will I remember this?" I couldn't believe I'd actually begun to consider time travel a viable option, but the dream theory wasn't working all that well.

"Who knows? Maybe it'll seem like a dream, but you'll have learned from it."

"What about you? Will you remember this version of me or the original one?"

"I can't say for sure, but maybe it'll be like when you wake up and you can remember feelings or images rather than specific details. We won't know until it happens."

"*If* it happens. I may wake up any moment now."

"It's possible. We're dealing with a lot of unknowns. Welcome to science."

"Welcome to life in general," I muttered, and flopped down on my bed.

"Can I ask a personal question?" Kelsey asked nervously.

"Really? More personal than asking if I'm gay and from the future? Sure, shoot."

She grinned sheepishly. "Do you have a history, or I guess a future, with Miss Hadland?"

I sighed and stared at the ceiling. "Not really. The night right before I came back, we connected. I hadn't seen her for years, but it felt like we'd always known each other. I don't know how to explain it."

"What happened?"

"Nothing. Everything's complicated with her. I live in New York, she lives in Darlington. I'm out, she's closeted. I need creative freedom, she's tied down by her job. I could have kissed her, I was so close, but…that's it!"

"What?" Kelsey asked.

"It's Jody."

"Who?"

"Miss Hadland." I sat up. "She's my missed opportunity. I should've kissed her."

"I don't think the universe bent time and space so you could get laid." Kelsey laughed, but I was already up and moving.

"She's more than that. She's miserable here."

"She seems to work hard, but I think she likes teaching."

"She's selling herself short. She put her own life on hold for everyone else. She made the wrong decision when she took the job. This wasn't my defining moment. It was hers."

Kelsey shook her head and tried to calm me. "You're the one who got sent back."

"You said yourself, no one really knows how this works, or why. All I know is I should have kissed her, I should have whisked her away, but I didn't. I let her stay in a bad situation. She told me what an awful time student teaching was for her, how it set her on the path that's still penning her in, and then I went back to that exact moment. Coincidence?"

Kelsey pinched her nose again. "So, what? You got sent back in time to make sure the best teacher we have doesn't actually become a teacher? That's what the universe wants?"

"Why does it always have to be about the universe, or the community, or some greater good? What about two people doing what's best for them? There'll always be other teachers. What if we only have one soul mate, and Jody and I missed each other?"

Kelsey looked like she wanted to disagree but couldn't formulate an effective argument. I took her silence to mean I was right and immediately began formulating my plans. High school went from a massive waste of time to the most important thing I'd ever do twice, and for once I actually looked forward to doing my homework.

CHAPTER SIX

I bypassed my locker completely, taking the stairs two at time all the way to Jody's classroom. She wore a maroon pantsuit today. What was with the Republican wardrobe? She probably believed the clothes made her appear more serious, but this one was a little too big at her shoulders, making her look like she shopped in her older sister's closet, which I actually found absurdly cute. I enjoyed the way her appearance melted my heart just a little.

"Good morning, Stevie," Jody said with a halfhearted enthusiasm. Her eyes crinkled slightly but didn't sparkle the way I knew they could. "Are you here for our daily dose of cryptic conversation followed by an abrupt emotional withdrawal?"

I laughed nervously. "I guess I deserve that. I meant what I said yesterday. I don't want to be a burden to you, but I also thought about what you said about using my voice."

"And what did you decide?" she asked with a wry smile. "Are you going to use it for good or evil?"

"I don't know if I'm qualified to make value judgments, but I do want to use my voice for the truth, or at least my truth, so I'm going to say what I think you already know."

She took a sharp intake of breath and seemed to hold it.

"I'm gay, and I know you are too." The words poured out in a rush. "I think that's what scared you in the locker room last week, and I understand why. I've been pretty scared this week too."

She exhaled loudly. "You're right. It's scary to say, especially here, but I prefer having it out there, and I'm proud of you for having the courage to face it."

"Me too," I said honestly. I'd felt immeasurably better after opening up to Kelsey yesterday, and now I felt almost ecstatic to have Jody regard me with the admiration currently emanating from her. She walked around to the front of her desk, once again removing the physical manifestation of her professional barriers.

"Are you okay?" she asked kindly. "Do you need any resources?"

"No, I'm good."

"So, this isn't a new development?"

"No, I've known for years, or I mean like a long time."

"What about your parents? Have you told them?"

"Not yet." I brushed off the question. "There's no need."

"Are you afraid of their reactions? If you're worried about safety—"

"No, not at all. They'll be fine."

She furrowed her brow. "Then why not tell them and let them help you?"

"I don't need any help. Telling them now will only worry them. I want them to enjoy my last few months of living at home."

"They'll worry about you being out in Darlington?"

"Of course they would. Just look at your own reaction. You're worried about me already. What if I slip up? What if I lose the pronoun game? What if someone else puts it together the way you did? There are very real consequences, but living in fear won't solve any of them."

"I'll admit I do worry about gay and lesbian students here, but I have a hard time imagining you making a silly mistake. You're too controlled."

"I've made plenty of mistakes, but coming out won't be one of them. I've got a plan. I'm headed to New York. I'll find many more supportive communities there, especially at NYU—gay student groups and gay-and-lesbian-studies courses. I'll study lesbian lit and political theater. I'll come out on my own terms, in a place where I'll get the best possible reactions."

Jody still looked proud, but the now-familiar sadness returned to the corners of her mouth and eyes. "You're very mature. You're handling a lot for an eighteen-year-old, and yet you seem to have it all together."

"Not everything," I admitted, "but my sexual orientation isn't a central conflict in my life right now, and I don't want it to be one in yours either."

She frowned. "What do you mean?"

"You have to worry about school and work and major life decisions. I don't want you to expend another ounce of energy worrying about my well-being."

"You're extremely sensitive to other people's plights. It's very noble of you."

"It's not noble. It's realistic. This isn't a safe place for a gay teacher. I know this town. I know these people. I lived here for eighteen years."

Her mouth curved up in amusement. "Your whole life?"

"No. I mean yes, eighteen years is my whole life. What I'm trying to say is I want to help you."

"Stevie." Her teacher tone returned. "I'm your teacher. I'm here to help you, not the other way around."

"Well, excuse me. Are we working on the banking model of pedagogy?"

Her eyes narrowed "Have you taken a course in liberation pedagogy?"

"No." *Not yet.* "I'm just saying yesterday, you asked me to use my voice to help the larger community, and I want to do that by helping you."

She toyed with a strand of fair hair resting on her shoulder. "You have lots of ways to help your community—"

"But we both know why I don't speak freely. I just thought if I could help you learn the system, the unwritten rules here, then you could help me give voice to my ideas. We could learn from each other."

Jody looked past me to the classroom, from the desks to the whiteboard to the bookcases. Did she see her dreams spread out before her? Did she feel so close to everything she'd worked for? Or had she begun to see the minefield of traps and pitfalls laid for her here? "I can't believe I've only been doing this for two months and I'm already overwhelmed."

I wanted to pull her into my arms. I wanted to carry her away with me. I wanted to save her from years of feeling this way. Instead I just nodded for her to continue.

"Mr. Owens is a nice guy. He approved all my plans before I started, but now he's checked out. He's got three months until he retires, and I think he accepted a student teacher so he could get an early start. He's supposed to supervise me, but I haven't even seen him since last Wednesday."

"Okay," I said calmly. "First of all, you're doing fine."

"I don't want to do fine. I want to do well. I want to make a difference, but I've got so much to learn, and I'm not sure I can do it alone."

"Then let this be your first lesson. You're already so much better than you know, and you're not alone."

She shook her head, but she looked like she wanted to smile. "I wanted that to be my line."

"It is." I grinned. "I stole it. It's a major theater faux pas, I know. Next time I promise I'll let you say it, okay?"

Her shoulders bounced in a silent laugh. "Okay."

"Now, we've only got a few minutes before the bell. Let's talk about your lesson plans. We're discussing *The Things They Carried*, right?"

"Yes. I'm starting to think I was overly ambitious in choosing it, but it's one of my favorites and raises so many important issues for high-school seniors."

"I agree. It blew my mind the first time I read it."

"Really? You've read it before? When?"

Shit, every time I got comfortable with her, I fell back into adult mode. Was that a sign we belonged together in another time? "I read it last summer. It's what made me want to write like that."

"Like what?"

"I want to make worlds feel so real you see their truth even when faced with blunt statements about their fiction. I want to write novels and plays where people see their most mundane impulses amid the surreal. I want to take the most stark realities and shape them into a magic mirror on the wall of people's minds." I stopped ranting in order to breathe and realized I'd just poured my heart's deepest aspirations out to Jody, who now watched me with a renewed color in her cheeks and a rekindled light in her eyes. "Sorry. I didn't mean to hijack your lesson plan."

"No, please don't apologize. That's exactly what I needed to hear. You reminded me why I wanted to teach this book in the first place."

I grinned in spite of the fact I probably shouldn't have just reaffirmed her desire to teach while trying to get her to run away with me. I couldn't help but be happy to see her so pleased. "Good. Carry that into class with you this morning."

"Thank you, Stevie."

I shrugged her off.

She touched my shoulder briefly, then looked a little chagrined for doing so. "I mean it, sincerely. Thank you. And for what it's worth, I think you'll be an amazing writer."

My chest swelled with pride both for this moment, and for all the moments, *our* moments, still to come. "Thank you."

I buzzed through the day. I greeted Señora Wallace in Spanish and took a turn conjugating a few verbs I'd relearned the night before. In trigonometry I took notes for the first time ever. In typing, I finished early, then set up a Hotmail account for Kelsey and sent her an e-mail telling her to buy stock in Google and Apple. She deleted it, but not before she got a good laugh. Several people turned to look at us, and I heard one student remark she'd never heard Kelsey laugh in the two years she'd been in Darlington.

I drove Nikki to Encarnacion's for lunch and paid for us to split a whole pizza. Maybe I should have done so sooner because Encarnacion's pizza offered the strongest argument yet against this ordeal being a dream. Thin crust, a sweet and rich sauce, and cheese so thick it stuck to everything it touched. Dreams never tasted this good.

My fear of being found out lessened with each passing minute. With Nikki's effervescent personality, I barely had to talk at all during lunch. Instead I took the time to listen to her for maybe the first time ever. She fit Darlington, and it fit her, but not in the close-minded or judgmental way. I sent up a silent prayer that her future really would be the one Rory recounted for her.

Back at school, I used my study hall to actually study and used my bench-warming time in gym to reread *The Things They Carried.* I made notes on things I could mention to impress Jody and glanced at my watch every few pages, counting the minutes until I'd see her again. Time transformed from purgatory to almost transcendental when in her presence. When I lost myself in her eyes, I almost felt like I wasn't stuck at all, as if you could have put us down in any time and any space without changing the way we connected. Those were the experiences I needed to create more of. After feeling lost and confused for so long, I craved the moments that gave purpose to this puzzle I was living.

By the time I got to theater class, I was almost enjoying myself. I'd had my first good day in over a week, and I had more time with Jody to look forward to. Our eyes met as soon as I strolled through her classroom door, and she smiled. I hoped no one else was paying attention because I probably looked like a crush-struck fool as I raised my hand in a little wave of greeting before ducking into my seat. Being an enamored schoolgirl certainly had its upsides. For instance, the way my heart did a little stutter step in my chest when Jody took the floor and called for the class's attention.

"You all have been working hard to learn your monologues this week, and I want to commend you on your progress. Memorization is a great first step in the acting process, so give yourselves a big pat on the back," Jody said, her smile exuberant. "Now you're ready for the next step in the assignment."

"We haven't performed them yet," one of the students said nervously.

"I know, and you will perform them, but not the words. You're going to go deeper and perform the meaning."

"What, like an interpretative dance?" one of the guys asked.

"No, that'll be your final exam." Jody's playful side sparked another twinge of joy in me. "For this week's task, you're going to perform the subtext of the monologue. You're going to stand up and not tell us the character's actual lines but what they mean, what they're thinking, what they're feeling."

I lowered my head and pretended to take notes in an attempt to hide my admiration. Jody was brilliant. She wouldn't be happy with a simple regurgitation of someone else's words. She wanted us to really know our parts, to understand what drove our characters. I made a mental note to try the exercise with some of the characters in my own play. Did their words truly reflect the essence of what I hoped to convey to the audience?

"That's not fair." Deelia sounded every bit like a petulant child. "We spent three days memorizing, and now you change the assignment on us?"

"The assignment hasn't changed," Jody explained calmly. "This has always been the end goal, but you can't dig into the subtext until you've built an adequate understanding of the text."

"My mom has been practicing with me every night, and she won't be happy to hear you tricked us into learning something we didn't have to know."

"Well." Jody sighed, a deep crease etching her forehead. "I don't think learning is ever something to regret, even if it doesn't yield immediate results. But in the context of this assignment, you couldn't effectively do the second part without completing the first. I'm sorry if I didn't communicate that this would be an ongoing project."

I ground my teeth together to keep from snapping at Deelia for being such an ignorant little twit or yelling at Jody to stop apologizing to her.

"Can't we just take a quiz or something?" one of the other students asked. "When we read books or plays in other classes, they always give us a quiz to prove we did the reading."

"I have faith in you. I assume you've done the reading," Jody said, clearly trying to stay positive. "That's why I'm asking for more from you. I want to challenge you to go beyond reading. I want you to learn, to comprehend, to internalize these lessons."

"A quiz would be easier to grade," another student added, causing me to snort. Of course a quiz would be easier to grade. That's why the other teachers assigned them. They didn't require any complex thought on the part of anyone involved.

"Yes, it would be." Jody agreed halfheartedly. "But we're not on the path of least resistance. We're going to move forward with our lesson on subtext."

I sat back and watched helplessly as Jody used Romeo's balcony monologue as an example for our subtext assignment. The students didn't help her. She had to pull them along every step of the way, nudging and pushing for possible interpretations of each sentence. I wanted to offer more support, but I was so angry I decided to keep my mouth shut except when called on. I hated to see the little bastards kill her joy, but I hoped this experience could help her realize she didn't belong here.

She'd fare much better in New York. She could teach at a magnet school or a performing-arts academy. She could work with students who actually wanted to learn instead of kids who wanted a shiny sticker at the top of their tests. Hell, she could work with me. With my skills as a writer and her understanding of the arts, she could make me a better playwright. She could direct my plays. We'd be unstoppable together.

I felt a momentary pang of regret for the students like me, the students who would never get a shot at seeing this assignment or this teacher. But did a handful of kids over the course of several decades outweigh all the assholes she'd have to face in the interim?

I couldn't get over the transition in Jody throughout the course of the day. She'd gone from cautious to open to exuberant to dejected, and my own emotions rode the roller coaster along with her. I was, once again, completely exhausted by the time I survived another family dinner. Thankfully, I'd completed most of my homework and could crash early. I had my hand on the doorknob to the basement when my dad halted my escape with a question I'd never expected to hear directed at me again.

"Stevie, did you do your chores?"

"Uh, what chores?"

He didn't look amused. "I think you're feeling well enough to start helping out around the house again."

"Sure, what needs to be done?"

"The trash needs to go out."

"Okay."

"And the dishwasher needs loaded."

"No problem." I wasn't a child. I wouldn't argue.

"And the baseboards need to be dusted."

"What?"

"Stevie," he said in his most paternal voice.

"Dad, no one looks at the baseboards." Okay, maybe I would argue.

"It's not about other people. It's about taking a little pride in your home. Trust me, when you have a place of your own, you'll understand."

"I won't," I said seriously.

He shook his head and tossed me a dust rag. "You say that now, but you'll feel differently in ten years."

I bit my lip to keep from shouting I knew for certain that wasn't true. I'd lived in my current apartment for almost two years now, and I'd only ever scrubbed the damn baseboards when he and Mom visited a year ago. Sure, I did dishes and laundry and took out the trash, but for all I knew I could be growing my own colony of penicillin on my baseboards. Come to think of it, maybe that's why my allergies had gotten so bad last winter.

As I set to work wiping the dust off the woodwork around our house, my mind wandered to my other life. Did winter still have a grip on New York? Spring had been teasing us with the occasional warm breeze. When I'd left a week ago, I'd actually seen some snowdrops blooming in the community garden near my loft. I missed New York. Winter was a bitch, and summer could damn near kill you, but spring and fall were stunning. The city came to life. Music streamed from open windows. Neighbors sat on front stoops. People went out of their way to amble through parks and gardens. Would Jody like it there?

I'd yet to let myself fully believe Kelsey's time-travel theory, but even if it wasn't logical, I enjoyed fantasizing about the prospect. Say for a minute I wasn't just working to make this dream more pleasant, and I actually could change our destiny. Would we transport back together? If we'd been together all along, I might never have come back to Darlington. She certainly wouldn't have served on any arts committees here. Would I wake up in our shared apartment in New York? Would I have memories of the last ten years of us together?

And what would be the catalyst for that quantum leap? Would we have some major defining moment to set our feet on a different path? Would it be like a fairy tale where one kiss could seal our futures? Would I wake up to a whole new world the moment her lips touched mine? I threw the dust rag in the corner and got ready for bed while internally chiding myself for entertaining such sappy sentimentality.

Then again, as long as I was considering the possibility of time travel, fairy tales weren't far off. Maybe a kiss could wake us. And honestly, was there a nicer way to be awoken? I drifted to sleep wondering if considering a life-shattering kiss with Jody made me Sleeping Beauty or Prince Charming.

CHAPTER SEVEN

I got to school more than half an hour early and in a great mood. A few days ago I couldn't imagine spending a minute longer there than I had to, but these quiet moments before the day got started gave me an opportunity to spend quality time alone with Jody without all the other pressures of the day. I thought about picking her up some coffee on the way in, but I didn't want to get too forward. We weren't dating…yet.

I walked through the halls with an added bounce in my step, but just before I reached the stairs, I noticed Kelsey alone at the end of the hall. She sat on the floor just past the last row of lockers with her knees curled to her chest and an open book in front of her. She seemed impossibly small and terribly isolated. I looked longingly at the stairs that would lead me to Jody as I passed them by.

Kelsey glanced up as I approached, her expression of apprehension fading into something almost resembling a smile when she recognized me. "You're here early."

"I was about to say the same to you."

"I get here early every day to get my stuff out of my locker."

"What, your locker only opens before seven thirty?"

She shook her head sadly. "My locker doesn't open with Michael leaning against it."

I rolled my head back, trying to ward off the tension rapidly developing there. "And that's why you're not in a hurry to get out of here in the afternoon. You have to wait for him to leave first?"

"It's not a big deal."

"He makes everything harder for you. That's got to take its toll over time."

"There's no use complaining about something I can't change."

"Have you tried?"

"Sure. I tried when I first moved here. The secretary in the office told me Mr. Phillips was the disciplinary officer for the school."

I groaned.

"He said he didn't like tattletales. Then he told me learning to work things out on my own would make me stronger and prepare me for the real world."

"What a pompous ass."

"He ended by saying he only wanted to help me fit in here, and people didn't get ahead at this school by assaulting the character of Darlington's finest young men."

"Finest young men?"

"Michael is an okay student and a good athlete. He's attractive and—"

"He's a white male."

"Please don't go there, Stevie."

"What? It's the truth. You're smarter and nicer and funnier than Michael, but he looks like Drew Phillips and you don't."

"It's hard enough to be one of the only minorities in town. I don't need you playing the race card on my behalf."

"Sure, 'cause somewhere along the way, racism became your fault too."

"Hey, how are things going with Miss Hadland?" It was a transparent attempt to change the subject.

I didn't want to drop the previous conversation, but her expression brightened noticeably at the redirection, and I didn't have the heart to drag us back to her own torment, so I sighed and took the bait. "They're going all right. We had a moment yesterday. I think we connected." I didn't want to overstate my position, but I needed to cling to the hope that something good could come out of this disaster.

"So what's next?" Kelsey asked.

"I don't know for sure. I'm helping her with some pointers on teaching this group of students, you know, to ease some of the pressure."

"And to convince her she shouldn't want this job long-term."

"Possibly, but I'm hoping she kind of sees that on her own. I mean, how can she not?"

Kelsey didn't seem convinced. "She didn't the first time around. If what you said about your return is true, then she not only survived student teaching, but she's stayed here for years. She's already made this choice once. Why not choose it again?"

I didn't want to consider the possibility of her choosing this school over me, and I didn't want to remember her noble reasons for doing so the first time around. "All I can do is offer her my best. If she doesn't want me, you'll just be stuck with me indefinitely."

"Go ahead and go see her."

"Do you want to come with?"

"No. You can't work your charms with me hanging around."

True, but she looked so exposed sitting there. I felt guilty about leaving her alone. Still, she'd perfected the skill of blending in. Maybe I'd only draw unwanted attention. Stuck in an impossible situation, I chose the option most likely to get me out of it and headed for Jody's classroom.

My guilt evaporated the moment I saw Jody in khakis and a navy-blue sweater set. She looked more comfortable than she did in the skirts, but I did miss the view of her athletic legs as she stretched her petite frame to write something across the upper part of the whiteboard.

"Can I help with that?" I asked, startling her once again. She jumped back, making a big slash across the board in bright-orange dry-erase marker.

"That's it, Stevie." She laughed so hard she held her hand to her chest while she caught her breath and stilled her shaking shoulders. "You've got a detention."

"What for?"

"For repeatedly scaring your teacher."

I laughed along with her. "I didn't mean to, I swear."

"Then why do you find it so funny? If I didn't know better, I'd think you were trying to get me to jump right out of my clothes."

I stopped laughing, and my cheeks burned with what must have been a dramatic crimson blush.

"Oh," Jody said a second later, her mind obviously not as dirty as mine. "That was inappropriate. I didn't mean to imply just because you're gay—"

"Don't worry." I raised my hand. "We won't speak of it again."

She turned back to the board, the lovely pink fading from her cheeks as she searched for a way to reassert her professionalism.

I ached for her. She was only twenty-two. At her age, I spent several nights a week in bars drinking and discussing literature with my wannabe beatnik friends until all hours of the morning. We were crass and loud, opinionated and absurdly full of ourselves, but that was our right. We were young and free and still learning about ourselves. Why did Jody have to be so together? Why did she expect to have all the answers? Compared to the age of a high-school student, twenty-two was light years ahead, but in retrospect, the distance seemed trivial.

"I'm writing some major themes on the board to try to stimulate class discussion this morning," Jody said, clearly trying to reappropriate her teacher voice. But a softness in her tone came up just short of authoritative. "I haven't been able to get the class to take over the conversation, and I don't want to be the kind of teacher who does all the talking."

"All right," I said, wishing we could discuss something more personal, but I'd meet her wherever her heart was. "What are the topics?"

"We've reached the part in *The Things They Carried* where we get the sense we're not dealing with the most reliable of narrators."

"Yeah. A lot of these kids will have a hard time with that concept. For them things are still very black-and-white. Something is either the God's honest truth or an outright lie."

"Right, but that sort of thinking limits their worldview, which is why I want to start exploring the idea of what's real versus what's true."

Jody might be naïve, but no one could accuse her of lacking ambition. "Pretty weighty subject for a group of students who want you to give them a reading quiz."

A deep crease appeared in her brow. "I know. I need to draw the connection with something they're more familiar with."

"What have you got so far?"

"I thought I might use the Bible as an example, since the vast majority of the students here believe the Bible's overarching message is true."

I nodded, hoping she wasn't going where I thought she might.

"But most people also believe in evolution, so we could talk about the overarching truths of the creation story even while we agree it didn't actually happen in seven days."

Yup, she went there. I tried to hide the horror on my face. What a terrible idea. To keep things in Biblical terms, the students would crucify her. This wasn't technically the Bible Belt, but you'd never know that without looking at a map. People in Darlington used the Bible more as a bludgeon than a guidebook, and while I wanted Jody to realize she didn't belong here, I didn't want her to take a beating in the process.

"I've got an idea," I said. "Why don't you let me make that point?"

"Why?"

"Well, I agree with it. I get the concept, and I'm a student, so maybe if I start the discussion, more students will jump in."

Jody considered the offer, then smiled so sweetly I would've agreed to catch a grenade for her. "You wouldn't mind?"

"Not at all." I faked nonchalance. "The book sort of hinges on them understanding the difference between truth and reality, but it's a complex concept."

"And yet you already seem to have a pretty solid grasp on both subjects," Jody said, sounding both impressed and a little suspicious. "You're got a lot more on your mind than most of your classmates, don't you?"

I met her eyes and said, "That may be the understatement of the year."

❖

After Jody did her morning classroom-maintenance routine of taking attendance and collecting homework, she had us rearrange our desks in a circle. I understood her reasons for doing so, but I silently cursed her dedication to student-centered teaching. A circle offered me nowhere to hide and heightened my suspicion that I was about to step into a gladiatorial area. I'd heard Christians were traditionally the ones fed to the lions, but I'd begun to wonder. Then again, didn't the Bible say, "Love knows no greater one than he who lays down his life for his friends?"

Maybe I was getting overly dramatic.

My life wasn't on the line here. I merely intended to give the mob more reason to make my life miserable. I hoped Jody would realize the significance of my gesture and maybe conclude I was also capable of more than friendship.

Jody introduced the topic of what's real versus what's true and then opened the discussion to the class. They responded with utter silence. Not even the sound of crickets chirping would disturb the students' absolute unwillingness to engage her. I looked around at my classmates. Were they dense? Surely not all of them. Were they apathetic? Possibly. It was only eight in the morning, and most of them had likely not yet discovered the joys of espresso. Still, they were used to being up at this hour. Were they afraid to speak? Afraid of Jody? Or more likely afraid of each other? I hardly blamed them for fear of public censure. At almost thirty, I still feared being called on the carpet. I probably wouldn't have said anything either if I were them. But I wasn't one of them. I had something greater at stake. I had my future on the line.

I met Jody's expectant azure gaze and suddenly felt like a tragic hero prepared to fall on my sword for her. "I think it's very possible for something to be true without actually being real." I started tentatively. Then, as if ripping off a Band-Aid, I screwed up my courage and plowed through in a rush. "Like the creation story in the Bible. I believe it's true a loving God made the world of His own will and then pronounced it good, but He didn't do it in seven days. So even, while the account in Genesis might not be real, scientifically speaking, it's still true."

I sucked in a huge breath and braced for the impact but refused to make eye contact with anyone other than Jody, who was currently looking at me like I was the sweetest, cutest, most articulate little puppy she'd ever met. I basked in her approval for the long, shocked minute it took my so-called peers to process the argument I'd just made.

As usual, Deelia struck first. "Are you an atheist?"

Amazing, really. She never seemed very clever when it came to comprehending a legitimate argument, but she was a mastermind at distorting one.

"No," I replied calmly. "Hence the part of my statement where I said God made the world and everything in it."

"You called the Bible a lie."

"Again, no. I explicitly said what the Bible says is *true*."

"You said God didn't create the world in seven days."

"Correct. That statement deals with what's real, not what's true."

"Real and true mean the same thing," one of Deelia's minions said. "Don't they, Miss Hadland?"

"Actually, it's not that simple. They can certainly overlap, and most often do, but truth is a much bigger concept than reality."

Deelia's head swung from me to Jody as if it were a mounted machine gun. I had to do something fast to draw her fire back in my direction. Without thinking, I took Jody's original point and began to spin it out with my own touches. "Something can be true without being real. That's why we read fiction in the first place. We learn truths through stories like the ones in the Bible."

"So now the Bible is fiction?" Deelia snapped back, assuming her ever-present pissy pose, pursing her lips and folding arms across her chest.

"The Bible is filled with stories, Deelia," I said, my voice rising despite my best attempt not to care about her opinion. "Jesus used stories all the time to make His points. They're called parables."

"I know what a parable is."

"Did you know Jesus used them over forty times? Probably because, unlike you, He understood storytelling is a better way to help people see the truth than impersonal facts and figures."

"Did you call Jesus a liar?"

I threw up my hands and sat back in my chair. "No. *You* called Jesus a liar."

Deelia's nostrils flared, and she raked her overdone nails across the top of her desk like she wanted to claw my eyes out. "I did not! You take that back."

"No. Everyone heard you. You said if stories didn't really happen, they're lies. And Jesus told stories all the time. So, *Deelia, you* called Jesus a liar."

"Miss Hadland." She whined like she always did. "This lesson violates my freedom of religion."

I laughed outright. "You need to stop using words and phrases you don't know the meaning of. Freedom of religion doesn't mean everyone has to agree with your religion. It means we're all free to believe whatever we want."

"I've never been more offended in all my life," she said. I found that pretty hard to believe, but she was no longer addressing me.

She fired her next salvo right over Jody's bow. "You should expect a call from my mother, or maybe she should call the school board."

"Or maybe she should call me." I leaned forward as far as my desk would allow, forcing myself between Delia and Jody both physically and metaphorically. "I'm the one who said everything you found offensive. Attacking Miss Hadland for something I did makes about as much sense as calling Jesus a liar for teaching truths through the use of parables."

I rested my case, leaving Deelia scowling but tight-lipped as I turned my attention back to Jody.

Her complexion had grown as pale as I'd seen it since the night in the locker room, and her normally clear eyes were covered with a cloud of confusion and disorientation. For a moment I worried she'd cracked completely, but she merely blinked a few times and cleared her throat. "Maybe we all need a few minutes to cool off. Why don't we table the discussion? I'd like for each of you to write a reflection on the difference between what's true and what's real for tomorrow."

Nice save. She did a convincing job of pretending she'd had the assignment in her back pocket all along, and maybe she had, but she hadn't wanted to resort to it so soon. Maybe I'd pushed Deelia harder than I should have. Even I hadn't expected her to go quite that crazy. Jody obviously hadn't either. Apparently, even after all we'd both experienced during our high-school careers, sometimes the extent of the venom could still come as a shock. Maybe that meant we hadn't resigned ourselves fully to living in their world.

My hands shook as the aftereffects of adrenaline pushed through my system. I tried to remember any other time I'd willingly confronted another person but couldn't recall one. The high was actually kind of exhilarating, but I found the comedown mildly nauseating. How did people like Rory face confrontation every day? Did they not feel the fear? Did they grow used to it with time? Or maybe their righteous indignation offered a reward greater than the risk.

As I packed up my things after class, Jody walked by my desk and said, "Don't forget you've got a detention today. You can serve it during your study hall if you need to."

Deelia snickered. "Looks like you're going to get what you deserve after all."

"Yes, ma'am," I said, trying to hide my smile.

This time I hoped Deelia was right.

Word of my morning antics must have made their way around the school quickly, because by the time I got to keyboarding class, several people stared and whispered. So much for laying low. I'd drawn more attention to myself in the last few days than I had in my entire four years of high school the first time around, and when I flipped on my computer screen I remembered why. The words **Jesus-hating dyke** splashed across my Word document.

Kelsey sat down at her workstation with little more than a glance at my screen. "You had to see that coming."

I shrugged. "I suppose. It could've been worse."

"It'll get worse," she said, with about as much emotion as one would give when asked for the time of day. "Hope it was worth it."

"Me too." I set to work on knocking out the day's assignment in ten minutes, then e-mailed my work to Kelsey so she could copy and paste it into her document.

"I'm trying to learn here," she whispered.

"I know, but I want to talk about Jody."

"Then write that in the e-mail instead of cheating."

I rolled my eyes. Mr. Glass never even looked at our assignments. He just asked if we did the work, then put a check in his grade book.

Besides, did copying and pasting a page about my dear Aunt Sally's trip to the grocery store count as cheating? Probably.

Why did Kelsey have to be so damn good? Aside from her quirks and her weird views on the intersection of science and fiction, she should have been seen as one of Darlington's best students. She was obviously brilliant and thoughtful and diligent, and she didn't want to make trouble for anyone. Why was she an outcast when goons like Michael Redly were considered Darlington's finest?

Because she didn't look the part?

Because she couldn't throw a football?

Sometimes life sucked.

"Hey, wanna go out to lunch with me and Nikki?" I asked.

"I can't."

"Sure you can."

"I have to eat in the cafeteria."

"Are you banned from open campus?"

"Kind of," she whispered, sounding embarrassed.

"Why? What did you do?"

"I didn't do anything, I just…" She lowered her voice even further. "I'm on the free-lunch program."

I recognized the code name for the high-school equivalent of food stamps. "No big deal."

"It is a big deal." She let her dark hair fall over her eyes like a child who believed if she couldn't see someone they couldn't see her. "So don't tell anyone."

"I'd never do that, but it's nothing to be ashamed of."

"I know. We haven't always been like this," she said so quietly I barely heard her. "My parents' store got burned down in St. Louis. They spent what little insurance money we got to move here. They wanted me to live some place safer, but it's taken longer than expected to get the new store off the ground."

My heart broke for her and her parents. They just wanted a better life for their kid, and they were sinking everything they had into it. Wasn't that the American way? Why should Kelsey be rewarded with trouble at home and trouble at school?

"Lots of people need a hand from time to time. Half the kids in here benefit from farm subsidies. How's that any different?"

"It just is."

"Right. Farm subsidies cost about three times what free lunches cost and give back to a much smaller group of people."

She shook her head. "You just don't know when to stop, do you? You're going to get your ass kicked if you say that any louder."

She was right. I'd never win this argument here, and I'd only make life harder for both of us. But that didn't stop me from feeling frustrated about it.

❖

There was no sneaking up on Jody this time around. She was clearly waiting for me. She stood with her back against the whiteboard, a smile on her lips and dark circles under her eyes.

"Stevie," she said, as soon as I took a seat, "I don't know whether to hug you or choke you for the stunt you pulled this morning."

Please pick the hug, I prayed. But honestly, I would've settled for any scenario that involved her hands on me. I trembled at the thought of her slender fingers cupping the back of my head and pulling me toward her.

"What were you thinking?"

"What do you mean?" I asked, afraid she'd read my inappropriate thoughts.

"You knew Deelia would snap, didn't you?"

"Oh, that." I laughed nervously. "Yeah."

"I didn't." She covered her face with her hands for a second. "Her reaction didn't occur to me at all. It was just a frame of reference, and I thought it would affirm their faith, not offend them."

"You've got a lot to learn."

"Obviously. And not just about Deelia." She eyed me seriously. "You surprised me every bit as much as she did. I didn't know you had that in you."

"Really?"

"I wasn't surprised by your logic, which was flawless, by the way. I know you're intelligent and capable beyond your age, but you've been in my class for two months and I can't remember hearing you say more than two or three words to one of your peers."

"Yeah. I don't talk a whole lot in big groups," I explained, worried I'd given too much away. I'd been so concerned about sharing some little detail that would reveal my secret, I hadn't stopped to worry someone might notice something like a complete personality transplant.

Then again, until this morning I hadn't acted any different from my first time in high school. I'd mostly stuck to the same patterns of sitting quietly in the background just trying to slide by until I could get out of here. That was the Stevie Jody knew. Hell, that was the Stevie I knew. I hadn't changed much over the next eleven years. Should that bother me? Should a twenty-nine-year-old see the world the same way she had at eighteen? "It's not that I don't have things to say. I have opinions, but it's just never been worth the fight to share them around here. I'm not real big on conflict."

"Then why did you do it this morning?" Jody asked, coming close enough for me to detect the scent of wildflowers in her perfume. "Why expose yourself, especially in a fight that should've been mine?"

I shrugged. I didn't have an easy answer, at least not one I could explain fully, even to myself. And yet I did want to tell her something true. "I guess I did it because you wanted me to."

She didn't smile like I'd hoped. Her lips parted slightly, and her chest rose and fell a little faster. I tried to read the cues her body broadcast. Had I said something wrong? Or had I said something right?

"I feel guilty," she finally said, "for leading you into such a mess, for pulling you into all of this."

"All of what?"

"All my problems, all my insecurities, all my...all my..." She bit her lip so hard the subtle pink turned bright white. "My emotions."

My heart rushed an echoing drumbeat through my ears. Was she hinting at what I hoped for? I tried to search her eyes for some clues but once again fell prey to the new depth of blue before me. Azure? Cornflower? Cerulean? Maybe no word could describe what I saw in her eyes, the same way she had no word for the feelings causing those blues to swirl around her expanding pupils.

"Miss Hadland," a harsh voice called from the doorway. I jumped so hard I hit my knees on the little desk with a loud clang.

Jody did a better job of remaining composed. "Mr. Phillips, what a nice surprise. How can I help you?"

"For one, you can send detention students to my office." He glared at me pointedly. "And during regular detention hours rather than pulling them out of class."

"I just had study hall," I said, but his scowl clearly said he wasn't talking to me."

"I'm the disciplinary dean for this school."

"I didn't know such a position existed," Jody said. "I thought you were a gym teacher."

His thick neck reddened around his too-tight collar, causing me to wonder if maybe he'd get more oxygen to his brain cells by loosening his noose of a tie. "All out-of-class discipline needs to come from me. I don't want students to get the wrong idea about rules being enforced unfairly."

I snorted and tried to cover it with a cough. He clearly meant that if rules were being enforced unfairly he wanted to make sure they favored his favorite redneck jocks.

"I'm sorry for the miscommunication." Jody remained steady. "And I think maybe I also used the wrong term for what's happening here. Stevie isn't being punished. She's done nothing wrong. She simply fell behind on her classwork when she suffered her concussion. I've merely asked her to put in some extra time to catch up on the lectures she missed."

Drew looked like he wanted to argue with her but couldn't think of a way to do so without revealing what a dick he actually was, so instead he turned his attention to me. "Stevie, go wait in the hall for a minute."

I didn't want to leave her alone with this douche bag, but what could I say that wouldn't undermine her in front of him? "Yes, sir."

I exited the classroom and leaned against the wall right next to the door so I could still hear everything they said.

"Jody." He used a patrician tone. "You've made some honest mistakes here, and I don't blame you. You're young, and you've been given entirely too much freedom, which may have led you to believe you're a real teacher."

A real teacher? What, like you, Drew? Gag me. She's got more educational bearing in her little finger than you have in your entire stubby little high-waisted body.

"I'm truly sorry for misusing both the term 'detention' and the procedure for assigning them," Jody said politely. "In the future I'll be more careful to include you in disciplinary actions that spill over out of class."

"Good, and it might be a good idea for you to run your midterm grades by me as well, since disciplinary actions are often assigned for athletes who aren't making the cut. I'd like to see those before you send them home."

Hell-to-the-NO. He couldn't change the grades of athletes to keep them eligible. Would she let him get away with that? Did she have any choice? I couldn't stand it. No matter how hard I bit my tongue, I couldn't stay quiet. I stuck my head back into the doorway. "Excuse me, but should I go back to study hall, or are we going to finish my lesson?"

"I think we're done here," Drew said in his cocky, wannabe-sheriff's voice. If he'd had a hat on, he probably would've tipped the brim to the little lady on his way out. I wanted to trip him and watch all the smug superiority fall right off his face.

Geez, I had to settle down. I sounded more like Rory every day. "Sorry about that," I said, settling back into my seat.

"Not your fault," Jody said sadly. "He's right. It wasn't very professional to pull you out of class just to chat."

"Please don't."

"What?"

"Don't let that guy make you second-guess yourself. You're better than he is. You don't deserve to answer to him for the rest of your career."

"I doubt he'll have much impact on my career."

"If you stay here, he will. He's next in line to be principal."

Her eyes widened, and she looked truly horrified. "He's wholly unqualified."

I laughed. "That's never stopped people around here before."

"But he teaches gym."

"He's a disciplinarian, he's a good ol' boy, and he's one of them. He enforces the status quo. That's what they value here."

"Administrators can't just be jocks who get bored with teaching. They have to have leadership skills and flexibility and a broad, long-term vision. That guy is nothing but a glorified bully. And what is it with wearing his pants up so high?"

I stared at her for a long, heavy minute before I burst out laughing. I laughed so hard tears streamed down my face and I clutched my side. I laughed because her little tirade was funny and true, and so very her. For just one moment, the professional completely disappeared, and the woman stood, bold and beautiful, before me. The instant was glorious but short-lived, and her passion gave way to embarrassment.

"I'm so sorry," she said, lifting her eyes heavenward. "That was entirely inappropriate. I don't know what came over me. I'd never intentionally denigrate another teacher to a student."

"Even a teacher who needs to be knocked down a peg?"

"Stevie, we can't do this. He's a teacher. You're a student. This whole conversation has to—"

"Okay, fine." I blew out an exasperated breath. "I respect the position you're in, but can you honestly tell me that's how you want to spend the rest of your life?"

"I don't know what you mean."

"I think you do. Do you want to spend your career kowtowing to him and dodging students like Deelia and watching your pronouns and always having to check over your shoulder for someone trying to kick down your closet door?"

Her eyes filled with tears, but she blinked them away stoically. "We've slipped into a zone that's just a little too personal for me. I didn't call you in here to discuss my life choices."

"Fair enough." I recognized how close she'd come to falling apart, and I didn't want to be another bully to her. "What did you call me in here for?"

She took a deep breath through her nose and released it slowly through her mouth. "I just wanted to say thank you for saving me this morning. You were very selfless."

I shook my head. My actions might have been brave or crazy or helpful or uncharacteristic, but they most certainly weren't selfless. "It was nothing."

"Well, it meant something to me. You saved me from a nervous breakdown by taking all the weight on your own shoulders. How can I thank you?"

I grinned. "What are you doing this weekend?"

Jody immediately took a step back toward her desk. "I can't see you outside of school. I'm sorry if I've given you the wrong idea. This is why I shouldn't speak freely with you. You may be an above-average student on every level, but you're still a student."

Shit, I'd sounded too forward and once again had to scramble backward like a crab trying to escape the crash of an impending wave. "I'm sorry. I didn't mean it to sound like a come-on. I just meant it's been a long week. I need to break out of the mold of Darlington a little bit. I thought since you deal with the same sort of thing, you could offer some suggestions."

She still seemed guarded in her posture, maintaining the distance between us, but the kindness in her eyes suggested she might be willing to give me the benefit of the doubt. "I imagine it's pretty hard for you to relax around here."

"You have no idea."

The corners of her mouth turned up a little. "I actually do. I know those feelings well."

"So what do you do? How do you break the tension on your days off?"

"I usually spend my Saturday in the city, but you can't do that."

"Sure I can."

"Your parents let you go to St. Louis?"

Parents' permission. Right. Forgot about that. Was there no legitimate way out? No wonder most of my classmates drank so much. Well, I refused to spend my Saturday night getting lit in some cornfield. "Yeah, I mean, they're going to let me live in Manhattan in a few months. St. Louis doesn't seem so challenging by comparison. Where do you go? A bar?"

She blushed. "Actually, yes, sometimes I do. But I never drink to excess, and I never drink and drive."

How cute. She thought I needed the drinking-responsibility talk.

"And the whole thing is a moot point because we're not talking about me. We're talking about you, and you can't get into the bars."

Holy shit, this wasn't easy. "Right, okay. No bars."

"There's a bookstore in the Central West End called Left Bank Books. It's near a coffeehouse, and it's gay-friendly."

I tried to hide my disappointment. Normally a gay bookstore would sound like heaven. Over the next decade our community would lose its bookstores at a sickening pace. I wanted to collect them all in my arms and hold them tight to my chest, but not nearly as bad as I wanted to hold Jody. "Okay, well, maybe I'll check that out Saturday night."

She smiled wistfully, and I wondered if she wished she could join me. I almost offered another invitation, consequences be damned, but the bell rang, foiling my plans...or maybe saving me from them? Only time would tell, and lately time had been a fickle mistress.

❖

"Hey, Dad," I called into his study after dinner, "can I have a little extra money, please?"

"Why?" He turned around in his desk chair, and I was struck again by how much younger he looked now. I didn't generally think of my parents as aging, but I couldn't help remembering how the gray around his temples would continue to spread until it covered his entire head, and the Florida sun would deepen the creases around his eyes but wouldn't make him any less handsome. "What's the matter, Stevester?"

I shook the image of his future from my head. "Nothing. I just wanted to take a friend out to lunch. Her family's going through a rough time, and I didn't want to leave her out of lunch with me and Nikki."

He reached for his wallet. "You're a good egg. Thinking about other people is an important quality. I hope you never get so busy or important you forget that."

"I'll try not to," I said, even while I worried maybe I already had.

He pulled out two twenties. "Here's one for your lunches. Go ahead and pay for Nikki too."

"What's the other one for?"

"Your mom and I are both on the night shift Saturday. You'll need to order a pizza or something for yourself."

Had I heard him correctly? Both my parents would be gone from six o'clock at night on Saturday night until six o'clock on Sunday morning? That only happened about once every three months, and I silently thanked the time gods for finally getting something right. My conversation with Jody replayed in fast-forward in my head. She went to St. Louis after a long week at work. Surely this week qualified, and I'd have an entire night to test that theory.

I reached for the money, almost gleefully, but he pulled it back. "Wait a second. You still have to finish the dusting, and you have to give your old man a hug."

I rolled my eyes to make sure I played the part of the reluctant teen, but I gladly wrapped my arms around him and squeezed tight. Not many things about high school were better the second time around, but having an appreciation for the things I'd miss someday ranked at the top of that very short list.

Chapter Eight

By Friday I'd worn every reasonable outfit I owned, and then some. I pulled every remaining item of clothing from my dresser drawers and stood in front of my closet for ten minutes, but I had no more butt-crack-covering jeans or tops that didn't make me look like I was headed to a Renaissance fair. It was way too early in the morning for this crap. I'd been here for over a week, and I'd grown no more used to functioning at ungodly hours than when I'd arrived. Without my mom's morning mental-fitness tests, Jody served as my sole inspiration for getting out of bed, and I refused to greet her dressed like a slutty pilgrim.

Surely I could find some long-sleeved T-shirts in this house somewhere. If only my dad were smaller I would've stolen one of his, but neither my brother nor I had inherited his broad shoulders.

My brother. Andy. Why hadn't I thought of him sooner? He'd been at college for two years now but still had a room full of stuff here for the summers. I snuck down the hall and opened his bedroom door slowly. Even though he would never catch me, he'd spent years of our childhood yelling at me for touching his stuff, and those lessons didn't fade overnight or, apparently, even after a decade.

The room was unnaturally quiet and clean. Mom must have picked up after his last visit, because Andy never made his bed. I'd heard his wife voice the same complaint about their son. They lived in Atlanta, and I hadn't seen my nephew in months. I felt a pang of regret for missing his fifth birthday. How many years would I have to wait to make it up to him?

I shook my head. It was too early for deep thoughts. I needed to focus on things I could control, like comfortable apparel. Opening Andy's closet felt like hitting a jackpot. I found a long-sleeve Cardinals waffle-weave shirt that fit me darn-near perfectly if I cuffed the sleeves. I also snagged a navy-blue V-neck sweater and a lightweight, olive-green army jacket to hold me over for a couple days.

I walked into school feeling more comfortable than I had in a week, and it must have shown.

"You look like you're in a good mood this morning," Nikki said as she took the seat next to me in English class.

"Yeah. I guess I'm getting back to my old self."

"Really? You don't seem like the pre-concussion you at all."

Warning bells sounded in my mind. "What do you mean?"

"You don't hang out by our lockers in the morning."

"I've just been working with Miss Hadland to get caught up in her classes."

"You seemed pretty caught up yesterday when you jumped down Deelia's throat."

I tried not to laugh. "She's been asking for that for a long time."

Nikki didn't disagree but frowned with concern. "Are those Andy's clothes?"

"I wanted a casual Friday."

"Are you sure you're feeling all right?"

"Yeah." I lied. The longer this conversation went on, the less sure I felt.

"Are you mad at me?"

"No. Why would I be mad at you?"

"I don't know." She tucked a strand of her sandy-brown hair behind her ear. "You just seem kind of far away lately."

Damn. I'd been so worried about not getting caught I didn't think about what that distance would feel like from her side of the friendship. "I'm sorry. Let's catch up at lunch today. My dad gave me some extra money. Wanna go back to Encarnacion's?"

Her eyes brightened. "Yeah, that sounds great."

"Do you mind if Kelsey comes with us?"

The clouds returned to her expression. "Why?"

"I've been working with her in keyboarding class, and people are kind of hard on her."

Nikki didn't look unsympathetic so much as cautious. "They probably are, but she doesn't make things any easier on herself."

"What do you mean?"

"She's kind of weird. She wouldn't dissect the frog in advanced bio last month. And remember when she passed around the petition last year to get vegetarian lunch options in the cafeteria?"

No, I didn't remember that, but I could imagine how well it went over. "What's wrong with liking animals?"

"Nothing. I'm not mean to her. I just wish she wouldn't make herself such an obvious target."

"No one should have to worry about being a target," I snapped. "She's just a kid trying to graduate. It's the school's responsibility to keep her safe. It's the teachers' job to make sure we all get a fair shot here."

Nikki looked surprised. "Are you sure you're not mad?"

I lowered my voice. "I'm not mad at you, but I'm frustrated with the system. It's set up to reward people who play the game, not people who actually do the right thing. You gotta remember that, Nikki. When you're a teacher, you gotta promise me you'll work with the kids who need you, not just the ones who are easy to work with."

She nodded solemnly.

"I mean it. It would mean so much to me if you remembered this conversation." I pleaded with her. "Being a good teacher isn't about getting good test scores or having a tightly managed classroom. It's about making sure you see every kid for who they could be someday, no matter how deeply their potential is buried."

"I promise." She spoke with so much conviction I believed her. "And Kelsey can come to lunch with us, okay?"

"Thank you. It means a lot to me."

"I see that." Nikki nodded and glanced over my shoulder in a way that caused me to turn around.

Jody stood a few feet behind me with a dazzling smile on her face. My heart pounded. I hadn't meant for her to hear that lecture. I didn't need her to be reminded of why she wanted to stay in this business. My argument to Nikki had probably reignited Jody's resolve to be the kind of teacher I'd described. I should've been mad at myself for undermining my larger mission, but I couldn't summon any disappointment while being simultaneously warmed by the glow of Jody's approval.

❖

Lunch went surprisingly well. I could tell both Nikki and Kelsey were worried, nervous, and not quite themselves around each other at first, but as time went on I was able to broker some common ground, and they eventually shared a few laughs on their own. I wasn't naive enough to think they'd become best friends overnight, or maybe ever, but at least they'd developed some sort of connection that gave me hope neither one of them would be completely alone if I did somehow manage to transport back to present life. I still wouldn't completely let myself believe I'd time-traveled, but the longer I stayed in my past, the more valid that option seemed. It would be irresponsible not to at least take some precautions.

I felt pretty proud of myself, honestly. I'd almost made it through another day without drawing any extra attention to myself. Best of all, the tension between Jody and me practically crackled with electricity. She'd been nothing but professional all day. She hadn't pulled me out of study hall or even called on me in class. She kept well clear of my personal space and only spoke a polite good morning to me all day. To an outsider it would've appeared she paid me less attention than any other student. She came across as studiously unconcerned with me, which made my heart tap a rapid beat against my rib cage.

Jody simply didn't do aloof. She didn't do detached. She didn't do distant. None of this was her natural state, which told me she was fighting her instincts concerning me, and she wouldn't be fighting them if they were telling her I was just another kid in need. A normal teenager might have misunderstood her withdrawal, but I'd been in her shoes. I'd tried to play off attraction. I'd lived enough of my life to recognize the difference between generic concern and genuine interest. I also had a writer's eye. I'd written women on the brink. I knew the subtle signs and how people fought them. Jody played the part with textbook precision. I almost cried with joy to see her turn away as soon as I walked through the door for theater class.

As we arranged our desks into a horseshoe, I made sure to position mine as close to her as possible. I'd always been the one to be pursued in a relationship, and while I certainly wasn't coming on strong, I enjoyed the knowledge that my presence affected this graceful, beautiful, driven woman. I got so busy stealing glances at her I didn't notice Kelsey until she collapsed in a heap into the seat beside me.

"Hey," I said cheerfully. "Long day?"

"Yeah," she whispered, hanging her head so her dark hair covered her face.

"TGIF, right?"

"Uh-huh."

"Kelsey," I said more softly, "hang in there. Just one more class, and then we get a few days off."

She nodded, but when she looked up, her eyes were red-rimmed and the stain of embarrassment or anger burned pink even under her tan skin. I'd seen her tired and resigned, even frightened, but I'd never seen her so broken down.

"What happened?"

"Nothing." She blinked away tears.

"Bullshit, Kelsey. Talk to me."

"I'm tired, but I'm fine, really." She raised her chin and took a long, measured breath. "And you're right. We're almost done for the day."

I didn't buy it, not a bit. I'd left gym before the rest of my class since I didn't have to change or shower, but locker rooms, like hallways, were battle zones where teachers either couldn't see and hear the abuse or simply chose not to. I could only imagine what Kelsey had gone through in the ten minutes since I'd last seen her. I resolved not to leave her alone there again, even if it meant participating in gym class from now on. I was about to tell her that when Jody called the class to order.

"Today we start our monologues," she said joyfully.

"You mean our subtexts." Deelia sniped like an expert.

"Yes, but lucky for us, the subtext of a monologue is still a monologue," Jody said with forced enthusiasm. "Isn't that exciting?"

The students grumbled, but Jody forged on, reminding the class of the parameters. We'd do three monologues a day for the next week. Each student would get a turn to perform, then lead the class discussion of the original piece, its subtext, and what they took away from it.

She looked around, clearly searching for another place to sit before taking the seat beside me, and called the first performer. She crossed her legs so her body angled away from me and gave her full attention to the student. The position caused her black skirt to ride up to reveal a distracting bit of thigh. I had to place my hand on my own cheek and turn my head away in order to keep from staring. I might have failed completely if not for my lingering concern about Kelsey.

I barely knew the student at the front of the class, but he seemed to do a fine job with the Saint Crispin's Day speech. I'm sure I would've held my manhood cheap for not standing with him, were I not utterly preoccupied with the women sitting on either side of me. My mood had shifted rapidly in a mere matter of minutes. Had I suffered visions of grandeur in believing I could make a real difference in either of their lives? I wasn't even sure anything I'd experienced in the last week had actually happened. And yet, the tension radiating from both Kelsey and Jody certainly didn't feel dreamlike. I wanted to reach out to each to them, hug them, protect them, shake some sense into them, make them see what I saw in their futures. I felt like I owed them each something, but could I really make a difference for either of them, or was I deluding myself?

I didn't know the monologue the next girl did. Something from *The Crucible* maybe? I doubted she'd ever read the play all the way through or understood its meaning. She was one of Deelia's friends, and I wouldn't waste an ounce of my attention on her. Everything to come in my life seemed to hang on one question: how could I get Jody to give up on the future she planned while at the same time convincing Kelsey to hold on to hers?

"Kelsey, you're up," Jody said.

Kelsey took a deep breath but didn't rise from her seat.

"Are you okay?" I whispered. "Do you want me to go?"

She shook her head and took another deep breath. "I can do it."

She slowly, almost painfully sulked to the middle of the room, then without introducing the piece began to speak in a clear, low voice I barely recognized, "To live or to die, that's my choice. Is it better to put up with the insults and injuries or stand up for myself, and in the process sign my own death warrant? To die, to sleep."

Her performance was no mere recitation of Hamlet's "To Be or Not to Be" soliloquy. She actually posed these questions to us, or more likely to herself.

"Death would stop all the pain of this life, all the trials and abuse. I wish for a chance to dream peacefully, but we don't know what death brings. If I knew I could find peace there, I'd take it freely. Who wouldn't? It's only my fear of the unknown that makes me endure the painfully slow passage of time, the bullying, the loneliness, the injustice."

I listened helplessly as she grew more animated, clenching her fists at her sides while pleading the case of death and lambasting life for its constant stream of horrors. On the pro and con list of death, the columns weren't even close to equal. Even if I didn't know the end of this story, I'd have no doubt which option she favored.

"If there was some way to end all this hellish torture, who wouldn't take their own way out? It's only the fear of what lies beyond that turns us all to cowards."

With that she hung her head, and the class applauded lightly, uncomfortably. How many of my classmates, if any, realized she'd cut the last few lines of the monologue? I didn't doubt the purposefulness of the edit. She'd ended on a line filled with disdain at her own cowardice, because that's as far as she'd progressed on her own journey into darkness. She wanted to die but was still too afraid to do so. I had time, but not much.

Kelsey barely sat down before I jumped into the yet-unstarted discussion portion. "First of all, you did a great job with that piece. You captured Hamlet's main conflict and put it into language we don't just understand but can also relate to."

"I agree," Jody added, seeming to understand the gravity of Kelsey's message. "I felt your words down to my toes, and I recognized that place, the position where you just want to ask yourself why you should even bother with the life you're living."

While Jody might not be contemplating the exact choice Kelsey feared, she wasn't in a dissimilar situation. She too had to decide whether to fight for a dream or let it die.

"Do any of you have thoughts about this piece?"

Deelia raised her hand, and Jody sighed heavily. She clearly didn't want to call on her, but she was the only one prepared to speak, so Jody nodded.

"If she was talking about suicide, I think that's inappropriate for class. It's a sin, and it sets a bad example."

"*Hamlet* is a classic piece of literature that's been taught in high schools for hundreds of years," Jody said, leaving no room for debate. "So, does anyone have anything to say that actually adds to this discussion?"

She looked around the class from one blank stare to another until her eyes finally met mine. I had to say something, but what? Could I change anything? And, if so, to what outcome? Either I could feed her some silly pep talk about how everything would all work out in the end, or I came down on the side of death. I needed to find some middle ground. Thankfully the happy medium is what I knew best.

I turned from Jody's pleading eyes to Kelsey's dark, haunted ones. "The problem I have with *Hamlet*, and so many of the others who've tried to dissect this piece, is it's always such a binary. Either he does nothing, or he kills himself and everyone else. It's a false choice."

"How so?" Jody prodded me gently.

"Maybe for the sake of a play you have to force everything to fit into a two-hour time slot, but in life, we don't have to resolve every conflict or follow some preordained script. We have a hundred other options in any given situation. Sure, if Hamlet fights, he makes himself a target. Maybe that's true for us. Maybe it's not. But he could've just gone about his business. Lots of people do. He was a student. He could've gone away to college. He could have legitimately gone crazy. Someone very smart once told me sometimes insanity is a survival skill."

Kelsey didn't budge at that allusion. "Yeah, but what do you do when death is the only dream left?"

"You get a new dream," I said emphatically. "There's always another way out. Maybe that way sucks. Maybe it's hard. Maybe you dumb yourself down for a while or drink yourself into oblivion or join a commune or a rock band, but do whatever you have to do to get to the next step. There's always a next step."

"Sometimes there's not. Sometimes you do your best and it's not enough. Why put yourself through it if you're going to wind up in the same place in the end?"

"There's always an alternative future. Hamlet says it himself. 'There are more things in Heaven and earth than are dreamed of in your philosophy.' You of all people know that, Kelsey. Just because you can't see a future doesn't mean it doesn't exist." She smiled faintly, but a smile nonetheless, and it caused the weight on my chest to lighten immensely. We might be living on stolen time, but perhaps I'd just bought a little more sand for the hourglass.

With Kelsey stabilized I turned to Jody, who wore a similar expression, her smile tinged with exhaustion and sadness as her eyes met mine. "Thank you, Stevie. That was remarkably eloquent."

"Eloquent?" Deelia scoffed. "I have no idea what anyone is talking about anymore. None of this subtext has anything to do with theater. How are you going to grade us on this?"

Jody rubbed her eyes. "I've told you several times, you'll be graded on how well you capture the essence of your monologue and how well you're able to discuss your character's underlying motivations and emotions, something Kelsey did very well today." Then turning to Kelsey, she added a sincere "thank you."

As class dismissed, I wanted to stay behind and talk to Jody. I wanted to know if anything I said had swayed her. I wanted to focus on her beautiful eyes, see her chest rise and fall with each breath, feel her body close to mine, but I simply couldn't leave Kelsey alone in the hallway.

I walked with her to my locker, then drove her home. Thankfully, everyone was eager to chase their own Friday-night plans and paid us little attention. Kelsey didn't talk much but seemed in higher spirits when I dropped her off at her parents' store. I promised to stop by sometime over the weekend and left feeling secure about her safety, then quickly turned my thoughts and my car back toward Jody.

I tore into the school parking lot and sprinted up the stairs to her classroom only to find the lights off and the door locked.

"Damn," I muttered, then glanced around the empty hallway to make sure no teachers had heard me swear. What could I do now? I could go stalk her at the college, but that seemed creepy. And I didn't even know if she lived on campus. I could go to St. Louis tomorrow night hoping to run into her. What were the odds of that happening? Waiting until Monday was the only responsible, measured approach. Two days apart wouldn't kill me. I could probably use some time to myself. A few days off would let me clear my head. I could play it cool or safe, the way I liked to.

Who was I kidding?

I couldn't wait for Jody even under the best circumstances, and certainly not when both our futures were on the line. As soon as my parents left for work tomorrow, I had to go after her.

CHAPTER NINE

I cursed the damned dial-up Internet for the fifth time in ten minutes. I'd finally managed to connect, but every search I ran took ten minutes to load and produced few results. Apparently small Midwestern bookstores didn't have a big Web presence eleven years ago. They didn't have Google Maps either, and my car had no GPS. Also, I drove a stick shift, which, incidentally, is not at all like riding a bike. By the time I reached St. Louis it was dark, and my nerves were frayed. It was a miracle I'd made it at all, but now I had no idea what to do next.

I had a vague recollection of where the Central West End was located, and when I got close enough, I ditched my car. I never drove in New York, and I felt infinitely more in control once on foot. The city—any city—was better than Darlington for my self-esteem. I enjoyed each strike of my heel on the pavement. The snug rise of brick and concrete to either side shielded me from the vast vulnerability of the open plains. The anonymity offered by faceless crowds always soothed me. I passed plenty of people without really seeing them. I wasn't out of place to them. They didn't care if I was gay. They didn't care that I might be a time traveler. They didn't even know I existed. People passing by were so oblivious to my presence it actually took me three separate tries to get someone's attention long enough to ask for directions to Left Bank Books.

I was only a couple blocks away and thanked my internal gay GPS for getting me so close. I practically jogged to the bookstore, which stood bold and proud on a well-lit street corner. Bright light spilled from the large windows, drawing me into their warmth and illumination. Each light shone down on a display of books. Kate Bornstein, Sarah Waters, Dan Savage, gay, lesbian, bisexual, and transgender writers sat right up front with mainstream bestsellers. I exhaled, all the tension slipping from my shoulders, rolling down my neck, and sliding off my back. The last ten days faded behind a dizzying wave of emotion.

This medium, these books, was timeless. Suddenly I wasn't lost or unmoored. This art form connected me to brothers and sisters from hundreds of years past—Virginia Woolf, Oscar Wilde, Radclyffe Hall—and tied me to yet-to-be-written books by yet-to-be-born writers hundreds of years into the future. Someday I'd take my place, however small it might be, among them. I noticed my smile in the reflection from the window. I was already there. This moment, this connection, this stirring in my chest was more than anything I could've conjured. I'd never felt so certain of my future as I did with my forehead pressed against the windowpane of Left Bank Books.

Then I noticed something else in the reflection, something completely outside myself and the future I knew, yet unmistakably intertwined with it. I stared first at the reflection, then turned to face the unfiltered beauty of Jody Hadland.

She smiled reluctantly, as though she didn't want to but simply couldn't stop herself. The expression held so much doubt, and so much hope, almost like a resignation to happiness. The depth of concern in her sapphire eyes negated any youthful qualities I might have found in her low-slung jeans and V-neck sweater. So many questions passed from her, unspoken, to my heart. So many dreams hung by the frailest of threads. If I cut those ties, could I use their tattered remains to bind us together? Could I weave a brighter tapestry for her, or did she deserve more than I could promise? Standing in the face of her untempered beauty, I began to doubt not only my abilities but also my worth. Could a weary time traveler ever offer a future to such a stunning, driven woman? Then again, did I have any choice in the matter? We'd both tried to deny this connection across the years and miles, but here we were in a place and in a time beyond coincidence.

"Hi," I said, my gift for prose momentarily overwhelmed by the weight of understanding.

"Stevie." She said my name as if she enjoyed it more than she wanted to. "I didn't want to interrupt. I just saw you and you looked so, I don't know…like you'd returned home after being gone too long."

"I don't know about home, but certainly standing here took me back to some place I'm not sure I've been yet." I shook my head. Why couldn't I just *not* sound like an idiot for once? "I'm sorry. That probably doesn't sound right, but have you ever just known something that defies reason, logic, and even the laws of physics?"

"Something you can't justify or explain or even believe, but you can't deny?"

Where could we go from here? What could I say to make her see what I envisioned for us? Finally, she turned away, and I grasped for any strand of connection. "Let's go look at some books."

"What?"

"We didn't come to a bookstore to stand outside, right? Come on. You can give me some recommended reading."

I held open the front door. She hesitated, but her reluctance lost whatever internal battle she'd waged, and she accepted the invitation. I followed her inside, trying not to get too far ahead of myself. I'd never known an English teacher who could pass on a bookstore, but I hoped at least part of her acquiescence stemmed from an interest in more than the novels we perused along the way.

❖

"Have you read this one?" Jody held up a copy of *Rubyfruit Jungle*.

"Of course," I said. "It's a classic."

"Have you read all the classics?"

I scanned the shelves. "Sure. *Patience and Sarah, The Beebo Brinker Chronicles, Stone Butch Blues, Bastard Out of Carolina*—"

"Stevie, I don't think I can give you any recommendations. You're way ahead of me in this genre. Maybe you should create a reading list for me."

"No." I caught myself getting ahead of my time. "I'm sure you've just got different tastes."

"I just turned twenty-two. I'm not sure my tastes are fully defined yet. There's so much I haven't even been exposed to."

I heard the questions behind the statement and thrilled at the chance to expand the horizons she was searching. "Well, I'm not sure of much right now either, but I do know these books. I'd be happy to make a few suggestions."

"Please do."

I scanned the shelves. "*Pages For You* is a beautiful read."

"What's it about?"

"A student has her first lesbian relationship with a graduate assistant. It's a very intimate coming-of-age tale."

Jody flushed a bright pink, and I realized I'd flown too close to the flame. I saw the book as a heart-twisting reflection on first loves, but from Jody's perspective the idea probably seemed creepy. "On second thought, this one is better in retrospect. It takes time to get under your skin."

"In retrospect?" She eyed me suspiciously. "It just came out. How much time could it take?"

"Right. I didn't mean like linear time. I just meant it's best saved for times of reflection, not times of transition."

"What makes you assume I'm in a time of transition and not of reflection?"

"Wishful thinking?"

She raised her eyebrows, but I pushed on, searching for another story to make a point with.

"Here, *The Swashbuckler*."

She examined the cover, then turned it over to read the back. "Why this one?"

"The main character, Frenchie, is a lesbian-literature icon. Lee Lynch paints her with a full brush. You see everything underneath the great butch façade, and you still think she's a total Mack Daddy. It's like you've peeked behind the curtain and still believe in the Great and Powerful Oz. Every baby butch in New York wants to be Frenchie."

"What about you?" She grinned. "Will you have a Frenchie phase when you get to the city?"

Will I? Future tense? Right. I'd never strolled the sidewalks of the Village, never celebrated at the Stonewall, never rolled through the dunes on the cape at night. "Only time will tell."

"I'd like to see that," she said wistfully.

"Really?"

"Yes. I shouldn't think that way. I shouldn't wonder what's in store for you, but I do. My path is set, but yours seems so open and full of promise. I like the thought of you in New York."

"What about the thought of you in New York?"

"New York and I aren't things anyone would ever put together. Can you really see me in a city that size? It would swallow me."

I did have a hard time envisioning her there, but maybe because I didn't have the imagination for it. Then again, shouldn't a writer be able to picture the end of her own story? If I couldn't, did that mean I'd lost control of the narrative? Or maybe I'd misunderstood the characters? I had no trouble seeing myself in the Big Apple because I'd already lived it. Couldn't Jody do the same? Isn't that where the phrase "beyond my wildest imagination" came from? I was living a stranger-than-fiction reality. Why couldn't Jody do the same? Wouldn't she have to if she transported back with me? Did she even want to?

"Stevie?"

"What?"

"Sometimes you're so close, so vibrantly here with me I can hardly stand the tension. Then the next minute it's like you're watching a play no one else can see. Where do you go in those moments?"

"Back to the future." I slipped in an unguarded moment of honesty.

"The movie?"

"Something like that." I grinned, then redirected the conversation "But that's a story for another day. Have you ever read anything by Sarah Waters?"

"No."

"Okay. I recommend all her work. *Tipping the Velvet* is my favorite from a sentimental perspective. It's lush and emotional with a beautifully idyllic happy ending, but *Fingersmith* is a wonderful lesson in craft and plot development."

Jody seemed to force herself to focus on the books I held for her inspection but clearly understood this conversation had become about much more than a simple reading list. "I can't seem to make decisions right now. Which would you start with?"

I handed her *Tipping the Velvet*. "Lead with your heart."

❖

I wished I could take Jody to a fancy restaurant, open doors and pull out chairs, order wine, and lean close over a single candle. Instead, I set a more attainable goal. Thankfully, she didn't require as much convincing as I'd expected to get her to agree to have coffee with me. She'd clung to her last tenuous boundaries in refusing to let me buy anything for her, but that didn't stop her from smiling broadly as she settled into the seat across from me at Coffee Cartel.

I regarded her over the brim of my robust Columbian blend. Her cheeks still carried a flush of pink to match her lips, which parted to blow a slow breath across the surface of her coffee. I'm sure the move was meant to cool her drink, but it only managed to raise my body temperature several degrees. I inhaled sharply and caught the scent of my coffee—strong, rich, and smooth. I closed my eyes and focused on the sensual scent, trying to block the surging tide of attraction swirling inside me. I leaned hard on my addiction to coffee in hopes it would supersede the chest-aching need Jody stirred in me, but when I opened my eyes to see her clearly fighting the same emotions, I felt certain we were destined to lose this battle.

I sat back and sipped my java. "Half caf, part skim, and total perfection. God, that's amazing coffee. I haven't had any for over a week. I almost broke down and drank the Folgers cardboard brew my parents use, but this is worth the wait."

Her amused smile crinkled the corners of her eyes. "You're full of surprises."

You have no idea. "Really?"

"You're more observant than most adults I've met. You're more centered than any eighteen-year-old has any right to be. You're better read than I am, and now I find out you're a secret coffee snob. I don't know what to make of all that."

"Clearly, you're to infer I'm a thirty-year-old Columbian spy," I deadpanned. "And I assume you're my Swedish counterpart, under deep cover as a student teacher."

She stared at me for a few seconds before she burst out laughing. "How do you do that?"

"Do what?"

"Know just the right thing to say to keep me hanging on without scaring me away?"

Relief flooded my chest, and wonder clogged my throat. I had no idea how I kept her interested. I couldn't believe she saw anything in me, but I silently thanked whatever deity would listen that she hadn't run yet. Surely her increased openness served as a sign we were on the right track. I decided to test this theory by pushing a little further. "Well, you've got the goods on me now. You've found my secret identity. But I don't know yours. It's your turn to surprise me."

Her smile faded, and she hesitated in a way that made me fear she'd close up, falling back on her position as a teacher or her age or simply her privacy defenses. Instead she hung her head and said, "I came here looking for you tonight. I shouldn't have. I should've gone to the bar or not even come to St. Louis in the first place. And when I saw your reflection in that window, so sure and proud like you'd found your place in the world, I should've walked away. But I couldn't."

I shook. My hands, my knees, even my chest trembled at the truth she'd finally given voice to. I had the unreasonable urge to run from her honesty, from her vulnerability. Simultaneously hot and cold, I forced myself to stand firm amid the swirling emotions as my every heightened sense burned raw and exposed.

"Thank you for telling me. I know it couldn't have been easy."

"Easy? No, nothing about you has been easy for me." She shook her head. "But until tonight I've been able to tell myself I was doing the right thing."

"And now?"

"Now, I'm terrified because I'm not sure what's right anymore." She raised her tear-filled eyes. "Do you know what that feels like, Stevie? Do you know what it's like to question every decision you've ever made? To go through everything you knew about yourself piece by piece wondering where you went wrong?"

"You probably don't believe me, but I do know that feeling. It burns your nerve endings until you want to rip out your hair or cut

open your skin to release some of the pressure boiling inside you."
I took her hand in mine, disregarding the public place or the social
taboos in the face of her anguish. "It makes you question your sanity,
your very sense of self. It's like finding out the air you breathe has
turned to water."

"I don't know what's real anymore. I feel like my body, right
down to some cellular level, has betrayed me. I've spent years working
toward a goal, a purpose that's sustained me through the most horrible
days and given me a reason to go on. It's made me who I am."

"That doesn't have to change. You're still yourself."

"Am I? I don't feel like myself. I've never in my life been attracted
to a high-school student. Not even when I was in high school."

"Oh." Not my most eloquent response ever, but I couldn't
concentrate with my heart doing its own version of Riverdance across
my rib cage. She wasn't just drawn to me out of curiosity. She was
attracted to me physically and to the point of distraction from her
lifelong goals. Part of me was elated, but guilt weighed heavily on my
shoulders. Her devastation was totally unfounded. I wasn't actually
eighteen, and all the things she'd admitted being attracted to were
qualities I'd developed well past my high-school years. I had to find
some way to lessen her anguish without extinguishing her desire.
"Being attracted to someone unexpected doesn't have to be the end
of the world."

"It's the end of my career, and before it even got started. What
kind of a teacher can't last until midterms without crossing boundaries
laid in stone?" She sighed and sat back. "I'm sorry. It's not your fault.
I shouldn't be dumping any of this on you. This whole conversation
is another example of how far I've strayed from the path I set for my
life."

"What if stepping off the path isn't a sign you've gone wrong?"
I asked softly. "What if it's a sign you were never meant to take that
road in the first place?"

She parted her lips, then pressed them firmly together until
they formed a thin white line. Closing her eyes, she took a couple of
slow, deep breaths through her nose, until the tension lines around
her mouth relaxed. "That's what terrifies me. What if I only deluded

myself to get through my own trials? What if I never had what it takes to make a difference, to make life better for anyone?"

"Please don't say that. You're an amazing teacher. You could change so many lives, and you deserve to be in a place where people appreciate you, where people see you the way I see you."

The corners of her beautiful mouth quirked up slightly, and I wanted to kiss them lightly just around the edges until a full smile broke through. "You deserve to teach in a school where you can be out, where you can teach the plays you want, where you can start a gay-straight alliance or run an anti-bullying program. And you deserve to go home every night to someone who can't wait to hear about your day, someone who wants to share every part of your life and hold you all night long."

"Stevie." She said my name like a prayer, asking me to stop and simultaneously begging me to continue.

"Jody." Her eyes widened, but she didn't reprimand me for crossing yet another boundary. "You're better than the life you planned. You might learn to be content here, but you deserve to be truly happy. Don't settle for less."

"I've spent my whole life preparing for this moment."

"Your whole life? You're twenty-two. I know it's hard to see, but your life is just starting. You're still in the in-between. You're going to grow into an amazing, strong, self-possessed woman. You can do anything you want."

"I've only ever wanted to teach."

How could that be? Sure, she seemed like the perfect teacher, but why would I be sent back in time to pull her from her right path? No, she was the one for me, and I was the one for her. Neither of us would be here now if that wasn't true. "You can be a teacher anywhere. This country is littered with high schools. New York is full of them."

"You're sweet and passionate, and you make me believe in possibilities that seemed almost alien a few weeks ago, but you can't just paint me into your life or your future."

"I disagree. Give me a chance to show you."

She shook her head and shrugged, but her eyes were clear and bright again. "I don't see that I have any choice. I can't summon any restraint when it comes to you."

That may have been the sexiest thing anyone had ever said to me. I wished I'd had some sort of sexy comeback, but I'd turned into a gooey puddle of romantic Jell-O, and in the time I'd needed to get my brain and mouth to work in tandem again, she glanced at her watch.

"It's after eleven. We'll never be back in Darlington before midnight."

"Do you have a curfew?"

"No, but I'm sure you do."

"No, I don't." *Did I?*

She raised an eyebrow skeptically. "Well, I'm exhausted, and I have a lot to think about, but I'd feel terrible leaving you in the city all by yourself."

"Fine." I rose and offered her my arm. "I promise I'll go straight to my car as soon as I walk you to yours."

This time she didn't hesitate. Whether she'd made peace with what was happening between us or was simply too tired to fight it anymore tonight, she looped her arm through mine and leaned close as we strolled through the Central West End.

I wished I could have made the walk last forever. Having her close enough to touch was a high like I'd never experienced. The subtle scent of wildflowers in her perfume magnified each breath I drew. Every other nerve ending in my body seemed to mute, diverting all their energy to the places where her skin brushed against my own. I didn't feel my feet even hit the pavement in the two blocks it took to reach her silver VW Beetle.

"Cute car. It suits you."

"Thanks," she said, unlocking her door. "Where's yours?"

"That's a great question." I laughed. "I parked near Westminster and Walton. I just need to find my way back there."

She rolled her eyes playfully. "Get in."

I did a miserable job of suppressing my grin at the prospect of even two more minutes with her.

"You'll have to do a better job of paying attention to your surroundings when you get to New York."

"Maybe you could help me out if you come with me."

She didn't reply, but I noticed her smile in the illumination from the streetlights we passed.

"That's mine there," I said, pointing to my little red Ford Tempo.

She pulled up behind it and killed her engine before turning to me. "I don't know what to say, Stevie. There's nothing appropriate— we passed that long ago. But I don't want to complicate things further. I need some time."

"I understand," I said, taking her hand in mine. "And I don't want to make things harder for you. I don't want to be something else you have to hide from or run from, but I do hope someday I'll be the person you run toward."

Her breath caught in an audible gasp as the words echoed across the years. The memory flashed so fiercely I actually felt myself in her car in another time, another place, another moment when I shouldn't have let her slip away. If only I'd seized that opportunity and kissed her then, we wouldn't even be here now. Then again, staring into her beautiful blue eyes, I didn't care when or where my second chance came. I was simply overwhelmed with gratitude for getting one.

I took her face in my hands, gently brushing a strand of fair hair from her cheek. She could've pulled away. She could've said no or asked me to stop. Instead, she closed her eyes and parted her lips slightly. I hesitated only long enough to savor the delicious buzz of anticipation running through me. Then I kissed her.

No more waiting, no more doubt, no more wondering. The instant perfection of her lips on mine, smooth and eager, yielding and giving, quieted any lingering questions. The warmth of her breath on my skin ignited a fire deep in my stomach that begged to be stoked. Unbearable lightness expanded my chest and pushed behind my eyelids as Jody pulled me closer, her fingers scraping lightly at my side. I might have come completely unraveled at the disorienting mix of physicality and sentimentality if not for my unwillingness to miss a single detail of her mouth against mine.

A million fairy-tale tropes combined to accentuate the sensation of waking, of coming home, of coming into being. My future, *our* future, sealed with a kiss. I could not, in all my imagining, conceive a more perfect ending to this epic adventure of bending time and space in my return to Jody.

The tension grew even as we released it and the fervor of our connection overtook timidity. We kissed with abandon until my lips were swollen. Our shared breaths, stolen in greedy gasps, fogged the windows. Finally, as exhaustion combined with a stirring of emotional awareness, Jody pulled slowly back.

We stared at each other, chests heaving, as the haze of lust cleared from my vision until I could no longer escape the realization we were still in St. Louis. I was still a teenager, and her eyes still shone with confusion and fear. Where did we go wrong? The kiss was exquisite, flawless, the best kiss of my life. It felt truly life-altering, and yet nothing had changed.

"God, what did we just do?" Pain raked sharply through Jody's voice.

"I hope you don't regret it."

"No." She touched my face gently before pulling her hand back. "Regret isn't the right word, but I don't know where to go from here."

"I've never felt anything like this." *Brilliant commentary.* I had to do better. But I knew even less than she did about what the kiss meant for either of us. I only knew what it didn't mean. It didn't mean resolution or escape or completion. This ripping at my gut felt nothing like the happy, sappy, flowery moments in books or movies. Where was our ride into the sunset or even our jump to present-day New York?

I should've comforted her, somehow, but I couldn't process anything clearly. I didn't have the answers either of us sought. "So much for not complicating things."

Her smile was weak and her eyes unfocused.

"Jody, I don't know what's happening between us. It's not what I expected." *On so many levels.* "But you don't have anything to fear from me."

She nodded grimly. "I believe you. It's me I don't trust. I'm so sorry. You deserve much more from your first time."

"My first time?"

Her eyes widened. "That wasn't your first kiss with a woman?"

"Oh, yeah, I mean I guess it was." I smiled in spite of the insanity of that thought. I'd just given myself a much better first kiss than my original drunken grope in a Greenwich Village bar. "Please don't apologize. You're amazing. It was amazing."

"It was, but I can't just enjoy it. I can't just spend the night getting lost on your lips. I can't call you tomorrow or ask to see you again. I can't even say who I am right now, much less who I'll be on Monday morning."

"I understand. I don't like it, but I understand. I don't ever want either of us to go back to Darlington. I want to drive you to New York tonight. I want the future to start now, but I understand you're not as far along as I am. Go ahead and take your time."

"Are you sure?"

I wasn't sure about much of anything right now, but I couldn't begin to tell her why, so I said, "Apparently, I've got nothing but time."

CHAPTER TEN

I watched the sun rise over a recently plowed cornfield. I'd been so caught up in having jumped back in time that I'd failed to fully process the shift in landscape until this moment. I wasn't in New York anymore. Sounds of morning birds and distant farm equipment rumbling to life filled the orange dawn. I lay back on the hood of my car as the cool morning air pricked my skin and the loamy scent of earth filled my nostrils. The enormity of open expanse made me feel insignificant and vulnerable, or maybe I'd done that to myself.

I'd let myself believe in the illusion of control, carried on by some mirage of a destiny, but all those fantasies of purpose or universal plans only served as a crutch to my unstable mind. I'd gotten my second chance with Jody. I'd done everything differently and enjoyed the reward of a perfectly beautiful moment, but the aftermath remained unaltered. No, that wasn't true. Our undeniable rightness had changed us both, but to what point? I remained stranded in my past, and she was still stuck with a future full of uncertainty. In an attempt to make our situations better, I might have actually made them worse. Where could either of us possibly go from here?

The slamming of a screen door drew my attention to a nearby farmhouse. A young woman stepped onto a wooden porch and lifted her hand to shield the sun from her eyes. I sat up to take in this vision of the early morning. She wore sweatpants and a long-sleeve nightshirt but somehow managed to project an image of elegance as she moved to the porch railing and smiled sympathetically. "Stevie Geller?"

"Good morning, Beth." I felt uncharacteristically calm as I hopped off my car and walked toward the most comfortable presence I'd experienced in over a week. "I hope I didn't wake you."

"Not at all. I don't sleep past dawn any more, if I even sleep at all."

"I'm sorry about your parents."

She swallowed and nodded but couldn't seem to speak, so she motioned for me to sit on the porch swing while she settled into an old wooden rocking chair. I watched her look out over the land her father had worked faithfully until two weeks ago. Her curls were tousled in the style of the sleepless, her blue eyes sunken with a sadness surpassing exhaustion. She was a shadow of the girl she'd been in high school and held only the barest hints of the woman she'd become. Still, her eyes were kind and her smile genuine, if subdued.

"What brings a high-school senior out to a barren field at sunrise?"

"Honestly," I said, "I don't know. I just sort of ended up here."

"Autopilot." She sighed. "I know it well."

"Do you think it leads to anything?"

"I hope so, but I can't imagine anything beyond this right now."

I turned back to the empty fields. They wouldn't be so stark in a few months. The seasons would change, seeds would sprout, rains would come and go, green would supplant brown, life lying dormant would assert itself once again. I turned back to Beth. The same would hold true for her. I didn't know how she'd survive this time, but she would. She'd blossom and grow. She'd push against the confines of the life she'd previously imagined to become someone she couldn't conceive of yet. Her story would unfold like the leaves of a cornstalk, rich and vibrant. Even in the darkness of this painful dawn, I could clearly see where she was headed. I envied her that.

"This too shall pass," I whispered.

"Will it?" Beth asked. "I don't know how."

"Neither do I," I admitted, "but it has to. Time may not be linear, and it may not always move forward, but I can say with relative certainty that it does always move."

She regarded me quizzically. "What else do you know about time?"

I shrugged. "Maybe nothing. In some ways it feels like I'm learning a lot, but then something happens to make me suspect it's all a lie. What do you know about time?"

"You can't store it up, and you can't get it back."

"What if you could?" I asked. "What if you could do it over? What would you change?"

Sadness creased her forehead, making her appear much older than she would eleven years from now. "I'd live every minute in present tense instead of always planning for some future I had no guarantee of."

I opened my mouth to object, to assert my certainty in her future and mine, but the words wouldn't come. How could I be sure of anything? What she'd said might be true, but then again I didn't even know if this exchange was really happening. Maybe everything I knew about this moment was a dream, or everything about our futures was pure imagination.

Thankfully I didn't have to explain myself, as we were both drawn out of our reflections by the sound of tires on her gravel driveway. A black Chevy Malibu pulled to a stop near the front of the porch, and a tall young woman with dark hair and serious eyes got out, balancing two cups of coffee. She eyed me suspiciously while I tried to place her.

"Good morning, Kelly," Beth said, brightening slightly.

Kelly's face transformed, all harsh lines fading away to reveal her youth and a sincere affection as she focused on Beth. I suffered a momentary rush of protectiveness on Rory's behalf and clenched my fist to hold it at bay.

"I woke up early, so I thought I'd come check on you," Kelly said. "I didn't know you'd have company."

"I need to get going." I wasn't sure what story was being written between these two, but I had no part in it.

"Are you sure?" Beth seemed torn between inviting me to stay and wanting to be alone with Kelly.

"Yes. I'll see you again someday. Okay?"

"I hope sooner rather than later."

She couldn't understand what she'd just said or how much I shared that desire, so I nodded even though tears filled my eyes. "Me too."

❖

I slept, or rather napped, fitfully until early afternoon. Sleep provided no more solace than it did answers, and even in my dreams, restlessness began to grow inside me. I'd always enjoyed my time alone. Time to think, time to recharge. I ran from conflict and avoided complications, so after a full night of both, why couldn't I force myself to remain still?

Was it Jody?

Was it me?

Was it time itself?

After tossing and turning in bed, I paced around my room until finally I gave in to the urge to move more freely and found myself standing outside the gas station owned by Kelsey's parents.

A tan-skinned man greeted me warmly.

"Hello, Mr. Patel. I'm Stevie Geller. I'm friends with Kelsey."

He raised his bushy eyebrows almost to his receding hairline. "A friend?"

"Yes, sir." I understood Kelsey probably didn't get a lot of visitors. "Is she around today?"

"Just a moment." He seemed skeptical but not unfriendly as he locked the cash register and put the key in the front pocket of his short-sleeve dress shirt.

I wandered around the store while he went into the back room, noticing some displays of chips and dip, a refrigerator full of sodas and sports drinks, and a shelf full of car products, but the bulk of the merchandise consisted of alcohol. Most of the walls held walk-in freezers full of beer and wine coolers, and the stands down the middle of the small store were loaded with liquor of every variety. Well, not every variety. Most of it was low-end and high proof, which said a lot about their average consumer.

"Hey, what are you doing here?" Kelsey asked as she emerged from the storeroom.

"I said I'd stop by."

"Yeah, but I didn't think you meant it."

I sighed because I wasn't sure I'd been sincere at the time either. "Sorry. I've been so focused on other things."

"No problem," she said. "You have a pretty good excuse."

"Yeah, but you've got a lot on your plate too."

She looked at the tile floor. "I don't want to talk about what happened Friday, so can we just leave it alone?"

I didn't want to agree. I wanted to tell her I knew how bad things were for her and beg her not to succumb to the pressure of her life, but I remembered her resolve to follow through on whatever I told her about the future. I needed to find a way around her prohibition on talking about her life, but I couldn't risk pushing her over the edge. Besides, I'd have to be at my best for a conversation like that, and I barely felt functional right now. "Fine. You don't have to talk about anything...yet."

She ignored the end of my statement and changed the subject to one I couldn't resist. "Have you seen Jody this weekend?"

"Actually, yes." I glanced over my shoulder at her dad.

She nodded and pulled me into a small office with an overcrowded desk and two chairs, then shut the door behind us. The only thing on the walls was a black-and-white TV showing live footage of the store's security camera. Kelsey glanced up long enough to watch her father return to his post at the front counter, then asked, "What happened?"

"I kissed her."

"Wow, for a writer you're not much of a storyteller."

I rolled my eyes. "What do the details matter? I ran into her in St. Louis. She admitted being attracted to me. When she drove me back to my car, it was exactly like the moment in present day, or the future, or whatever. It was exactly the do-over I thought we were meant to have."

"And?"

"And I kissed her, like a knock-your-socks-off-and-curl-your-toes kind of kiss. Fireworks, angels singing, but then nothing."

"Nothing?"

"No transformation, no quantum leap, just a student teacher making out with a time-traveling student in her car. I did everything right this time, and it was perfect, but nothing changed."

"So now you're freaking out?"

"Of course I'm freaking out!" I shouted, then realized anyone on the other side of the door could probably hear us and lowered my tone. "What's not to freak out about? I've put us both at risk, and for what? To justify my mental break?"

"Are you back to considering mental illness as a valid possibility?"

"How can I not? I've changed everything and changed nothing." My throat tightened. "I'm not going to wake up from this nightmare no matter how many alternate endings I write."

"Well, to be fair, you haven't changed everything. You tried only one option," Kelsey said in her clinical voice.

"How many more options are there? I mean, do I need a complete personality overhaul? I don't want that. I did just fine with my life the first time around without putting my neck on the line. All I want to change about my future is Jody's role in it."

"Then why are you ready to abandon your plan so easily?"

"Easily? I put Jody's career in question. I took a knock on the chin from Deelia. I put myself at risk of being institutionalized by even talking to you."

"Yeah, but did you do anything differently this time that wasn't an attempt to get out of here?"

"Why would I?" Bile churned in my stomach again. I didn't like where she was headed with this. "The whole point of this experiment was trying to wake up and get back to where I belong."

Kelsey shook her head. "What if you belong here?"

"I don't."

"Maybe not forever, but you need to consider the fact that for right now, you're where you need to be. Whether it's a trick of your own mind or some greater plan, there's no fairy-tale ending at the moment."

I flopped into a chair, exhausted. "I guess I don't have much choice in the matter, but what the hell am I supposed to do now?"

"Just keep trying," she said.

"Keep trying what? Trying to win Jody? Trying to get her to quit her whole life for a high-school senior? I can't provide for her. I can't offer her anything but scandal. I can't even go to NYU if I don't finish high school, and what is she supposed to do if she stops student teaching? Just hang around here until summer? We can't be together. What if we got caught? We'd face the condemnation of the whole town. We'd be big gay symbols of everything they despise. I can't do that to her. Hell, I can't do it to me. I don't do conflict. I'm not that person." *I'm not Rory.*

The idea of being outed in Darlington caused a pain to throb right between my eyes and the roar of my own pulse to rush through my ears. I felt like I had on the podium back at the awards assembly, and I feared a similar outcome. "I've been deluding myself into thinking I'd find some way out. I don't see any good way for things to end anymore."

She hung her head and allowed her dark hair to cover her eyes. "Tell me about it."

Something twisted painfully in my chest. God, what was wrong with me? I'd given voice to her worse fears. "Kelsey, I'm sorry. I didn't mean that. I don't want to dump all my problems on you."

"It's fine. You're not saying anything I don't know."

"Really, I didn't mean anything. I just had a bad weekend. I'm sure there's another way."

"No, you're not," she mumbled. "You don't even believe you've time-traveled."

I exhaled forcefully. No, I wasn't sure I believed in time travel. Maybe I didn't know anything about our futures, but I did believe she was headed for trouble. Even if my mind had only made up a story about her killing herself, it likely did so because of all the evidence in front of me now.

I didn't know what to say, so I stared at the security monitor, watching a young man in a Cubs hat wander around the store. I enjoyed a mundane distraction, everything in black-and-white, literally, and with no controversy. I wanted to lose myself in the distant simplicity of this soothing play.

Then all of a sudden the tenor of the performance shifted completely when the guy on the screen grabbed a fifth of whiskey and stuffed the bottle under the flap of his denim jacket.

"Hey, Kelsey," I said.

"What?"

"That guy. He just swiped a bottle of liquor."

She glanced at the screen to see the man push out the front door.

"Hey, he's getting away." I jumped up. "We have to stop him."

She snorted. "This from the person who doesn't do conflict."

"Yeah, well, we can tell your dad."

"I don't want him to try to chase the guy down. I'll tell him in a minute." Her lack of concern worried me. Had she stopped caring about anything anymore?

"Should we try to get his license-plate number for the police or something?"

"The police won't do anything. We report stuff like this once a week. We have the video footage and plate numbers. Sometimes we even know their names, but the police act like it's our fault. They hope we'll give up and move."

Anger and frustration burned my skin. "But why?"

"For the same reason I get bullied at school, the same reason Jody can't come out, the same reason Mr. Phillips protects his rednecks and lets other kids suffer. The cops all grew up here, went to school here, and played sports here. Why would they act any different than the rest of them? Hatred is a learned behavior. It's passed down, taught."

I ran my hands through my hair until they got stuck in the tangle of thick curls. I wanted to rip them all out or scream or throw something. "Surely someone out there doesn't feel that way."

"Sure, lots of them," Kelsey said, sounding sadder than ever. She opened the door, then looked back at me before saying, "The good ones probably outnumber the bad, but it's just, well, they *don't do conflict*."

I followed her out and waited silently while she told her dad about the theft. I quietly watched his resignation as he viewed the tape and called the police station. I waited for an officer to arrive and added what information I could to his report. Helplessness weighed me down, causing my shoulders to sag the way Kelsey's often did. I stood off to the side, trying not to draw attention to myself. I would've slipped out if not for the sickening rock of guilt in my stomach.

I at least owed them the decency not to run away without telling Kelsey's father how sorry I was that people would steal from his store. He thanked me and said he hoped this incident wouldn't keep me from coming back to see Kelsey again. I assured him what I'd witnessed hadn't changed my opinion of them at all, but as I drove home, I feared the incident had lowered my opinion of myself.

CHAPTER ELEVEN

S tevie," Mom called as she knocked firmly on my door, "are you up?"

"No," I called back, and buried my head under the pillow.

"You better get moving."

"No," I said, softer.

"I heard that."

I groaned and pushed myself into a sitting position, then swung my feet onto the floor. "I'm up."

"Good," she yelled, and I promptly fell back onto the bed. The lethargy consuming me now stemmed from more than merely the early hour and another restless night. My weariness encompassed more than sandpaper eyelids and muscles too listless to perform basic functions like getting out of bed. My lassitude was born more from emotional exhaustion than physical.

How could I face another day in high school knowing what I now knew about my prospects for breaking out of this existence? Replaying some of the most frustratingly worthless experiences of my life had barely been sufferable under the impression that my plight held purpose, that I had some modicum of control over its final outcome. Now, with nothing left to gain, I no longer had the strength to hold myself upright long enough to face the onslaught of the day ahead.

I closed my eyes and let myself drift back to the last time I'd felt something other than turmoil. I was in St. Louis again, my lips against Jody's, her slender fingers running along my sides. My breath grew quick and shallow at the memory of her body against mine. I fought the urge to slip my hand down the flat plane of my stomach and under the waistband of my pajama pants. What was the point of having a teenager's body if I didn't get to enjoy the libido that came with it? Then again, why waste a perfect first kiss if I wouldn't get to relish the memory of it or chase a follow-up. It wasn't that I didn't want to. My body was on fire for Jody to the point I feared combusting when I saw her this morning. I wanted to go in early, close the door to the classroom behind me, and pin her against the wall. I wanted to lay her back on her desk and—

No.

This had to stop.

None of these fantasy scenarios would bear fruit. I forced myself to remember the confusion creasing her forehead, the anguish cracking her voice, the dark circles of worry under her blue eyes. And why? Because I thought I could save her? I couldn't even save myself. How the hell could I face her today and tell her I couldn't handle the pressure any more?

"Stevie," my mom called, "if I don't hear you moving around in thirty seconds, I'm coming in after you."

I considered telling her I was too sick to go to school, but my mom the doctor and human lie detector wasn't nearly as likely to fall for that as other parents. I rolled out of bed and braced myself on the wall until certain I wouldn't fall back down. Then I worked my way over to the mirror. I looked like I'd been on a tequila bender. My eyes were red and bloodshot, my skin pale. Worst of all, my hair stood out like a Chia Pet on steroids. I needed to pull myself together, but instead of asserting control over my life in some reasonable way like drinking coffee or taking a cold shower, I reached for a pair of scissors I kept in the top drawer of my desk.

The first cut came before I fully realized what I was doing. The second one brought more awareness as I watched several inches of black curls flutter to the floor. The next snip echoed through my ears with a metal snap, satisfying in its finality. With one more slice, I reduced the length of my hair by a third, so it hung just above my shoulders. I then set to work thinning the remainder with a few well-placed cuts to the under layers near the base of my neck. The end result was a shorter, shaggier style, a compromise between the Chia Pet and the closer cut I'd favor in a few years. It wasn't fashionable but an infinite improvement on how it'd looked before. A shower with some extra conditioner subdued the frizz, and when I added a pair of khakis and one of Andy's hunter-green pullovers, I felt almost human again.

In less than half an hour I'd transformed myself from awkward teenager to burgeoning baby dyke. I might not be able to control anything about my life, but if I had to face the daily hell of high school, I could at least look like myself while doing so. I wouldn't win any points for fashion, but I arrived at school feeling a little less helpless.

Nikki intercepted me as soon as I came through the door. "What happened to your hair?"

"I cut it."

"Yourself?"

"Yeah, can you tell?" I glanced at my reflection in the glass front of the main office. "I thought I did a passable job."

"No, it's actually pretty good, but why did you change it?"

"Because it looked like a blimp that dropped its toaster in the bathtub."

She laughed, then caught herself. "And Andy's clothes?"

"They're much more comfortable."

"That's all?"

"That's all." I lied, unable or unwilling to explain I was fighting an overwhelming sense of vulnerability.

"All right," she said, but didn't move out of the way of my locker. I glanced from her to my watch, then back to her.

"You in a hurry to get to Miss Hadland's class?"

"What? Why?" My stomach felt like I'd swallowed a bucket full of rocks. Why bring Jody into the discussion? Did she suspect something, or was I paranoid?

"You're spending a lot of time with her before school, and now you show up with a new haircut and wearing someone else's clothes."

So she didn't know what was going on, but she'd figured out something was up. "Maybe I've just got senioritis. I'm getting excited about New York, you know?"

She nodded. "Okay, but if there's anything you want to tell me, you know you can, right?"

The offer was sweet, and I was so tired of hiding I almost took her up on it. Maybe I should give her a chance to be a closer friend than I'd let her be the first time around. I entertained the possibility of coming out to her for about thirty seconds before she added, "You could tell me where you were all night on Saturday."

My chest tightened. "What's going on, Nikki?"

"I saw you drive out on I-55, and I started calling at eleven, then again at one a.m. By sunrise I got worried and drove over to check on you just to see you pull in at six in the morning." She waited quietly for a few seconds while my mind spun like a hamster wheel.

I had to say something, but what? It wasn't just about me. I'd put Jody at risk too. If someone noticed me heading to St. Louis, maybe they'd seen her also. Then again, Nikki didn't seem to know anything about Jody's involvement.

"Stevie," she prodded me, "are you in trouble?"

"No." *Maybe.*

"Then why won't you talk to me?"

"I'm just not really sure what's going on." It was the only truth I could voice at the moment. "But you're a good friend, and I appreciate that. As soon as I figure some things out about myself, we'll talk. But right now, can you not tell anyone about Saturday night?"

She looked torn between her desire to know more and her natural instinct to uphold a friendship. I pushed a little harder. "Please. It would mean a lot to me."

She sighed dramatically, blowing a strand of hair off her forehead and stepping away from my locker. "Fine, but please promise me you're not doing anything that could get you hurt."

I smiled weakly. I wasn't sure that was true in every sense, but I chose to believe she was only talking about my physical well-being. "I promise."

The bell rang, and I kicked myself for missing my chance to talk to Jody before class started. Then again, with as much trouble as I'd had facing Nikki, maybe I needed a little longer to decide what I intended to say to Jody.

❖

"Good morning, Stevie. Nice haircut," Jody said as soon as I walked in. She looked terrible and tired and so damn beautiful as she scanned me up and down appreciatively.

"Thanks." I tried not to make it too obvious that I wanted to unbutton her white oxford shirt with my teeth.

She seemed as though she wanted to say more or hear more from me, but neither one of us had the words or the privacy to express what was happening between us. Students took the seats behind us, and Jody did a commendable job of calling them to order. I doubted anyone else noticed the distracted way her eyes kept meeting mine or that she didn't appear to have a detailed lesson plan like she usually did.

Instead she declared the period a reading day for us to catch up or reread challenging parts of *The Things They Carried*, followed by a one-page reflection. She didn't engage us again for the rest of the period. I opened my book but never turned a page, instead wondering if she'd checked out of today's class because she was too upset to focus or if she'd simply lost her will to care.

I would've been thrilled with her lack of commitment three days ago but now found it troubling. I glanced at her over the top of my book and found her watching me too. In the second our gazes connected, I noticed her eyes were red rimmed but bright. She likely hadn't slept any more than I had, but she didn't seem nearly as downtrodden. I quickly buried my nose back in my book.

The aftermath of the kiss we'd shared should've been more gut-wrenching for her than for me. With the way she valued the boundaries of a teacher/student relationship, she shouldn't be able to reconcile what we'd done with the teacher she hoped to become. Why wasn't she avoiding me? Why wasn't she terrified of me? Why did she seem to want contact instead of distancing herself behind her professional façade?

I set to work writing a reflection on truth versus reality. It was basically the same paper I'd written last week, and I could barely bring myself to acknowledge that reality or truth even existed. Nothing felt real right now, and truth seemed such an idealistic concept when I couldn't believe the basic laws of science. I certainly didn't trust my own judgment enough to decipher the difference between it and reality. It took everything I had not to blurt that out after class when I handed my paper to Jody.

I waited until all the other students had left before asking, "Are you okay?"

"I am." The corners of her mouth quirked up. "Or I will be soon."

"Really?" I asked, distracted by the memory of her mouth against my own. How in the hell would we mange to last three more months without ripping each other's clothes off? And why wasn't she more upset about that prospect?

"I've made some big decisions." She shook slightly as though she'd just suffered a chill.

The hair on my arms and neck stood on end. Something wasn't right, something I couldn't place yet. "Do you want to tell me about them?"

"We can't talk now. If we're going to do this, we need to do it right."

"Okay," I said, not at all sure what she meant.

"I have to make it through the day, and so do you."

"Do you want me to come in after school?"

"Please." She reached out as if she intended to take my hand, and I wanted to give it to her, but I couldn't. Not here, not now. Someone might see, so I stepped back. Her smile faded, and the spark left her eyes.

"After school, okay?"

She pursed her lips together and nodded. Then I left quickly before either of us said or did something we'd regret. I had to stay strong, but as I neared the door she called out, "I really do like your hair."

I turned to see her looking so very young and hopeful, as though she were the schoolgirl instead of me. My heart twisted sharply because, of course, she was. I couldn't shake the feeling I was destined to break both our hearts.

❖

I spent the rest of the day in a stupor. I have no idea what happened in any of my classes, and I spent lunch sitting in my car in the school parking lot. After all I'd been through, it seemed weird to say, but something wasn't right, and not just the time-travel business. My every sense seemed deadened, as if I had cotton in my ears and mouth. Maybe I was in a coma and nearing the end. Or maybe everything else felt dull and colorless compared to Jody's touch.

Jody. What big decisions had she made? Why did she get to be clear-eyed and smiling while I muddled through a gray fog? I would've resented her peace if I didn't care about her so much. I wanted her to be happy, and even more, I wanted to be part of that happiness, but I didn't want to risk public condemnation in the process. Maybe we could be friends until we were in a better position. Then again, isn't that what we'd done the first time around? Why couldn't that be good enough for God, or the universe, or my coma?

I slammed my gym locker in frustration.

"Not eager to get back to gym class?" Kelsey asked.

"Something like that."

"Well, it's basketball day. That should be easy on you."

"Why?"

She shook her head and whispered, "You're on the basketball team."

"Right," I said with all the confidence I could muster, then under my breath added, "eleven years ago."

Drew Phillips set up the girls on one half of the gym and the boys on the other. I still wasn't cleared for contact sports, so he relegated me to retrieving balls that went out of bounds.

"And try to pay attention this time, Geller," he instructed me.

I rolled my eyes and jogged to the other side of the court before I said something inappropriate. I spent the next fifteen minutes chasing out-of-bounds plays while Drew settled himself comfortably in the first row of the bleachers and proceeded to watch only the boys' game. I found the entire exercise tedious, with the exception of the sarcastic remarks I occasionally whispered to Kelsey, who mostly ignored me in favor of trying not to trip over her own two feet. I didn't think anyone could be clumsier than I, but somehow she managed.

Of course Deelia didn't help anyone on the court with her overblown belief in her own athletic abilities and her insistence on playing the annoying role of ball hog. She missed shot after shot, at least half of them air balls, then managed to blame her teammates for a bad setup or insufficient block while growing embarrassment fueled her sharp tongue. I glanced at Phillips, wishing he'd realize she needed to be taken out, but women's sports apparently deserved even less attention than the dirt he was currently scraping from beneath his stubby fingernails. I tried to ignore Deelia's mini-meltdowns until she stomped her foot as she threw another ball so hard it ricocheted off the backboard and bounced into the boys' game.

"You shoulda got that one, Stevie," Michael barked as he picked up the ball.

I ignored the comment and extended my hand for the ball, but instead of passing it, he turned to Deelia. "Here ya go, babe."

In true show-off jock form, he inbounded the ball too hard, and Deelia took an abrupt step backward, which sent her directly over Kelsey's feet. She went down dramatically on her backside, hitting the floor so hard it jarred her whole body onto the court. She let out a high-pitched yelp and glared at Kelsey. "You tripped me!"

"I didn't," Kelsey said, her eyes wide with panic.

"You did. You did it on purpose."

I started toward them but wasn't fast enough to beat Michael. He flew across the court and towered over Kelsey. I watched helplessly as she cowered in his shadow and began to apologize profusely.

"I'm sorry. I didn't mean to. I mean, I didn't know she needed to back up."

The entire gym class stopped to watch the exchange, and even with several yards between us, I had no trouble hearing what came next. Michael reared back and shouted, "Shut up, you worthless sand nigger!"

A violent shake caused my stomach to lurch painfully. I don't know where I found the strength, but I charged through them all until I pushed my way in front of Kelsey to face Michael. "Take it back, you ignorant, racist asshole."

"Stay out of this, you fucking dyke."

He spat the word down into my face with more venom than anything I'd ever had directed at me. I fought the acidic tide of bile in my throat but didn't step back. Maybe I was frozen in terror or shock, but I didn't move until Drew Phillips put his arm between us.

"Break it up, you two. What's going on here?"

"Kelsey tripped Deelia, and Stevie snapped on me."

"Liar. I snapped on him because he used a racial slur."

Drew turned to Michael, who rolled his eyes.

"He did. He called her the n-word." I couldn't even bring myself to repeat the comment. It hurt bad enough just to think about. "And then he called me a dyke."

Drew rubbed his forehead. "All right, everybody needs to cool down. Deelia, go to the nurse. Michael, get back to your own game."

"What?" I exploded. "Did you hear what I said? He used a racial and a homophobic slur. That's hate speech, and the school is *supposed* to have a zero-tolerance policy. You can't let him walk away without any punishment."

"Fine." Drew shrugged. "Michael, if I hear you cuss in class again, you'll have to run some laps."

"Okay, Coach," Michael said, then smirked at me before jogging back to his game.

"Cuss?" I couldn't let it drop. "Racial slurs aren't cuss words! Do you not understand that, or do you not care?"

Drew's face turned red, then purple. "He got his warning, and here's yours: if you don't want people to call you a switch-hitter, maybe you should dress a little nicer."

Several of the students snickered or laughed outright at the comment, and my face burned so hot I feared passing out again. I'd never considered hitting another human being in my life, but my hands balled into fists at my side, and I had to grind my teeth in order to restrain the terrifying flash of rage pushing up from my core.

"Now hit the shower," Drew ordered us. "All of you."

The others made a break for the locker rooms, but I stood, feet cemented to the floor, until Kelsey and Nikki flanked me on either side and pushed me toward the locker room. I let them lead me blindly, shuffling through a red haze of hurt and anger.

I sat on the bench and kicked off my shoes, then pulled off my shirt, all fear of high-school locker rooms gone. I couldn't see anything but red, anyway.

"Are you okay?" Nikki asked.

"I don't know." I pulled on my khakis. "I guess. What about Kelsey?"

"I'm fine," she said from behind me. I turned to see her dressing quickly, her head down and her hair covering her face.

"Really?"

"Yeah," she mumbled. "I'm sorry I got you in trouble."

"You didn't." I jumped up and grabbed her by the shoulders. "That wasn't your fault."

She lifted her chin and shook her dark locks from her eyes. The pain and embarrassment I saw there were more terrifying than Michael's wrath. She looked haunted or, worse, dead. I dropped my hands to my sides, fear turning the embers of my fury to ice.

"Hey." Nikki nudged us both. "Everybody's okay. It's not that bad."

I stared at her in disbelief, and she shifted awkwardly from one foot to the other.

"Really," she continued nervously, "I'm sure he didn't mean it. Besides, he's a jerk and no one likes him anyway."

Some of the girls around us nodded. Others looked away nervously. Nikki plastered a fake smile on her face. "Everything's all right. Just let it go and get to class, okay?"

Kelsey nodded, and I did the same, even though I knew neither of us would be able to let it go. We'd carry the trauma of those words with us for the rest of our lives, no matter how long or short they might be.

I stumbled more than walked into Jody's classroom, and her eyes darkened immediately. She scanned me up and down, then looked past me to Kelsey, who slumped into her chair and put her head down. Jody joined us immediately and crouched between our desks. "What's the matter, you two? What happened?"

"Nothing," Kelsey said into her hands

I inhaled sharply at the low monotone of her voice, catching the scent of Jody, so close, so comforting. We couldn't do this on our own. I wasn't strong enough, and neither was Kelsey. The words spilled out of me. "Michael Redly called Kelsey the n-word, and he called me a dyke."

Jody gasped. "That's it. We're going to the office right now."

"No! Please, no," Kelsey pleaded.

"We have to. That's harassment—it's *abuse*. It can't be tolerated."

"It already has been," I said. "Mr. Phillips heard him say it and didn't do anything."

She eyed me seriously, silently asking for the rest of the story. "And he told me if I didn't want people to think I was a switch-hitter, I needed to dress nicer."

Her blue eyes turned dark and stormy, and her face flamed red. She pounded her fist on her own leg. "Unacceptable. I'll go over his head."

"Don't do something to make it worse," Kelsey said in a trembling voice.

Jody glanced at her and froze. Maybe she saw the extent of her pain or her own fear mirrored in Kelsey's eyes, but her expression softened drastically.

She took a deep breath before smiling at Kelsey, then back at me, all hints of her anger fading under a mask of compassion. "Okay, you're in control of this situation. I know it may not feel like it at the moment, but you aren't alone."

Kelsey nodded, and her chin quivered before she flipped her hair back into her face.

"Stevie, you can sit out your monologue today if you need to."

I couldn't collapse. I had to stay strong for her, for Kelsey, maybe even for myself. "I think I can do it."

Jody smiled sadly and squeezed my shoulder. "Okay, the floor is yours."

I stood on weakened legs and took a few tentative steps to the front of the room. "This is the subtext from Zubaida Ula's monologue from, um…" I closed my eyes and composed myself. "It's from *The Laramie Project.*

"I was at a memorial service for Mathew Shepard, and it made me feel better to know I wasn't the only one who felt terrible. I'd thought maybe I didn't have a right to be so upset because it hadn't happened to me. Then someone said, 'We have to show the world we're not the kind of people who do stuff like this.'"

I snorted bitterly, a rusty taste like blood coating my tongue at the memory of Michael's words and Nikki's attempt to whitewash them away.

"It's a lie. We are the kind of people who do bad things because we let them continue. How can we pretend we're not? We already let it happen. What kind of backward thinking are you deluding yourself with to be at the place where bad things happen, where you see them with your own eyes, and hear them with your own ears, and then you say, we're not really like that?"

My voice picked up and so did my pulse. I was moving away from the script, away from the subtext, away from acting. I looked from Kelsey to our classmates, then to Jody, pleading with them all to give me some answers. "We have to address this, we have to admit we're part of it. We can't look the other way or sweep it under the rug. We need to take responsibility for our own part in all this hurt and pain. We have to admit part of it is our fault. It is *our* fault."

My voice echoed loudly through my ears and rattled into my chest. "It *is* our fault."

I didn't wait for their reaction. I didn't look at their faces or listen to their delayed applause. I took three steps and collapsed into the nearest empty desk. Jody was on her feet in an instant standing beside me.

"Thank you, Stevie," she said, looking intensely into my eyes. "Thank you, very much. I know you're supposed to run the discussion, but I'd like to say a few things first, okay?"

"Okay," I croaked gratefully.

"A teacher has to think about so many things, and they're all important. At any given moment, I'm worried about each one of you. Will you understand the reading? Did I challenge you enough? Will you pass the state tests? Have I prepared you for college? Will I make it through all the course material in time? Did I remember to take attendance?" She sighed, then smiled. "It's so easy to get overwhelmed that sometimes I forget the most important things we can learn will never show up in a textbook or on a test or on a college syllabus."

She walked around the room as she spoke, making eye contact with each student she passed. "Our responsibility as human beings far outweighs our responsibility as students or teachers, and Stevie's monologue reminded me that each time we fail in those human responsibilities, we hurt not just ourselves, but everyone around us."

She pulled up a student desk and turned it to face us all. "Let's circle up and talk for a while."

The students looked nervously at each other before moving their desks into a circle. "We're not going to do the rest of our monologues?" one of them asked.

"We'll have time for monologues later. Let's focus on creating a dialogue," Jody explained gently. "I want to hear your thoughts on bullying."

The room was dead silent, and everyone struggled to avoid eye contact by staring at their shoes.

"I understand it's not an easy topic," Jody said. "I was bullied pretty badly through middle school and high school. I even considered killing myself for a while."

I expelled a breath of air like I'd been punched in the stomach, and Kelsey looked up with wide eyes and rapt attention.

"I complained to the administration, but they were too busy to listen or too overwhelmed to care, and bullies are smart. They learn early what they can get away with and when and where." Jody continued, her complexion pale without the flush of anger that had marred her skin earlier. "I used to wonder why no one ever stopped them, why otherwise good people let the taunting and harassment continue, but then I realized they were being bullied too."

Jody's eyes grew piercingly bright, and as she talked her natural coloring also returned. I watched, transfixed as she came more fully alive than I'd ever seen her. "You see, a bully doesn't have to actively terrorize everyone. They just have to make one person so miserable no one else would dare cross them for fear of becoming a target themselves. All those other students who stood by and watched me drown were just as scared as I was. Do you know what I'm talking about?"

One of the students raised her hand, and Jody acknowledged her with a gracious smile.

"I just, I wanted to say sorry to Kelsey." The girl stared down at her desk, as her voice grew thick with emotion. "I don't agree with what Michael said, but I didn't know what to do."

Kelsey's tan skin lightened with a pink tint as she mumbled, "It's okay."

"It's not really," the girl said. "I just didn't want it to happen to me, and then when he unloaded on Stevie, I got even more scared."

"That's important to admit," Jody said, getting up and moving over to stand beside the student.

A boy near her raised his hand, then said, "I didn't hear it. I only learned what happened on the way to this class. I've been sitting here telling myself I would've said something, but that's probably not true. I'm fighting to keep my grades up and stay on the baseball team. I don't have the energy to fight other people too. And I feel guilty about that."

Jody regarded him with nothing but compassion as he struggled to find more words. She'd opened up to them, so naturally they couldn't help but respond. She hadn't pressured them. She'd merely met each student where they were and gracefully led them to a better place. I'd never seen her so at ease with her role or with herself. Not even when she'd surrendered to my kiss.

Especially not then.

"But we've all got our own problems, and if I don't stand up for what's right, how can I ask anyone else to?" the boy asked.

"I think this is where I need to remind you all you aren't alone," Jody said, taking the floor again. "Bullies thrive by isolating people, but you don't have to face them by yourself. You have friends, you have parents, you have teachers."

One of the students scoffed. "The teachers don't help."

"Some won't, you're right," she admitted sadly. "But some will, and you know who they are. You have coaches and pastors and school counselors and the nurse too. You may have to try more than one option, but you have to keep trying."

Why didn't she just tell them to come to her? They clearly wanted to. I saw it in their eyes—even Kelsey's. They were pulling strength from her the way she'd always hoped they would. She'd just done exactly what she became a teacher to do. Why not embrace that final step? Why not encourage them to lean on her?

Then her words rushed back to me. *"I've made some big decisions."*

She'd decided to leave with me. She refused to tell the students she'd be there for them because she wouldn't. I should've been thrilled. I should've jumped over my desk and pulled her into my arms. I should've wanted to carry her out the door.

Instead, the weight of guilt pinned me to my chair. It held me down and choked out my voice. It clogged my ears and drowned out the remainder of the conversation. She'd just found her purpose. I'd watched her transform from a girl into the woman I'd already known she'd become. In setting aside her own needs to meet those of her students, she'd actually become a more full version of herself. A better version than I'd ever inspired her to be.

I couldn't let her quit.

I couldn't let her leave these kids behind.

I couldn't let her settle for me when she could have something so much more meaningful.

The bell must have rung because everyone else packed up their things and left, but I never heard it. I didn't move either. Not even when Kelsey said she was headed out. I should've gone with her, but I couldn't.

When Kelsey was gone, Jody closed the door. She turned to me looking tired and conflicted, but smiling. "You were magnificent today, Stevie."

"No." I shook my head. "You were. I'm so impressed with how you stood up for those students. How you guided them through those emotions. I'm so sorry I didn't see it sooner."

"See what?"

I stared at her for as long as I dared, trying to memorize her features one last time, to pack away one more happy moment. I let my eyes caress the slender curve of her hip and trace the arch of her neck. I ran my gaze along her jawline and lingered at the corner of the lips I'd kissed. Then I glanced up and met the deep blues that called to me across time. "You belong here."

"What?"

"You're where you're supposed to be. These students need you."

She looked at me with wide, wounded eyes as if I'd betrayed her. "What about what I need?"

"You need them too. They're part of you." My voice cracked, raw and broken, an outward sign of how my heart felt. "I was selfish to tell you otherwise. I wanted you for my own. I thought I could give you a better life, make you happier, but I saw the way you connected with them today. I can't give you anything better than that."

"I'm not asking you to give me anything. I'm offering myself. I'm ready to walk away." She glided her hands through her light hair and shook them out. "I've written my letter of resignation. I'm giving it to my advisor tonight."

"No." I jumped up. "Jody, you can't. Where would you go? Think about your future."

Her eyes were frantic, like a wounded animal's. "I did. I wanted you to be a part of it. And I can't have a relationship with a student. I won't be that person, but I won't be without you either. I thought you wanted me too."

"I do. God, I do…but there's no way. Maybe someday, but not now. Do you have any idea how much trouble we'd get in if someone caught us? It'd be worse if they found out you resigned for me." I paced around the room, trying to make her see the consequences of following me down the path I'd advocated days ago. "You'd never teach again. We'd be in the papers. We'd never get out from under a scandal like that."

"All I'm hearing is you talking about what everyone else needs or wants or will do." She came closer, dangerously close, so close I broke into a sweat at the physical battle to keep myself from falling into her arms. "What about your monologue? What about taking responsibility for what you want, for what you know is right?"

"I don't know what's right any more."

She froze, then, looking heavenward, shook her head. "I can't believe this. You're a liar."

"I'm not."

"You are. You're a liar and a coward. You're so afraid of making a scene, of taking a stand you're even lying to yourself."

The words stung.

"I thought you were different. I thought you'd changed. Then when you kissed me…" She covered her face and stifled a scream into her hands. "I let you kiss me. Damn it, I can't undo that, Stevie. I have to resign now."

"You don't. No one will ever know."

"I will know!" She staggered, and I reached out to steady her, but she pushed me away. "I will know, and I've made my peace with that. It wasn't easy, but for you I did. I believed you would do the same for me."

"I'd do anything for you, if I could. Please believe me." I begged frantically for her to understand me. "If I knew of any way out of this situation, any legitimate option or alternate reality, I'd take it."

"Alternate reality? This one isn't real enough for you?" Her shoulders sagged, and she leaned against the wall to support herself, or maybe to bear her disappointment in me.

"What do you want me to do?" I pleaded.

"Create your own reality."

"I can't."

Jody hung her head, then looked back up, her eyes meeting mine before she said, "Fine. I can't make you take responsibility for your own story, but if you want to be a writer, you'd better learn to craft better endings than this."

I opened my mouth to speak, but the words wouldn't come, and it didn't matter anyway. Jody had stopped listening. She turned her back to me and stared out the windows of her classroom. I wanted to go to her, to touch her, to comfort her. Instead, I ran.

I tore through the hallway and down the stairs, intending to blow past my locker. Everything had backfired. Lancing, piercing pain tore at my chest and burned my lungs. The first time I'd done something for the right reason, or at least for selfless reasons, I'd ended up feeling worse than ever. My breath rasped in harsh gusts, raw against my throat and shaking all the way to my stomach. I'd destroyed Jody. I'd wrecked her dream, then failed to provide her with a new one, and in doing so I'd cut off my one refuge in this endless nightmare. I saw no relief, no solace, no hope left anywhere on the horizon, no future for either of us. No future at all, only the constant downward spiral of the past.

Blinded by tears, I careened around the corner only to draw up short a few feet from a group of students. Michael and Deelia led the horde, and I took a step back. What where they still doing here? It didn't matter. I was already running.

Then I heard Kelsey's voice, small and scared, over the pounding of my own heartbeat.

"I'm so sorry," she said.

"Sorry's not good enough when my girlfriend has a sprained wrist." Michael sneered.

I skidded to a stop. White-hot rage boiled up inside me and lent so much force to my voice I hardly recognized it as my own. "Leave her alone."

The crowd turned to look at me. Michael's eyes narrowed to angry slits. "Excuse me?"

"Leave. Her. Alone."

"Why should I? Because some dyke bitch says so?"

"Go ahead and call me a dyke if it makes you feel better about yourself. It must be hard for you to see people like me and Kelsey headed for bigger, brighter lives, when you know you're barreling toward a dead end."

"What are you talking about?" Deelia snapped.

"Oh, come on, Deelia. Even you aren't that dumb." I circled closer to them now, something I couldn't explain taking over and subduing the fear inside me. "You know how this story ends."

"I don't know what you mean," she said, raising her nose in the air.

"I'm going to NYU in the fall. You're going to cosmetology school."

"Michael's going to State."

"Where he'll major in drinking until he accidentally knocks you up and has to marry you." Once I'd started spinning this narrative, I couldn't stop. The words poured out, each one like a boulder being lifted from my shoulder. "Then he'll work a series of dead-end jobs until he gets so resentful he'd rather make love to a bottle of whiskey than you."

"That won't happen."

"It will," I said smugly, while their eyes bulged and a thick vein popped out on Michael's neck. "And you'll both get fat."

Kelsey laughed, and they all turned menacingly to her, but I got between them quicker this time.

"Don't even try to pin any of this on Kelsey. She's not responsible for your failings or your insecurities. She's moving on to better things than you can even imagine."

"Stevie," Kelsey whispered, "don't say anything else."

I turned to see her shaking her head and backing away. "I have to."

"I don't want to know the ending."

The ending. Jody's voice rattled through my memory. *"Learn to craft better endings."* Kelsey'd already said she'd be stuck with whatever I told her about the future. I could tell her anything. I could create a new reality. "Kelsey, you have to listen to me whether you want to or not, because you're going to get through this. You're going to make it through three more months, and then you're going to find a whole new world for yourself in college."

"I can't."

"You can. You have to. You have to go on to become a scientist."

"A scientist?"

"Yes, and an amazing doctor who blends traditional medicine with new technology and ancient wisdom. You'll help people in ways other doctors won't even consider."

Kelsey continued to shake her head, but she was smiling now, a smile like I'd never seen, one of disbelief but also of wonder. It changed the shape of her entire face and lifted the corners of her big brown eyes.

"She's crazy," Michael said, then shouted again, "Stevie Geller is crazy."

"Yes, I am," I shouted back with equal force, drawing the attention of everyone up and down the hall.

Doors opened, and Drew Phillips stepped out of the administration office. "What's going on out here?"

"Stevie's yelling at everyone," Deelia complained. "And she's lying too."

"Yelling, yes," I admitted, "but not lying."

"Is this still about the name-calling?" he asked sternly.

Footsteps fell rapidly on the stairs behind me, and I glanced over my shoulder to see Jody approaching. "This is about taking ownership of my own story, and since everybody's here now, I'll only have to say this once."

"Say what?" Drew asked through clenched teeth, his face turning a disgusting shade of maroon.

"I'm gay," I said resolutely, then for emphasis added, "very, very gay."

Gasps echoed through the hallway, and Drew looked like he might be physically sick. "I won't have that kind of talk in my school."

"Would you rather I call myself a 'switch-hitter'? That's the term you used, wasn't it?"

"Stevie," he shouted.

"What? You don't want everyone to know you directed a homophobic slur at a student? Or maybe you don't want them to know you're really bad with sports metaphors because I'm not a switch-hitter. I bat for the other team."

"Get out of here right now, all of you," Drew snapped, then turning to me specifically added, "You tell your mother to expect a call from me."

I raised two fingers in a Boy Scout salute, then whirled on my heel, immediately locking eyes with Jody. The disappointment had vanished from her expression, replaced by sheer pride, accompanied by a dazzling smile. I took one step toward her, but as I did, my foot connected with someone's leg.

I had plenty of time to process the fact that someone had tripped me and to wonder why I hadn't expected it. The fraction of a second before I hit the ground was also enough to see the admiration on Jody's face transform to fear as she reached out for me. I wanted to catch her hand, to pull her close, to touch her one more time, but the last thought that pushed through my mind was that I was about to hit my head.

Hard.

CHAPTER TWELVE

I recognized the familiar hum of hospital activity and the smell of antiseptic, along with the IV running down my arm. I didn't have to open my eyes to know I'd suffered another concussion. My head throbbed, and my neck ached. I sighed heavily and braced myself for the surge of pain I knew would accompany the act of opening my eyes.

"Stevie?" Jody asked, and I turned my head toward the sound of her voice, sparking a wave of nausea. "Can you hear me?"

I nodded and opened my mouth to speak, but my throat was too dry.

"It's okay," Jody said, laying a hand on my shoulder. "Lie still. I'm going to get the nurse."

I relaxed into the pillow, trying to discern if I'd sustained any other injuries from the fall. I wondered which one of those assholes had tripped me when I was on such a roll. Probably Deelia—she'd been standing closest. So much for sliding through my senior year a second time. Everything would be different now. At least Jody'd come to the hospital with me. I still didn't know how to make peace with whatever we were to each other, but hopefully coming out to the whole school constituted taking a stand. Was it enough to make her stay?

"Hey, Stevie," a vaguely familiar voice said. "I paged the doctor, and I'm trying to keep your friends from getting too excited out in the waiting room. I don't want you getting worked up, okay?"

I nodded and managed to croak out an "okay."

"Can you open your eyes?"

I tried, only to have my eyelids flutter enough to let in a sliver of painfully bright light before clamping them shut again. "Hurts."

"Sensitivity to light is not uncommon with a concussion. Miss Hadland, will you close those curtains?"

I heard the soft pull of industrial-grade fabric against metal, and the white light trying to penetrate my eyelids lessened to a grayish pink.

Do you remember where you are?" the nurse asked.

"Darlington."

"Right."

"And do you remember what happened?"

"Someone tripped me."

I heard some rustling, then silence, and I wished I could see the nurse's expression.

"What about the date?"

"Um, March eleventh, 2002?"

"Did she just say 2002?" Jody asked, fear creeping into her voice.

"Okay, Stevie, you took quite a hit, and you've been out for a while. Why don't you just stay still and quiet until the doctor gets here, okay?"

She wasn't telling me something. The surreal sense of déjà vu pricked at my skin. "Did I get the date wrong?"

"Don't worry about that now. I'll be right back."

I waited for the soft click of the door closing before asking. "Jody, are you still here?"

"I am," she said, and I felt her hand cover my own.

"What year is it?"

"Stevie…" she said, conflict thick in her voice.

"Please, tell me. Am I a senior in high school?"

"No."

My head spun, and I fought to keep from throwing up.

"Are you okay?"

"Yeah," I lied, then forced a smile. "Just hibernation sickness, I guess."

I squinted my eyes a little until I acclimated myself to the dim light of the room. I searched for her face, but everything was still a blur. "How long have I been out?"

"You've been in a coma for almost twenty-four hours."

"That's all?"

"That's all?" She laughed softly. "It's been the longest twenty-four hours of my life."

I heard the door open and a man's voice say, "Hello, Stevie. I'm Doctor Lohnes. How you feeling?"

"Pretty bad at the moment."

"I bet." He took my wrist between his thumb and fingers. "Your pulse is okay, and your vitals are strong. How's your noggin?"

"A little fuzzy," I admitted. "I think I told the nurse I was a senior in high school."

"You sure did," he said, not unkindly. "Have you rethought that answer?"

"Yes." I hesitated. "I think I'm twenty-nine."

"Where do you live?"

"The Village. New York, New York."

"That sounds exciting. Do you remember what landed you in Darlington Regional Hospital?"

"I was at an awards assembly, and I got so nervous I passed out."

"Well, that's not the medical explanation, but it's close enough."

"What's the medical explanation?"

"Do you want me to step outside?" Jody asked.

"No," I said, and managed to open my eyes a little more. "Please stay."

"You're fine," the doctor said. "It's nothing too serious. You had very low blood sugar complicated by a good bit of dehydration. Add a bona-fide panic attack, and your body couldn't keep up with your accelerated heart rate or shortness of breath. You lost consciousness, and when you fainted, you sustained a pretty significant concussion. Your body needed some time to recuperate."

"Sorry," I mumbled.

"It's okay," he answered.

"Not to you, to Jody."

"Hush. What's done is done," Jody said. "I just want you to get better."

"I'm feeling a little better." I opened my eyes again, this time all the way to meet hers. They were every bit as blue as I remembered. Her hair was shorter but still fair and fine. The subtle appearance of lines across her forehead might have been from age, or maybe concern, but they did nothing to detract from her beauty. I trembled and squeezed her hand tighter.

"What is it?" Jody asked, leaning closer. "Does it hurt?"

"No, it's you." I caught my breath and tried to let it out slow and steady. "You're still so beautiful."

Her lips parted, and her cheeks turned crimson.

"Well," the doctor said awkwardly, "you must be feeling better."

Oh shit, did I say that aloud? Had I just outed her? I let go of her hand quickly and tried to sit up, struggling against the bass drum of pain pounding through my skull. "Sorry. I just…I'm still a little out of it."

"It's okay. I see nothing to worry about long term, but given the amount of time you were out and the level of your disorientation, I want a specialist to look you over."

"Sure." Maybe that wasn't more warranted than he realized.

"Can the others see her now?" Jody asked.

"Yes, as long as they keep it quick and quiet."

He closed the door behind him, and I stared back at Jody. "I'm sorry for saying that. I don't know what came over me. I'm having a hard time getting reoriented to the future."

"The future?" Rory asked, coming in with Beth right behind her. "That's a heavy topic for a moment like this."

"Not really." I tried to explain. "Not when you've spent the last ten days living in the past."

Beth raised her eyebrows. "That doesn't sound very fun."

"It was awful. Mostly." I laughed. "I was back in high school."

Rory agreed. "That does sound awful."

"It must've been a dream, but it didn't feel like one. You were there," I said to Beth, then turned to Jody, "and you were there."

Then I looked at Rory. "You weren't there."

"Good." She grinned.

"It just felt so real and so long, so detailed. I feel different now, like I'm not sure which of my memories are real and which ones aren't."

"Are you sure you're okay?" Beth asked.

"Yes. I'm a little sad though. I mean, I even considered the possibility I might be dreaming because of the circumstances, but I don't know…I expected things to be different when I woke up."

"Like what?" Rory asked.

"I'm not sure. Maybe a happier ending." My chest throbbed at the thought of Kelsey, and tears filled my eyes. I missed her already. "I let myself think I could make a difference, like my actions could make someone else's life better, only to find out I didn't actually take the chance, ya know?"

Everyone stared quietly, either at me or the floor. Were they thinking about their own missed opportunities or mine?

A gentle knock on the door caused us all to look up as a striking Indian-American woman entered carrying a clipboard. She had long, straight black hair and big espresso eyes. "Stevie, I don't know if you remember me, but I'm Doctor Patel."

My heart jumped painfully, and I fell back to the bed with a sickening thump that caused pain to flash red and white behind my eyes.

"What's the matter?"

"What happened?"

"Are you okay?"

Everyone talked at once, but Dr. Patel was the first to act. She was over me in an instant, cupping one hand behind my head and the other on a pressure point on my neck. "Stevie, can you hear me?"

I nodded, shocked into submission by the touch of her very strong, very capable hands. "Kelsey?"

"That's right. I've got you. I need you to take a deep breath," she said calmly. "Breathe through the pain."

I sucked in a deep, gasping breath and shuddered it out through a clenched jaw. Then I attempted another one, this time a little slower.

"Okay," she said, "let me see your eyes."

I met her intense gaze, so unlike the cold, disillusioned expressions I'd come to expect from her. "I bet that hurt pretty badly. Care to tell me what happened?"

"I don't know what happened," I said honestly. "You, you startled me."

She glanced at the monitor wired to my arm. "Your heart rate is worryingly elevated, but your oxygen intake is still good. You've had enough excitement for one day."

I'd probably had all the excitement I could handle for a lifetime, but I couldn't begin to explain that now.

"I'd like you all to say good-bye for the evening," she said to the others, then turned back to me. "And I want to run a few more tests on you. I'll be back in a few minutes."

As soon as the door closed, everyone turned to me, looking worried and confused.

"Jesus." Rory rubbed her forehead. "What was that?"

"I don't know." I blinked and rubbed my eyes.

"You looked like you'd seen a ghost."

"I did."

"What do you mean?" Jody asked, her voice strained.

"I saw Kelsey Patel. That was Kelsey Patel, right?"

"Yes."

"Rory?" I asked. "Don't you remember what I told you about her before the assembly?"

She seemed to search her memory. "No, I'm sorry. I don't remember ever hearing her name until today. What did you tell me?"

"That she killed herself when we were in high school."

I didn't need to decipher the looks the others traded. They thought I was crazy. I'd begun to suspect as much myself.

"I'm an anti-bullying advocate," Rory said, slowly, softly. "I'd remember hearing about a Darlington student committing suicide."

"Jody." I was pleading. "You remember her, don't you?"

"I remember she was in your class. That's all." She shook her head. "But Rory's right. If one of my students took their own life on my watch, it would've consumed me. I would never be able to forget a loss of that magnitude."

"Are you sure that wasn't just part of your dream?" Beth asked

"I have a clear memory of our conversation, and it was before I passed out. I know it was. Or I thought I knew. Now I'm doubting everything."

"Like what?" Jody asked.

"Like you," I said, examining her more closely. If Kelsey was alive, had I also altered Jody's path. "Did I kiss you in your car?"

"Last night? No." Her blush returned. "I thought you might, but you didn't."

"What about when I was in high school?"

Rory blew out a low whistle. "Wow, that must have been a hell of a dream."

Jody shook her head. "You most definitely did not kiss me then. I'd have never survived student teaching."

"But you did survive, didn't you? You've been a teacher in Darlington for all these years?

"For better or worse," Jody said, her voice softened with exhaustion.

"It's for the better." I squeezed her hand. "Please, trust me."

"Okay." Worry creased her features. "I trust you, but you need to rest."

"Will I see you again?"

"Of course. None of us are going to leave you alone. You know that, right?"

I nodded. I didn't know much else, but I did know that.

I lay in the hospital bed and stared at the ceiling. I'd woken up. I'd returned to my life, to my future, or the present. I'd hoped for this transition, prayed for it, and changed so many things in my own mind to get here, but now reality felt less real than my dream. Or had it been a dream? If so, when had it begun? And had it ended yet?

As if summoned by my musings, Kelsey entered my room tentatively. "No fainting on me, okay?"

I smiled in spite of my confusion. No amount of disconnect could temper my happiness at seeing her alive and well and apparently successful. "Sorry about earlier."

"It's okay. The nurse told me it was 2002 for you earlier today."

I sighed. "It sounds pretty crazy."

"Maybe, but people thought Galileo was crazy too."

I eyed her suspiciously. "Do you believe in time travel?"

"I don't know. Do you have a Tardis?"

"I think we've had this conversation before."

She shrugged and took the seat beside my bed. "It's not impossible."

"Really? Do you remember it?"

"No, but I can't imagine all the conversations I've forgotten since I last saw you."

"I feel like I just saw you yesterday but also a very long time ago. What kind of doctor are you?"

"I'm a neuropsychologist. I deal with the intersection of brain functions and psychological processes."

"Wow. I have a hard time believing there's much call for that in Darlington."

"There's not. I'm based out of St. Louis University Hospital. I only see patients for consult here once a month, but when I heard you were in, I had to come check on you myself."

"Why?" I sat up and tried to search her eyes for any clue as to what connection we had to one another. "What do you remember about me?"

"Honestly, it seems like so long ago now I'm having a hard time recalling a single specific encounter. It's like waking up after a dream. I remember how I felt rather than what happened. Still, I think you were nice to me in high school when no one else was."

"And that's enough for you?"

"The mind is a funny thing. We understand only a small part of our brain functions and even less about our emotional response patterns or their triggers."

"So you don't think it's impossible for me to have time-traveled, but you think it might be impossible to know for sure what happened while I was unconscious?"

"It's a funny, funny business, and those aren't the answers I generally look for."

"Right. You wanted to run some more tests."

She smiled, an expression I didn't think I'd ever tire of seeing from her. "I just did."

"And? What's the prognosis, Doc?"

She rose and patted my hand. "The only thing standing between you and a full recovery is your willingness to open your mind to experiences that defy logic."

I snorted. "You have a prescription for that?"

"Yes." She chuckled. "Time."

CHAPTER THIRTEEN

I slept fitfully, each time I roused fearing I'd awake in a different decade. I frequently startled myself into awareness with a lurch that caused my stomach to revolt and my brain to hammer against my skull. Somehow, reentry to the present was even harder on my body and mind than going backward had been. I didn't recover nearly as quickly or painlessly this time around.

Perhaps it was harder to face all the inconsistencies in this transition. At least when I'd gone backward, I'd done so all the way. Jumping forward seemed to change parts of my life while leaving others untouched. Trying to figure out which things fell into which category left me fighting a kind of emotional whiplash to accompany my physical symptoms. Then again, maybe I continued to struggle physically simply because I wasn't eighteen any more.

I stared down the neck of my mint-green hospital gown to see that my breasts and stomach had lost both their form and firmness. Frowning slightly, I glanced up to find Jody watching me, amusement curving her mouth and crinkling the corners of her eyes.

I grinned sheepishly. "You caught me comparing my present-day body to the one I had yesterday. You know, when I was eighteen."

"Ah, well, we've all been there."

"Really? You don't look very different than you did then."

"I doubt that. It feels like ages ago."

"Not to me."

She pulled a chair right up next to my bed and sat down. "I can't imagine what you must feel like. You're jumping from one point of your personal history to another, losing people and picking them up again along the way."

"That's very sympathetic of you, especially since none of that actually happened."

"But you believed it did. I could see that so clearly yesterday. You were completely convinced Kelsey had died, and you mourned the loss no less than if she had."

"You don't think that makes me insane?"

"No more than me feeling sad or lonely when a good book ends."

I searched her eyes, finding signs of exhaustion and frustration similar to the ones I felt. "Are you all right?"

"Yes." She smiled, then shook her head. "I'm just tired."

"Why do you always do that?"

"Do what?"

"Pretend you're okay when something's bothering you."

"Occupational hazard, I suppose. If I'm going to be there for my students, I need to focus on their needs. I have to be fully present for them both in the physical sense and the emotional one. I can't take my problems into the classroom, especially personal issues that might come to the attention of the administration."

"But I'm not one of your students. Not anymore. You don't have to pretend with me, and you don't owe me anything. I don't want to be any more of a burden than I've already been. Let me help you."

Her lips parted silently, and her chest rose with a deep inhalation. "No one's ever said anything like that to me."

I smiled sadly because I thought I'd said something like that to her, but this moment wasn't about me. "Then this conversation is long overdue. What's on your mind?"

She stared at the ceiling. "This is going to sound crazy."

"Crazier than my coma dream?"

"Actually, in a way, yes." She sighed. "Because I spent all night lying awake wondering what you saw in your dream to make you so happy I'm still a teacher."

"Why?"

"I know it wasn't real, but right now I'm looking for any reason, any sign to tell me whether I should keep putting myself through this, and you seemed so certain about my place as a teacher yesterday when you weren't certain about anything else."

"Jody, believe me when I say you're saving lives." I wanted to cup her face in my hands, to pull her close and make her feel my sincerity. Instead I reached for her hand. "You said it yourself. You would remember if you'd lost a student on your watch. It would rip you apart. You remember every student who ever struggled in your classroom. I bet you've even considered adopting a handful of them."

She grinned shyly. "I may have looked into the foster-parenting a time or two."

"See, you're made for this work, and you love those students like they're your own children."

"You're right," she said, not sounding overly happy about it. "I can't imagine who I'd be if I weren't teaching. Thank you for reminding me."

"It's the least I can do." I eyed her more carefully, stifling the urge to brush a stray strand of blond hair that had fallen from her ponytail. "A few days ago you seemed so much more resolved, or maybe resigned. What happened to bring on a new bout of questions?"

"I don't know if they're new questions. They've been lingering since…well, forever, but I thought things would get easier with time."

"And they didn't?"

"They did until Drew Phillips became principal three years ago. Things have gone steadily downhill, and then—" She seemed to catch herself.

"Then what?"

"He's just been on a tear for the last few days. It'll blow over."

My stomach knotted. "What you mean is he's made your life hell since I passed out and ruined the assembly you worked so hard to plan."

"It's not your fault, and if not for this, he would've found something else."

What a son of a bitch. Two days ago I'd worried about him finding out I'd kissed her. Eleven years later I still felt guilty for putting Jody at risk for his wrath. No matter what the date or circumstance, the thought of him hurting her made me nauseous. "He's a bully, the worst kind, because he's actually got the authority to hurt you. People in a position of power should have a higher standard of care, not a lower one. I honestly don't know how you've survived for ten years. I didn't even last ten days before I snapped on him."

"What do you mean?"

"In the past, or whatever, I couldn't stomach his attitude, which is strange, because he didn't bother me any more than any other redneck the first time around, but this time he seemed much more oppressive. I felt like I'd been stuffed into a pressure cooker and had the heat cranked up until I blew my top."

She scooted closer, her eyes attentive. "What happened?"

"I totally unloaded on him and anyone within a fifty-foot radius. I drew quite a crowd in the high-school hallway. I called them losers and said I was headed for a better life. Then I told Drew I was 'gay, very, very gay,' and he needed to get used to it." I smiled at the memory. "I also told him he was bad at sports analogies."

"That doesn't sound like you at all."

"A week ago it wasn't."

"What changed?"

I blushed and stared at my lap. "You did."

The room suddenly turned unnaturally quiet for a hospital. When I finally glanced up, the blue in her eyes had turned dark with emotions I couldn't read. "I wish I could've been there."

My chest ached. "It's strange now, because I spent most of my time in the past praying everything was a dream, only to wake up and find myself wishing it had been real."

"Why does that matter if everything ended well either way?"

She was right of course. She'd remained a teacher, and Kelsey had lived to reach her full potential. From what I'd been able to discern since waking up, all appeared right with my world. Soon I'd return to New York, to the life I'd longed for, the life I'd been content with a week ago. "I guess it doesn't matter. I just…I felt like a different person when I woke up. It's disorienting to find out I'm not."

"Aren't you?" She sounded concerned. "You don't think this experience changed you?"

"That's the problem. I don't know if it did or not. I had a moment of courage and purpose while knocked out, but that's over.

Once I woke up, I returned to confusion, or at least uncertainty, about who I am and what I want. Any changes from the experience were temporary."

"They don't have to be. You're in control of your own story. You can edit it any way you want."

A tingle of excitement ran up my back and tickled my neck. "You actually said something like that in my dream."

She smiled playfully. "Dream Jody sure sounds smart."

"Only because Dream Jody is based on real Jody. The rest of the experience was much more fictional. Kelsey was never in any real danger, you never quit teaching, and you never…we never." I blushed profusely. "I never kissed you."

Jody turned a delicious shade of pink. "Well, I suppose there is that."

"Yes." I pushed on awkwardly. "It's hard enough to make life-altering changes even when you've got all the reason in the world to take the risk, but it's virtually impossible to maintain that kind of courage when you're not even sure your reasons for doing so are real."

Jody nodded slowly, pensiveness creasing her brow before she reached into her school bag and pulled out a book. "I brought some reading for you."

"Oh?" I didn't understand the abrupt shift in topics.

"I initially picked it because I remembered you saying you liked it a long time ago," she said, then added, "but now I'm wondering if something more wasn't leading me to this choice."

"Why?"

She laid the book on the bed beside me, revealing her old, weathered copy of *The Things They Carried*. "Because I think maybe you need to exert a little less energy trying to figure out what's real and focus a little harder on trying to determine what's true."

I stared at the cover, a hundred different thoughts spinning through my pounding head.

Why this book?

When had I told her I liked it?

Was this a sign?

From her? From the universe?

Thankfully, Jody didn't expect any answers or even any response. She simply smiled as she rose, letting her hand rest lightly on my shoulder before saying, "Happy reading."

I was so lost in thought I barely looked up to see her go, but when I did I got the sinking feeling I'd just let the last tie to my sense of purpose walk out the door.

CHAPTER FOURTEEN

I rocked back and forth slowly. My feet never left the ground but simply rolled from heel to toe with the rhythmic ebb and flow of Beth and Rory's porch swing. I inhaled the cool, crisp breeze filled with the scent of earth and impending rain as if it held some healing property. The symptoms of my concussion had faded considerably in the last three days. Movement and light bothered me now only when sudden or excessive, and reading provided more solace than pain. If only I could sleep without fear of the past, I'd probably feel at least as good as when I'd arrived.

"Hey, McFly," Rory called as she bounded up the porch steps. She'd taken to employing a wide and varied arsenal of time-travel nicknames to keep our conversations light. "Can you answer an honest question for me?"

"Sure."

"When you went back into the past, did you kill John Connor?"

I rolled my eyes and stifled a laugh. "That's a new one."

"I just thought of a bunch of *Terminator* references while on my run." She perched nimbly on the porch rail, leaning against one of the large support columns with her feet crossed casually in front of her. "Don't worry. I'll spread them out over the next few days."

"Well, that's something to look forward to." I'd been released from the hospital yesterday but wasn't cleared to fly for two more days. "Are you sure you don't want me to get a hotel room? You know what they say about guests and fish starting to smell after three days."

"Not at all. I haven't gotten to use any of my *Peggy Sue Got Married* jokes yet."

"What a way to pass the time."

"Did you finish your book?"

I glanced at Jody's copy of *The Things They Carried*, which hadn't been out of arm's reach since she'd lent it to me. "I don't know if I'll ever be finished with this book, but I'm having a hard time processing it in my current context."

"Cut yourself some slack. You've been through a lot. You're going to need some time to reorient yourself."

"Time. I've got more time than I can handle until I go home."

"What does it matter where you are? The questions will be the same in New York as they are here. I'd venture a guess that the answers will be the same too."

"Any ideas what those answers might be?"

"Sorry. I've got nothing for you there, but if the dream was a product of your imagination that might be a good place to start looking for some resolution."

She made the comment casually, her logic seeming effortless, but I got the message. Whether unintentionally or subconsciously, I'd created a variety of worlds for myself to navigate. I was the only person who could map the meaning of those experiences. "I suppose you're right. I've got a lot to sort out. I might as well start now."

She stood and stretched her lean form. "You're a writer. Don't you people lock yourself in a room and wax philosophical about the greater lessons of life until your eyes bleed?"

I shook my head. "You give me too much credit. My eyelids droop or turn to sandpaper, but I always stop before they bleed."

"Fiction writers." She shook her head as she went inside. "Must be a cushy life."

I remained on the swing, pondering her suggestion. I'd spent the last couple of days trying to figure out if I should go back to what I used to know or create something new from my experiences, but maybe I'd given myself a false choice. Perhaps I needed to combine what I knew with what I wanted to make sense of.

I pulled out my MacBook Air. Typing still gave me a headache, but maybe I could talk about my experiences as a way to construct some meaning. I doubted any coherent work of literature could stem from such confusion, but at least the exercise would help kill my remaining time in Darlington.

After opening my dictation software I stared at the blank page. Where to start? The first sentence of any project was always one of the hardest, but here it involved more than prose. I needed to figure out how I'd gotten off track, or maybe put back on track, which meant I needed to figure out how the whole ordeal started.

Did everything begin when I fainted at the assembly? Perhaps it started when I chose not to kiss Jody, but even that moment needed context. Maybe the adventure began when I saw Jody at the restaurant and the rest of the world faded around us. No, even that memory seemed incomplete, or at least not mine to own. Out of so many pivotal moments, I needed to find the one where I'd made a decision, the one where I'd had the ability to choose another way completely and didn't.

I closed my eyes and sifted through the memories until I heard a question, a statement. No, a command. *"You've got to put yourself out there more, Stevie."* Edmond's voice burned through the haze of my mind and plunked me down in a specific time and place, the last one left untouched. I replayed the conversation, speaking to my computer, and watched the story unfold on the page before me. I spoke my version of the events that led me here, not just reliving them but examining them from the perspective of a viewer, or a reader, a personal historian.

Darkness fell, and the air turned chilly. Rory opened the door wide enough to toss me a hooded sweatshirt. I continued my narrative through dinner. Beth smiled sweetly but said nothing as she placed a plate of home-cooked food on the swing next to me. One by one the lights downstairs went out, followed shortly by the ones upstairs. I wrote until I had nothing left to write about, except the act of writing itself.

Then, finally, I slept.

❖

Jody exited her little black car and raised her hand to shield her eyes against the low-hanging sun. "You look much improved."

"Thanks," I said from my near-permanent spot on the porch swing. "I think."

I enjoyed the view of her as she strode across the yard and up the porch steps. She'd clearly just come from school in her white oxford shirt, navy blazer, and sensible heels with her hair pulled back in a gold clip. She filled out the ensemble better than she had as a student teacher, and she carried her authority naturally, more from her grace and air of capability than from her fashion choices.

"I wanted to make sure you were still on the mend."

"I think I am." I scooted over and patted the spot next to me. "Both physically and mentally."

"I saw Beth this morning," Jody said, taking the seat and falling into the gentle rocking of the swing. "She said you'd been writing."

"I went on a binge all day yesterday and most of the night."

"Is it a new book, or a play?"

"I'm not sure. Right now it's therapy."

Jody nodded thoughtfully before affecting her best therapist voice. "And how does that make you feel?"

"Actually, a lot better. I worked through most of my major conflicts about what was real, or at least what reflected truth."

"Care to share?"

"Well, I don't know if the time travel itself actually happened, but you helped when you said everything turned out right in the end. When I was under, I got wrapped up in Kelsey's survival, and that worked out exactly how I wanted. Then I got worried about you and your career, but you're right where you need to be in this moment." I sighed and thought about the last remaining questions, the ones that took me back to the start, the ones that tripped me up every chance I let them. *You've got to put yourself out there more, Stevie.* "I've resolved two of my three major plot points and am trying to work up the courage now to face the third."

"And what's that?"

My heart beat faster but without the crippling self-consciousness I'd felt in the past. "Will you go to St. Louis with me tonight?"

"What?"

"I want to test a theory. No, that sounds too clinical. I'd really like to take you on a date. The kind of date we may or may not have had before, the kind that builds memories and makes meanings regardless of what comes next for us."

She smiled brightly, her eyes shimmering with emotion. "I'd love to have that kind of a date with you."

I fought the urge to give a fist pump and instead revealed my eagerness by saying, "Can we go now?"

She gestured to her clothes. "I'm still dressed for work."

I indicated my worn jeans and Rory's hooded sweatshirt. "I'm still dressed for the porch. We'll balance each other out. Let's live this moment in present tense."

"All right."

"All right?"

She nodded. "Let's go."

She shed her suit coat as we crossed the Darlington city limits. We flew down I-55, laughing, talking, touching tentatively, the brush of a hand against a knee or a shoulder. As we crossed the mighty Mississippi, Jody unclasped the clip from her hair and shook out the fair strands. She pointed out new Busch Stadium in the shadow of the Arch, the corners of her mouth curving so deliciously they crinkled the corner of her eyes. The St. Louis scenery was impressive from the riverfront to Forest Park, but I couldn't take my eyes off Jody. Any affinity I'd held for the city paled in comparison to the emotions she stirred in me.

Without the shifting walls of time or the rigid responsibilities of her job to constrain us, thoughts I'd previously fought finally flowed freely. My attraction to her strained every muscle and tendon in my body, but even more so I felt drawn to her on a deeper level, as though my heart pressed against my ribs in an attempt to be nearer to hers. Surrendering to her allure both thrilled and terrified me. The last time I'd been in this city with her I'd focused on the future I believed in. But now I refused to consider even the idea of a tomorrow.

"Where are we going?" Jody asked.

"I don't know."

She raised her eyebrows, and I realized she hadn't meant for the question to be about my long-term intentions but rather about driving directions. "Oh, sorry. Head toward the Central West End."

She slowed as she turned onto North Euclid, leaving the speed and congestion of the larger city behind. Trees shaded the road from the lingering light of dusk as the muted streetlamps cast dancing shadows across wide sidewalks. I had the overwhelming urge to be outside with her, strolling hand in hand while soft music wafted on the breeze around us. Well, maybe the music played only in my head, but I still directed her to the first open parking spot. Then on a whim I jogged around the front of the car and opened the door for her.

Jody flashed one of her heart-swelling smiles. "Thank you."

Normally I would've felt cheesy in any sort of romantic lead. I was a New Yorker, for goodness' sake, a modern lesbian, aloof and suspicious. But Jody had met each chance I'd taken tonight with openness, and even joy, so I decided to try for one step further and held out my arm. She took the offering without hesitation and looped her arm loosely through my own. An unusual lightness spread through my chest as we strolled along window-shopping and soaking up each other's company.

While she stopped to examine some antiques in a storefront window, I surveyed her. I marveled at the complete sensory connection, from the gentle touch of her hand on my arm to the scent of her perfume in every breath I took. Her beauty filled my sight, and the sound of her voice thrilled my ears. The only sense left unsatisfied was taste, and the memory of her mouth on mine begged to be renewed, but I wouldn't rush or push like I had before. The moment was no longer mine to command. The time we shared tonight would be an offering, an opening of myself for her to accept or reject of her own accord.

We ambled along until we reached the large plate-glass windows of Left Bank Books, and the hair on the back of my neck stood on end.

"I love this place," Jody said, her reflection smiling brightly at me in the glass. "Whenever I need to escape the small-mindedness in Darlington, I usually head here first."

I eyed her seriously, wonder building in my chest. "I knew that."

"Really?"

"Yes." I answered emphatically and turned back to the books on display. The familiar sense of belonging enveloped us. We might have years and miles and jobs and a whole society between us, but we found solace in the same things. Surely that counted for something.

"Stevie, look." Jody tightened her grip on my arm as she stared at the upper right corner of the display. There atop all the others sat my most recent release.

The thrill of seeing my own work on someone else's shelves never got old, but this time it carried a different kind of excitement, of purpose, of belonging.

Belonging tied me to this spot in the past, and now the connection spilled out from the window to the woman beside me. I was through considering coincidences. She'd seen me here with her twice now, and as I stared at her reflection covering my name in the window, I couldn't deny the two fit together somehow.

I untangled my arm from hers and looped it around her waist, lightly pulling her closer. The choice was hers, but I wouldn't shy away from my desire to hold her. That desire grew tenfold as she fulfilled it by leaning closer, connecting her hip with my own and resting her head on my shoulder.

"What are you thinking about?" she asked.

"About us, how nicely we fit together."

She hummed a little noise of contentment. "That's a very nice thing to think."

"What about you?" I asked, meeting her eyes via our reflection. "What's on your mind?"

"I like it here in your arms very much, but I don't trust myself."

"Why?"

"Because you feel too good. It all feels too right in a way nothing else has felt right in my life for a long time." She shivered. "But there's also a sense of urgency. When I see your book there, I remember you're not tied to this place, or even to me. You're going back to New York."

My chest ached at the thought, and I tried to force it from my mind. "Not until tomorrow. We've got all night together. Let's make the most of it."

"One night." She sighed. "Then you'd better distract me with a pretty nice dinner, because if I let myself dwell on everything I might like to do with the remainder of our time together, we'll to find some place much more private than a city sidewalk."

The heat in my body quickly spiked to a level akin to a brick oven, expressing all the air in my lungs and zapping my throat dry. I opened my mouth in the suave manner of a fish snatched from water and stared at Jody. Amusement spread across her twinkling eyes and impish grin.

"Come on," she said, pulling on my arm. "Duff's is right across the street, and I think that's our safest option…for now."

I nodded mutely, trying to focus on steadying my legs as we crossed the street even while the echo of her "for now" rattled around my chest before settling someplace decidedly lower in my body.

❖

Duff's was an Irish-American pub with high-backed wooden booths and low lighting. The color scheme was overwhelmingly dark with the occasional brass accent, and I worked hard to study the details instead of losing myself in Jody's eyes. If I didn't stare at her, maybe I could lie to myself about how consuming my attraction to her had become. She seemed to be waging her own internal battle, but she'd chosen the weapon of our impending separation to combat her feelings.

"Tell me about your life in New York."

"It's, well, pretty standard. I live in the Village, down by…Wait. Have you ever been to New York?"

She shook her head.

"Then you wouldn't know the cross streets. How else should I describe it?"

"Can you walk to the Statue of Liberty? Central Park?"

"Not really. Mostly I walk to Starbucks."

She laughed, and then her eyes brightened even in the low light of the pub. "Do you go to Broadway?"

"A couple of times a year."

"I'd love see a Broadway play," she said wistfully.

"Come with me." I reined in my enthusiasm and sat back in the booth. "I mean, come visit. We'll go see whatever play you want."

"I don't know."

"Come on. What kind of theater teacher has never seen a Broadway play?"

Her smile turned sad. "One who will probably never leave Darlington."

The warmth in my stomach went cold and empty. Why did she have to keep reminding me I was leaving tomorrow and she would never leave? How would I stay present in the moment if she insisted on reminding me this might be our last moment together? "You have all summer off. You wouldn't come to New York for a visit?"

"Just a visit?" she asked in a voice so soft I barely heard her. "I'm not sure I want to be a tourist in your life."

The words struck me like a punch to the stomach. Is that what I asked of her? To play a bit part, a walk-on, a cameo? Was she saying she couldn't play any part in my life, or that she'd accept only a starring role?

Our food arrived, perfectly cooked, perfectly plated, perfectly delicious, but neither one of us did much more than push it around our dishes. Maybe tonight hadn't been such a good idea after all. Could we really repeat the past, especially a fictional one?

I struggled with the silence and tried to reignite our previous conversation. "I do live close enough to walk to the Stonewall."

"That's exciting," she replied, her interest sounding genuine, if subdued.

"Yeah." The novelty of the historic landmark had impressed me when I'd first moved to the area, even though I didn't particularly identify with the Stonewall rioters. I'd never had much emotional attachment to the gay foremothers and forefathers who'd fought there. Even now I saw no part of my life as belonging to their legacy, except for a few moments in the halls of Darlington High School that might or might not have actually happened.

"Are you okay?" she asked. "I'm sorry. I didn't mean to kill the mood."

"No, you didn't. I just realized the only part of my life I considered worthy of the Stonewall lineage probably wasn't real."

She turned her attention back to not eating her chicken marsala. "I know how you feel."

"Really?"

"How could I not? I'm closeted. Everything I've ever done for our community has been a covert operation."

"But you do so much good for your students. Your whole life is about making things better for the next generation. You offer them hope and protection."

"Do I? Or am I only protecting myself?"

I reached across the table, and she met me halfway, interlacing her fingers with my own. "At least you're doing something. I can't say the same for my life. I've taken the easy road, the selfish road, and what do I have to show for it?"

"You have a successful career."

I shook off the platitude. "I observe, I sit on the sidelines, I comment on fictional lives without ever taking a risk myself."

"I've avoided risk too, Stevie."

"But at least you did so for an honorable cause. Every student you reach goes on to help make the world a little better." I squeezed her hand, trying to anchor myself though my faith in her. "And the world *is* changing. You have nondiscrimination laws in Illinois now, federal hate-crimes legislation. Gay marriage has even made its way to the Midwest. The generation you've educated made those changes."

"But have I changed with them, or am I the same person I was ten years ago?" The creases in her forehead caused her brows to furrow over darkening eyes and made her appear older than ever. "And more importantly, do I want to be the same person ten years from now? Because that's where I'm headed."

My chest constricted, and I sat back, breaking the contact between us. "I think that's the biggest question I've had left after my whole ordeal. Am I the same person I was in high school?"

"Maybe the more important question is do you want to be the same person you were in high school?"

"A week ago I would've said yes. I liked my life, myself, just fine."

"And now?"

"I don't." It was the first time I'd said those words aloud, but the parts of my life or my personality I'd been content with now seemed weak and drab compared to the person I'd let myself become during my date with the past. "I'm ready to change. I'm just not sure how."

She nodded, a strand of hair falling into her eyes. I wanted to slide it through my fingers, to run my thumb across the smooth skin of her cheek, to cup her face, to pull her in. I worried she'd pull away, but I still ached to take the chance.

"Jody." I breathed the word more than said it. "I want to be the person I became in the past. I want to hold onto the good things I saw in myself. And one of the things I most liked about the new me was you."

"Me?"

"Yes, you. Or at least the person you made me want to be. That's why I asked you out tonight. Regardless of whether those moments were actually real, I needed to know if the feelings they'd inspired in me held true."

She inhaled a slow, deep breath as if steadying herself. "And?"

"They do. You inspire me. You make me better. The best version of me is the one with you, and I don't want to lose you."

She stared at me, eyes focused, lips slightly parted, chest rising and falling slowly while I waited, attempting to remember to breathe. Seconds passed like hours. God, why wouldn't she say something? Anything? Preferably something nice or reciprocal. Maybe she was trying to formulate a gentle letdown. As an English teacher, she hated clichés. So perhaps she wanted to formulate a more original version of the "we're better as friends" speech. But with each second spent in painful silence, I began to suspect I'd prefer a slap across the face to the suffocating tension.

Finally, Jody held up one finger and signaled the waiter. Before he'd even fully approached the table she said, "We're going to need the check now."

"Would you like me to box up your—"

"No, thank you. Just the check, please."

He reached into the pocket of his apron and produced the bill. I reached for it instinctively, still uncertain what had happened. Was she walking out on me? Had I offended her? Her expression remained controlled, neutral, unreadable while I counted out a couple of twenties and shakily tossed them on the table.

She rose slowly, took two steps, then turned back and drained her glass of merlot before wordlessly heading toward the door.

My heart hammered relentlessly as I followed her to the car. Clearly, I'd blown everything. How had I misread the situation so badly? I thought she'd sent me signals of her interest all night long. Maybe I'd gotten too emotional, too personal. Maybe she didn't like me hinting at a future we couldn't have. What if she had only expected a night of fun, and then I turned serious on her?

She got in the car, and I hesitated at the passenger-side door steeling myself for a long, awkward ride home. My heart felt like someone had fastened a metal clamp around it and begun to tighten the screw. So much for putting myself out there. I'd obviously misread the moral of this story, and damn, it hurt.

Jody reached across the car and pushed open the door. "Get in, Stevie."

Uh-oh. She'd used her teacher voice. In no time, place, or situation did I dare refuse the teacher voice. Taking a deep breath, I climbed inside and closed the door behind me.

"Jody, I'm sorry."

"You should be," she said, then held up a hand to cut off my next attempt at apology. "You put me in a terrible position back there. I mean, really, you say something like that in the middle of a restaurant. What did you expect from me?"

"I didn't expect anything. I didn't think it through. I didn't consider the fact that you might be uncomfortable or feel pressured to respond."

"Or what about the fact that we're in the middle of a city thirty minutes from my home with no privacy or space for me to respond freely?" She pushed her hands through her hair. "No one has ever said anything so perfect to me. It took every ounce of fortitude and self-restraint I've developed over the years not to grab you by the collar and drag you across the table."

"I know. I'm sorry. I didn't anticipate—wait, what?"

She smiled brightly and took my face in her hands, then pressed her lips to mine, instantly eliminating my confusion. There was no lag time, no shock to register or catching up to do. We came together effortlessly. Our mouths found each other—insistent, passionate, explosive. In a second we were fully intertwined, her hands on my waist, mine tangled in the fine hair at the back of her head. She opened her mouth, searching, gasping, grazing her tongue along mine. Her lips were impossibly soft, but she didn't yield to me, or me to her. We both pushed on in tandem, neither willing to slow the surging tide of escalation.

The kiss was nothing like the one I remembered, not tentative or exploratory. This time we knew each other. We'd grown into each other, or toward each other, our bodies recognizing what our minds had refused to acknowledge. This was right. We were right. She tasted of sweetness coated in red wine, and I grew drunk on the combination. A fire started at my core and spread out, consuming us both. She grasped for more, tugging at the hem of my sweatshirt and slipping her hands underneath. I dragged my lips from hers, along her jaw and down her neck. I wanted more. I desperately nipped and sucked as much of her exposed skin as I could reach in the car.

"Stevie," she gasped, her lips close to my ears, "we have to stop."

"Yeah." I panted but made no move to lessen the pressure of my mouth against her shoulder.

She extracted one hand from my shirt and ran it up my arm to my neck. Cradling my head, she held me in place, baring her neck for my continued exploration. "Really, we can't do this here."

"Uh-huh," I mumbled.

She tugged on my hair lightly to break the contact of my mouth long enough for me to register her concerns. I sat back, dazed, and glanced around. People passed by the intersection just ahead of us. Headlights flashed to the side. The amber glow of a streetlamp illuminated the patch of sidewalk I'd occupied moments earlier. I took a shaky breath, then looked back to Jody.

The moment our eyes met her hands were on me again, immediately followed by her lips. We kissed fervently, her mouth persistent, demanding, exhausting. Quickly losing my grip on the situation, I eased back slowly, understanding we had to regain control while simultaneously wishing we never would.

Jody gave one last press forward, following me halfway across the car, before grazing her teeth across my bottom lip as she released me. "Wow."

"Yeah," I replied breathlessly.

"Was the kiss in your dream like that?" she asked, lifting her fingers to her swollen lips.

"It was good, amazing even, but this one was better."

She blushed, momentarily bashful. "I got a little carried away."

"We both did, but a good kind of carried away, right?"

"A very good kind."

I grinned.

She grinned right back, and I worried if we stayed there staring at each other as if waiting to see which one of us devoured the other first, we'd end up arrested for lewd behavior in a public space.

"Maybe we should head back to Darlington now," I said reluctantly.

"Probably." She sounded equally displeased with our options as she fired up the engine and pulled out of the parking space.

We rode in silence back to the interstate, both of us breathing a little heavier than usual. As she crossed the bridge to Illinois, I took her hand in mine, caressing her wrist with my thumb. "It's going to be a lot harder to get on a plane tomorrow."

She nodded. "It's going to be a lot harder to let you."

The silence grew thick again as the suburbs faded behind us. The farther we got from the city, the further she slipped from me. I hated the chasm growing between us and struggled to think of a way to bridge the divide.

"Will you come visit me this summer?" She pursed her lips together, and I added, "Please?"

"A lot can change between now and summer."

"I know, but I want to try."

She nodded but didn't agree, leaving me to wonder if she doubted my resolve or hers.

She slowed the car as she neared an unfamiliar exit twenty-five miles from Darlington.

"Are you okay?"

"I think so," she said shakily. "This is my usual exit."

I looked at the upcoming sign. Oquendo. Right, she didn't live in Darlington. "Sorry you have to drive me all the way back to town." I lied. I wished we would keep on driving, forever.

"You could…I mean it would be easier if…" She stopped, swallowed, then started again. "Would you like to spend the night with me?"

My answer was simply and painfully honest. "Yes."

She squeezed my hand and took the exit, pulling onto a state road, then a town street, followed by a gravel driveway.

Without another word we exited the car, and I had to force myself not to rush us to the house. I took her hand in mine and brought it to my lips. "Are you sure about this?"

She touched my face, gently guiding me into a sweet kiss that hinted at much more with the lingering brush of her lips. Then she turned and opened the door, drawing me inside with her.

I wanted to see her home, to notice her personal touches, to compliment the warmth and charm the décor would certainly exude, but I couldn't see anything other than her—her eyes glistening in the dim light, her hair falling down across her shoulders, her shirt wrinkled, and her cheeks flushed. I marveled that this beautiful woman who had avoided relationships and risks and invasions into her personal space had invited me into her sanctuary. The wonder was almost too much, leaving me momentarily speechless. A writer finds few things more frustrating than a loss of words, but in this case they weren't lost as much as unnecessary.

Wrapping my arm around her waist, I held her close, then hooked one finger under her chin and lifted it gently until her eyes met mine. Suspended on the same breath with her, I imprinted her image in my mind. I took in the sight of her perched on the edge of desire, eyes heavy with need, lips parted, the pulse of her heart beating rapidly enough to reverberate through me. I burned her perfection into my memory. Then when I couldn't stand the suspense a second longer, I captured her mouth with mine.

Years of doubt faded away along with our careers, our homes, and the very idea of a tomorrow. We met in our purest form—bodies, heat, energy. The sweetest intentions devolved into the basest of needs as gentle caresses gave way to touching, clutching, and groping. Jody's hands were under my shirt, sliding up my ribs until she cupped my breasts. Holding them in her hands, she ran her thumbs around the curve at their sides, drawing circles ever closer to the center but refusing to capture them fully. My breath came sharper, harder, with the delicious tension of anticipation until she finally took what we both wanted, palming me fully and running her fingers over my nipples. We broke the kiss, gasping, and she used the separation to push the hoodie and undershirt over my head.

She kissed my shoulders, my neck, my collarbones as I began working at the buttons on her shirt, fumbling through a random pattern. One from the bottom so I could touch the smooth plane of her abdomen. Then two from the top so I could taste the skin between the cups of her bra. I became so entranced with that spot I popped open the next two from the bottom simply because they were the easiest to reach without lifting my head. I'd lost track of how many more I had to undo as a desperate need to have her unwrapped fully before me pushed at the back of my eyes. Clutching each side of the starched, white fabric, I meant only to test the restraints, but instead I pulled it open fully to the clatter of buttons breaking free and scattering across a hardwood floor.

Jody looked up at me, then down at her shirt, now open from her throat to her waist. Stepping back, she slid it from her shoulders and down her arms. Then reaching back for the strap on her bra, she released and guided it to the floor as well. I stood momentarily paralyzed, my mind rebounding enough to register that I'd never held anything so beautiful. I wondered only briefly if I was worthy of such a gift before my body regained control and asserted its ability to handle this situation.

I pulled her back to me, relishing the warmth and softness of her skin, flush against mine. We kissed passionately, tongues searching as we explored newly exposed territory with trembling hands. Her breasts were small, firm, and amazingly responsive to my touch. Dipping my head, I sucked a trail down her neck and across her chest. Kissing every spot of flesh along the way, I covered her breasts, taking one in my mouth quickly and then releasing it, then drew a path back to the other. She stumbled two steps until her back found the wall, and I followed eagerly.

She moaned, arching her neck and letting her head loll back. Her body was one smooth, graceful arch reaching out to meet my mouth, her skin a flawless canvas to paint with my lips. I bent lower, then knelt, kissing a scattered path along her stomach, varying pressure and depth as each space dictated. I wanted her to feel me, to know me, to always remember me against her body. I wanted to mark her, to see the evidence of this connection, to leave proof that I had really been here, to leave something of myself behind…but tears stung my eyes at the thought of marring such a perfect work or art. Pulling back to view her fully again, I chose instead to imprint *her* on me, both real and true. The overwhelming clench of my heart contented me with the knowledge she was as much a part of me now as the blood rushing through my veins.

Threading her hands through my hair, she guided me back to her body and held me fast to a spot just above her navel while I unbuttoned her slacks and lowered the zipper. Her pants fell to the floor, and I kissed a line above the waistband of her navy bikini briefs before peeling them away slowly to reveal the last piece of perfection.

Jody's legs trembled, or maybe I did. The weight of what we were about to do wouldn't allow either of us to remain upright for long, but I couldn't wait or separate long enough to relocate. Breathing her rich, heady scent, I kissed lower over the final curve of her, through soft, blond curls and into liquid heat.

Jody cried out, clutching me to her center, her fingers digging into my shoulders, my neck, my scalp. Her body opened easily, so receptive, her hips rocking forward first to meet my mouth, then my fingers as I pushed inside her.

"Stevie, please," she called out.

Chills danced across my bare skin followed fast by a fire stoked with the need she poured into my name. I pushed in more fully, something primal taking over as I rode the erratic rhythm of her hips. Searching the contours of her body, mapping her arousal, I refused to surrender to the incoherency threatening to cloud my mind and blur my sight. Instead I opened my eyes and, still holding her tightly to me, watched her muscles contract and shake. Kneeling before her felt almost religious, a thank offering for the gift of her body, the gift she'd bestowed for the sole purpose of my adoration.

"Yes," she breathed, the most beautiful word I'd ever heard, and contracted around me. A strangled sob escaped her throat as she groped for something to anchor her while a final wave of passion crested around us.

Then her body went limp and slid slowly down the wall. Guiding her descent, I cradled her in my arms, pulling her head to my chest, offering what rest and comfort my own shaking limbs could afford.

Kissing her hair, her temples, her forehead, I rocked us softly together while her breathing slowed. "You're so beautiful, Jody. Even more so than I dreamed."

She squeezed me tighter, another tremor radiating from her body and through mine.

"What is it?" I asked

"I need you," she said.

"I'm right here."

She pushed back to arm's length with both of us kneeling bare-chested before each other. Dark emotion swirled around her expanded pupils, holding me suspended in the intensity of her gaze. "I need you in my bed. Now."

The air left my lungs in a rush, but she gave me no time to recover before taking my hand and leading me toward her bedroom.

Even in the shadows, her naked form made my mouth dry and my fingers twitch. No hallway had ever felt so endless or alluringly adorned. Finally, she pushed open a door, revealing a queen-sized bed with a rich cream comforter. I didn't have a chance or the desire to examine anything further before Jody nudged me onto the bed. I sat on the edge, feet planted firmly on the floor in an attempt to keep grounded amid the dizzy wave of lust surging through me. I held my breath as she nestled her hips between my spread knees, then released it in a rush when she popped open the button atop my jeans.

She kissed me soulfully as she lowered the zipper, then dragged her lips to my ear and whispered, "I've dreamed of this moment since your first night back in town."

Goose bumps spread down my arms as the words fluttered against my cheek and spread into my chest. "God, Jody, I've wanted you for so long."

"You've got me." She kissed my cheek and, with her palm splayed across my lower back, urged me into a standing position until my jeans spilled down my legs. Then without wasting any time, she sent my underwear to join them.

I watched her eyes rake over my body, a pink flush spreading across her chest as her eyes caressed my body from top to bottom, then up again. Under other circumstances such an inspection would've left me cowering, shaken to be exposed, fearful of being found lacking. But in Jody's care, I summoned the courage to stand vulnerable and comfortable.

Pressing close again, she eased me onto the bed. I scooted back on my elbows toward the pillow. She crawled over me until she'd straddled my waist, her breasts taut against my own and her lips fastened to my mouth. The kiss wasn't rushed, but it didn't allow me to catch my breath either. Her tongue stroked mine, edging me higher even as she worked her hands lower. She scraped her fingernails down my chest and across my ribs before circling my stomach and turning back up just before she reached where I most wanted her to be.

On the second pass, my hips rocked up involuntarily to facilitate more contact. She smiled against my lips but didn't acquiesce. Shifting her weight to her knees, she repositioned her hips firmly against me, both relieving the pressure and accentuating it. We moved together in the subconscious dance of giving and taking. I reached for more, wanting to pull her entire body into mine, clutching her hips, digging my nails into the soft flesh there. I rocked her against me, rolling, surging, and then retreating together. Clinging to her tightly, I relished the way her weight settled on top of me—firm, solid, undeniable. Sweat beaded between us, slickening our movements and immersing us in the scent of arousal.

Her mouth never left mine as she worked her graceful fingers between us and then between my legs. I bucked under her touch, so very close already, but she refrained from taking what could have been an easy end and moved lower, encouraging me to open and moving inside with one slow, steady push. I closed my eyes, my head rolling from one side to the other across the cool pillow, but she wouldn't be content with the physical and withdrew almost completely.

"Open your eyes, Stevie."

My eyelids fluttered, heavy and uncoordinated, but she waited until I focused, my gaze as clear and steady as hers before she moved forward again.

"I'm here," she said. "I need you to know that."

"Yes," I gasped.

"It's not a dream."

I bit my lip to keep from shouting when she pushed deeper, her thumb grazing my clit.

"Let it out," she urged me. "I'm not going anywhere, I promise."

My body believed her. My muscles contracted, holding her in place.

"I'm all yours tonight, Stevie. Don't hold back."

My breath came in harsh, uneven bursts. Fire spread across my cheeks and flashed behind my eyes. My hips jerked, and my fingers tightened around any piece of flesh they could grasp.

"So close."

"I know, baby. Let go for me." She gave one more emphatic thrust, and lightning flashed through my body. I shouted a string of incoherency as I lifted us both off the bed, every muscle contracting, twisting in my abs, and shaking through my limbs.

Jody rode, and stroked, and kissed me until I collapsed, wasted, beneath her.

"God, you're amazing."

She smiled as she rolled to the side and snuggled into the crook of my arm.

"I mean it. I've never felt anything like that. It's like you saw right through me."

"If I did, it's only because you let me."

"I did." A sense of wonder floated through my consciousness. "I opened to you completely."

"You were perfect."

"No, we were perfect together. We *are* perfect together." I rolled onto my side, a new feeling exploding in my chest. "Jody, I…I think I…"

She kissed me quickly, silencing the word on my lips but doing nothing to crush its existence.

"Shh," she whispered when we parted, her eyes glistening with tears that froze me in fear.

"What is it? What's wrong?"

She placed her palm over my heart, and I wondered if she understood it beat for her now. "Don't say it. Just show me again."

The request seemed somehow inconsistent, but my body recognized what she'd asked of me, and I was no longer in a position to deny her anything.

CHAPTER FIFTEEN

I felt Jody's absence the minute she slipped from my embrace, and I reached for her instinctively.

Catching her arm without even opening my eyes, I asked, "Where are you going?"

"I have to get ready for work."

"Work?" The word didn't make sense.

"It's a school day."

"We just fell asleep," I mumbled, my body refusing to come fully awake even for this conversation.

"School starts whether I'm well rested or not." She still lay warm and soft and close to me, but her voice conveyed none of those things. Finally, I forced my eyes open, squinting against even the faint light of dawn. She lay on her back beside me, the thin sheet doing little to hide the perfect shape of her body. Even in my exhaustion, she stirred a fire in me, one that might have given life to my aching limbs and bruised muscles if not for the ice in her eyes.

"Jody, what's wrong?"

"Nothing."

Why did women always say the word "nothing" in a way that suggested they meant "everything"?

I rolled onto my side and tentatively pushed a strand of hair from her face, savoring the silky, light texture. "Last night was amazing."

The corners of her mouth quirked up.

"You're amazing."

She glanced at me out of the corner of her eyes. "Don't."

"Don't what?"

"Be sweet and sexy and charming right now. It's already hard enough to get out of bed this morning."

"Then don't." I stroked her cheek with the back of my hand. "Call in sick."

She sat up abruptly. "I have to go to work."

"You really won't stay with me?" I tried to tamp down the hurt in my voice, but her distance stung. I hadn't expected a marriage proposal, but what we'd shared the night before had shaken me. How could she face this morning like any other school day?

"You won't be here. You're flying back to New York. You have a whole life to return to today, and I—" She finally turned and looked at me fully, pain crossing her beautifully delicate features. "All I have to cling to then is my work. So forgive me if I'm not eager to give up the one thing that might keep me sane when you're gone." She headed for the bathroom while I flopped back onto the bed.

I had a five o'clock flight out of St. Louis. After counting the hours, the weeks, maybe years of trying to get out of here, I was finally headed back to New York. I needed to go back. I couldn't just abandon my life, my apartment, and the opportunities for my career. I liked New York. I liked my apartment. I liked the freedom to be whoever I wanted. I didn't like the person I'd been there a few weeks ago, but if I wanted to test the changes I'd made, I needed to do so in my real life, and in the future, not clinging to the past or to Jody's skirt. We'd shared an amazing night, but much like my time-traveling odyssey, how could I trust anything I couldn't carry back into the real world?

Still, this morning didn't have to be good-bye. Not the permanent kind. Why did Jody insist on putting a period where I wanted a comma? We didn't need to end the exploration we'd begun. No, we'd done more than explore last night. I'd found all the important answers. She belonged in my future. What did the details matter? We could work them out along the way.

The bathroom door opened, and the woman I'd spent the night with was gone. Ms. Hadland stood in her place, her hair pinned up, her smile polite and professional, the perfect expression to complement her respectable skirt and sensible shoes.

"Jody," I said, swinging my feet over the edge of the bed but refusing to drop the sheet, second-guessing the vulnerability I'd welcomed last night. "Can we please talk?"

"Of course. We can talk on the way back to Darlington, but not until you put some clothes on and have some coffee." More distance. She wanted to expand the divide between us even as I tried to close it. "I'll be in the kitchen."

I listened to the sound of her heels clicking on the hardwood floor as she walked away. The sinking feeling in my stomach was worse than the one I'd had when passing out. Part of me wished I'd lose consciousness now if only I could guarantee I'd get to relive last night in my dreams.

I showered quickly, trying to wash off the feeling I was losing the only thing I'd ever really needed to hold on to, but the ache in my muscles served as a constant reminder of how we'd claimed each other the night before. I wasn't naive. I hadn't thought making love meant we'd rent the U-Haul, but I hadn't expected her to unceremoniously dismiss me. We had to find some sort of middle ground.

I exited the bathroom and found my clothes from last night folded neatly on the freshly made bed. I wanted to wreck it all. I wanted to rip the sheets off and throw the pillows to the floor. I didn't want her to erase the evidence of my existence so easily when I carried her in every part of me. Instead, I bit my bottom lip to keep it from quivering while I roughly pulled on my jeans and Rory's hoodie.

Jody met me at the front door. She held out a travel cup nervously as though it were a peace offering. "Half caf, part skim milk, right?"

I froze mid-step. "How did you know that?"

She shrugged. "You must have said something sometime."

"We didn't get coffee last night."

"No." She raised her eyebrows.

"We haven't gotten coffee at all this week, or before I passed out."

"I guess we haven't. Maybe it's just a coincidence."

A now-familiar chill raised the hair on my neck. "We got coffee together in my dream. I ordered half calf, part skim, and we talked about what a coffee snob I am. It's not a common order."

Her lips parted, and for a second her eyes lightened within the dark circles of sleeplessness. Then she shook her head. "Maybe you told me that."

"I didn't, Jody. You know I didn't."

She opened the door, and I followed her across the porch. "This is a sign."

"You're grasping at straws, and I won't join you." She sighed. "I can't do it. I can't stretch for a reason to hold on while you walk away."

"You're the one walking away."

She spun around fiercely. "Don't pin this on me. Tomorrow morning I'll wake up right here, right where I have every morning for ten years. Where will you be?"

"In New York, but—"

"But nothing. You're doing what you have to do. Don't you dare judge me for doing the same."

"It doesn't have to end this way," I said halfheartedly. "We could find a compromise."

"I don't want to be your compromise." She got in the car, and I followed reluctantly, the ache in my chest spreading into my limbs.

She pulled onto the county road leading toward Darlington as the sun broke free over the cornfields. "I didn't mean it that way."

"I know you didn't mean I was the compromise, but I also know that's what we'd end up being to each other with nothing but miles between us. Maybe an established relationship could handle the strain of separation, but you're still finding yourself, testing everything. You're still not sure what you believe is real, and I don't want to be one more piece of a puzzle you leave behind."

"I could stay a few more days, try to figure a few things out."

She took my hand. "A few days would only give you time to get into my system deeper. Then what?"

"Then we can talk on the phone. Get to know each other. Take things slow."

She grinned a little bit. "I think the slow ship sailed the moment you took me up against my living-room wall."

I sucked in a sharp breath at the memory of being on my knees in front of her, but she pressed on. "Could phone calls and e-mail be enough for either of us any more? That doesn't sound like a relationship. It sounds like a long good-bye."

"Maybe," I said, sadness settling into my core at the realization she was probably right. I thought about everything that had changed in the past two weeks. Who would I even be in three months?

"Then come with me," I pleaded. "You said yourself, Drew is on your back. Your students have changed. Maybe it's time for you to change too."

"And you said I'm meant to be here, at least for now. I can't leave my students in the middle of the year. What kind of message would that send if I gave in to a bully?"

"Okay, stay and finish the year, but then reevaluate."

She didn't reply as we pulled into Rory and Beth's driveway.

"We can write old-fashioned love letters. It'll be romantic. And it's only three months. Then this summer you can come stay with me in New York for three months."

"The three-month compromise," she said sadly.

I didn't want to compromise, but I didn't want to let her go either. I lifted her hand to my lips and kissed it gently. "I waited eleven years for you. What's three more months?"

She shrugged and sighed. "Fine. Let's just see how it goes."

I should have felt better. It should have been a victory for the side of hope. Instead, it felt like a surrender to the inevitable.

"It's not perfect, but it's better than nothing, right?"

The tears in her eyes suggested she wasn't sure she agreed with my assessment, but she nodded anyway.

I took what little comfort I could find in this moment and kissed her softly, slowly, sadly. She returned the kiss in much the same fashion, without opening to me the way she had before. She was trying to guard our hearts, and I didn't want to hurt her more, but I had nothing left to protect. She already had the best parts of me.

"I'll call you tonight when I land, okay?"

She sat back, then gripped the steering wheel as if to keep herself from reaching for me again. "Travel safely."

"I...I—" The next word stuck in my throat, the word I shouldn't be ready to say, the word she didn't want to hear, the word that would only make this harder on both of us. I swallowed it. "I will, thanks."

I closed the door and jammed my hands in the pockets of my jeans. Clenched fists, clenched jaw, the muscles in my back rolled and rippled with the urge to chase her as she pulled away. I stood rooted like an oak tree to the open plains while the winds of pain and sadness swirled around me. I remained there long after her car faded on the endless Midwestern horizon. I stayed fixed to that spot of prairie even when I heard the porch door slam behind me and footsteps fall along the gravel driveway.

Rory clasped a hand on my shoulder and stood beside me in the silence for a few minutes before nudging me toward the house. "Come on, Dr. Who. Breakfast is ready."

I smiled sadly and followed her inside. What else could I do?

❖

"You ready to get home?" Beth asked as I dropped my bag by the front door.

Home. That ever-elusive concept. Was I ready for it? Maybe, but I wasn't sure I was headed there by going back to New York. "I suppose so."

She hesitated like she wanted to say something but didn't know how, or if she should. Instead, she hugged me tight.

"Thank you for everything. I've been a pretty high-maintenance house guest, but you've been wonderful, and welcoming, and such a good listener." I thought of sitting on the porch with her, both over the last few days and in my time travels. As I wondered how long it would be before I saw her again, her words came back to me. *I'd live every minute in present tense instead of always planning for some future I had no guarantee of.* A spike of dizziness rushed to my head, and I held her tighter to steady myself.

"Hey," she said calmly, "you okay?"

"Yeah." I took a deep breath. "Just the past rushing up through the cracks again."

Rory and Beth exchanged one of the glances that suggested they could communicate telepathically.

"I'm fine, really. I just remembered something Beth said in my dream."

Beth teased me. "Was it very wise?"

"Actually, yes."

"Good. I hope you listened."

"I did." I turned from her to Rory. "At least for a while."

"How'd that work out for you?" Rory asked.

Images of Jody with her head thrown back in abandon flashed through my memory—the taste of wine on her lips, the warmth of her body pressing down on me. "It worked out...perfectly."

They both smiled like they were already two steps ahead of me.

"Then I got scared and started looking for a middle ground. Shit." Energy surged through me, fueled by a sense of purpose I hadn't experienced since..."High school."

"What about it?"

"Would you drive me to the high school instead of the airport?"

Rory pumped her fist triumphantly. "Yes!"

Beth kissed me on the cheek, then pushed us both out the door.

We flew through town with Rory pushing her Prius faster than any hybrid had the right to go until we skidded to a stop, throwing rocks across the school's gravel lot.

We both jogged through the double doors, but as I rounded the corner into the main hallway, I collided with Drew Phillips. Damn. How did he manage to always be there when I most needed him to go away? Did he have some sixth sense for detecting gay people approaching his building?

"You two can't be here," he said sharply. "Distinguished alumni or not, this is school hours, and I'm the principal."

"Stevie's just here to pick up some paperwork from Jody," Rory said quickly.

"Then you can wait here while I walk her up."

Double damn it. I couldn't say what I had to say with Drew listening. Even if I wasn't afraid of him, Jody had good reason to be.

"Actually," Rory interjected, "I wanted to talk to you while she runs up."

"Make an appointment like everyone else," he said through clenched teeth.

"Or maybe I should just go right to the school board with my idea for a gay-straight alliance at the high school," she said nonchalantly.

It must have taken a second for the comment to sink in, but once it did, his neck turned a deep maroon, and the veins in his forehead stood out markedly. "A what?"

She grinned like a kid who'd been told she got to go to the candy store and the ice cream parlor in the same day.

"Why don't you go on up, Stevie, while Drew and I step into his office."

I didn't wait for Drew's explosion. I knew she'd keep him occupied for long enough, so I turned and jogged down the hallway. Taking the stairs two at a time, I was almost to the second floor when the bell rang. Students flooded the corridors, and I struggled against the crowd. The universe wasn't making this journey any easier on me, but I no longer expected it to. Forging on through a sea of adolescents, I finally made it to Jody's classroom before freezing in the doorway.

She had her back to me as she stared out the window. My heart lurched at the sight of her in profile. It was the same angle I'd enjoyed this morning in her bed, but this time she looked so stable, so stoic. She knew her place, she knew her role. This was her arena. Once again I felt like a bumbling teenager nervous and unworthy in the shadow of her gracefulness.

She turned and met my eyes with a sharp gasp. "God, Stevie. You startled me."

"Sorry." I grinned at the tiny thread to our past. "You were just so stunning standing here I forgot myself for a second."

She blushed. "I was lost in my thoughts."

"A penny for them?"

She glanced past me to the students still milling about in the hallway. "It's my prep period. I need to go over my lesson plans."

My hopes sank a little. She wouldn't jump into my arms simply because I showed up. She needed more from me. I needed to give her more, but the prospect of complete vulnerability caused me to tremble and hesitate, lost in fear once again. What if I couldn't do it? What if the words I'd choked back this morning failed to come? What if I passed out again? Or even worse, what if I managed to say everything in my heart and Jody still rejected me? Sweat prickled my skin, and the blood whooshed through my ears.

Jody refused to throw me a line as she continued to cling to her own lifeboat. "The students are doing monologues this week, or monologue subtexts. I'm not sure if you remember that lesson—"

"I do," I choked out. "I remember it twice."

"Because it was doubly agonizing for you?"

"Yes, and for more reasons than you can ever know."

She rolled her eyes. "No, you've made yourself clear. I believe you said exposing yourself on paper was nerve-racking enough and you could never lay yourself bare in front of any audience."

Did she remember everything I'd ever said to her? No wonder she doubted my staying power.

"What are you doing here, Stevie?" she finally asked. "Saying good-bye once in one day hurt badly enough. If you stopped in to rip my heart out one more time, you've done that. Why are we still talking about subtexts and your fear of public exposure?"

"Because I have something to say to you."

"I don't think I can take any more discussion. Just seeing you is enough to wreck me. I still have one more class to teach today. I can't give you any more of me if I'm going to survive. I need to be a teacher right now."

"Okay." An idea formed slowly in my mind. "Then don't say anything. I'll do a monologue."

"A monologue?"

"Yes. You can sit there in the front row and listen. Grade me if you have to."

"Why?"

"Because I want to audition for you."

"You want to audition? For what? The high-school play?"

"No." My heartbeat raced like a thundering herd of wild horses. "I'm hoping for a bigger role."

She arched an eyebrow.

"I wanted to try for the part of your leading lady."

A hint of amusement crinkled her eyes, but her lips formed a tight line. "Fine."

"Fine?"

She took a seat at one of the student desks in the middle of the classroom and motioned to the open space in front of her. "The stage is yours."

"Okay." I blew a long, slow breath and shook out my hands in the hopes of stopping the tingling sensation in my fingers. Then, closing my eyes, I said a silent prayer that I wouldn't have a stroke. "So, for my audition today I'll be performing the subtext of, well, of the last two weeks of my life."

She nodded for me to continue, her expression devoid of emotional indicators.

"I've always been okay. My life, my career—it's all been lukewarm, and I liked that, which is why I didn't want to come back to Darlington. This town unsettled me and made me feel things I couldn't compartmentalize. When Edmond talked me into coming back, I swore I wouldn't let myself go there again. In and out, that's what he promised, and I clung to that promise even when I shouldn't have. My first night back I wanted to kiss you, but I was afraid of all the things you made me feel, not just the depth of connection, but also the embarrassment of seeing my life of convenience next to your passion and purpose. I felt like a coward, so I took the coward's way out."

I rubbed my sweaty palms on my pants. I hadn't planned to relive all of this. I hadn't planned anything. My stomach twisted, and my head grew light, but I wouldn't faint this time. My pain held a purpose now. "I paid for my cowardice in a hell only my own mind could have conjured into existence. I did my penance by reliving a past to which I'd convinced myself you were the key. Pinning all my hopes for escape on you seemed so much easier and more enjoyable than facing my own faults. But it didn't work. You helped me see that, and you inspired me to be a better person than I could have imagined possible."

She leaned forward. "Stevie—"

"Monologue," I said, holding up a finger. I waited until she sat back again.

"When I finally got back to the present, I couldn't face the prospect of leaving you behind. The depth of our connection gave me the courage to be vulnerable last night, and the reward was greater than any dream." Emotions stirred, tightening my throat, but I forced the words through. "In your arms I felt raw and exposed and whole."

Jody's cheeks turned crimson, but she remained completely still, passive. I shifted from one foot to the other, nervously.

"Then this morning, everything came crashing down." I bit my lip, trying to stem the rush of emotion ripping at me, but the battle was worthless and warrantless. I couldn't hold back anymore, and I didn't want to. "When you pulled away, I experienced the flip side of allowing myself to feel. Your composure made my turmoil all the more terrifying. I went from feeling perfectly fitted with you to being agonizingly alone. I wanted to beg you not to leave me, but I wasn't brave enough to give you the last piece of my heart for fear you'd crush it too."

I hung my head. "So I retreated back into my old defenses. I took the safe path instead of the right one, and in doing so, I failed us."

I paused, waiting for some reaction, another interjection, anything. But Jody sat politely impassive, her legs crossed and her hands folded neatly on the desk in front of her.

"The last few weeks left me with more questions than I'll ever be able to answer, but one thing I've learned for sure is that time, like life, is messy and scary. There's always an easy way out, but that's not the future I want anymore. I waited eleven years to get you back. I don't want to wait another day to have you in my arms, in my life, again."

I crossed the room and dropped to my knees before her, no longer even trying to hide my shaking hands or shallow breathing. "Jody, I love you. I think I've always loved you. I know that complicates things, but I'm here now, completely open, completely vulnerable, completely terrified, because I think you're worth it."

I took her hands in mine and stared up at her, my breath shallow and my throat scraped raw with emotion. "So there's my monologue. It's the best I have to offer. Do I have any chance of getting a callback?"

Jody finally allowed a crack in her stoic façade and blinked back the tears forming in her eyes. "No."

The word cut through me like a knife, its sharp point crushing my ribs and piercing all the air from my lungs. "No?"

"No. There's no need for a callback." Jody smiled sweetly. "I don't need to hear any more to know you're the romantic lead I've been looking for. You've got the part."

A thousand fireworks exploded through me. I jumped to my feet, pulling her up with me. Encircling her with my arms, I lifted her off her feet and spun her around, dizzy with exuberance. I pressed my lips to hers and kissed her possessively.

"What the hell?" Drew Phillips stood seething in the doorway.

"Sorry," Rory said, looking simultaneously proud and apologetic. "I held him as long as I could."

I set Jody down and took a step back, but she caught my hand and squeezed it tight in hers. All the blood had drained from her already-fair complexion, but she didn't shake or shrink from the disgust in his eyes.

"I can explain," I said, completely unsure about the truth of that statement.

"I saw you kiss her. What else is there to explain?"

"He's right," Jody said calmly. "There's nothing to explain. Not that I owe you an explanation, Drew, but just in case you're confused, I'm gay."

She waited a second to let her words sink in, then turning to me with a bright smile added, "Very, very gay."

"You…you…you." Drew sputtered. "You can't stay here. I won't have a lesbian in my school."

Rory and I both began to speak at once, but Jody raised her hand and silenced us with her best teacher stare. "Drew, I suggest you go check that demand with the school district's attorney, because I believe you'll find that statement puts you in violation of the State of Illinois's nondiscrimination laws. In the meantime, Stevie is going to stay to speak to my last-period advanced-theater class."

"I am?" I asked.

"Yes. You owe me and my students after passing out last week, and now that you've overcome your fear of public speaking"—she grinned playfully—"it's time to pay up."

"Yes, ma'am."

"Rory, you can stay too, if you'd like, but Stevie won't need a ride home tonight."

Rory shook her head, admiration plainly written across her face. "In that case, I'll walk Drew back to his office. You know, just to make sure he gets there."

Drew glared at her, then back at us, but clearly didn't know what else to say without talking to his lawyer. He chose, instead, to storm dramatically out of the room. Rory nodded her approval, then trailed after him at a more leisurely pace.

I turned back to Jody. "I can't believe that just happened."

"I can. It's time to stop running, and I love you too."

My heart pressed against my ribs, suddenly feeling too big for my body. "And Drew? And the school board? It's going to be a fight. Are you ready for that?"

"Actually"—she wrapped her arms around my waist—"I am. What about you? You've already been through so much today. How are you holding up?"

"Me?" I laughed and pulled her closer. "I'm having the time of my life."

Epilogue

I caught Jody's sparkling blue eyes across the crowded auditorium. She smiled gracefully as she accepted the praise of another happy parent, but her gaze kept wandering to me. I leaned as casually as I could against the high-school desk we were using as a prop onstage and enjoyed the time to watch her interact with people who appreciated her fully.

Well, maybe not fully. They loved her for the care she invested in their kids, for her gentle way of drawing them out, for the confidence she fostered in them, but none of them could fully share my awe of her. She'd consumed every part of my life for the last six months. First in Darlington, then in New York, she'd left her mark on my career, my life, my body. I popped open the collar of my baby-blue oxford shirt in an attempt to stem the rising heat that always accompanied thoughts of her in my bed every night.

She arched an eyebrow my way as if she could tell I was thinking about what we'd done together that morning or our shared promise of an encore when we finally made it back to our loft. Despite the shot of attraction that passed between us, or maybe because of it, we kept our distance until all the students had left. None of the kids in the summer theater program needed to see their playwright ravishing their director.

"Job well done, Stevie," Edmond said, approaching cautiously.

"What's that?"

"The play," he said, then added, "and what you've done for Jody."

"I haven't done nearly as much for her as she's done for me."

"Well, you've both done a lot for the youth theater program and for all the kids involved."

I smiled thinking of the fun we'd had over the last few months. We'd toured New York from Broadway to the Stonewall, but the joy of sharing the city I loved with the woman I loved couldn't compare to sharing the work we loved. Who would've expected the words I'd written on Rory's and Beth's front porch to become the basis for a play directed by Jody and performed by teenagers from my own neighborhood? "It's been more fun than I could've imagined. The kids are fantastic, and watching Jody work with them to bring my words to life—I don't know how to explain it. It's the surreal in the mundane, truth in fiction. They've reminded me why I wanted to do this work in the first place."

He smiled sadly. Why wasn't he happier? "What did you think of the adorable little gay boy we have playing you?"

"I thought the director was very flattering with that casting."

The response, like all the others since he'd arrived just before showtime, was too subdued for Edmond.

"All right, what gives? I gave you a new play. I did the press gleefully. Hell, I spoke at the program fund-raiser last week, and you haven't even hugged me yet, much less told me what else you have lined up for my fall publicity stunts.

"I'm so sorry, Stevie."

"What? Why?"

"It's all my fault. I pushed you too hard." He crumpled dramatically onto my shoulder, his product-filled hair smelling of lavender and mint. "I'll never forgive myself for putting you through that assembly and the concussion and your nightmare. It was so painful to watch the character playing you go through all that awful torment in high school."

"Oh, Edmond." I wrapped an arm around him and patted his back. "Is that why you've been so distant lately?"

He nodded, sniffling quietly. "I wanted to wait at the hospital with the others, but I knew you wouldn't want me there when you woke up. Ever since then I've been waiting for you to fire me."

"Fire you? That trip back to Darlington was the best thing that ever happened to me."

"Really?"

"I've got a new play, a new purpose, and the love of my life. I know the stage show doesn't go past the high-school stuff, but that's only because it would be inappropriate for teenagers to act out the vast of amounts of sex I've had lately."

His shoulders shook with laughter.

"I'm not going to fire you. Hell, if Jody sticks with me long enough, I might just make you the best man at our wedding."

He looked up excitedly. "I'd rather be the flower girl."

I shoved him playfully away from me and caught sight of Jody headed toward us.

"What are you two plotting?" she asked suspiciously, "and should I be worried?"

"Not at all." I wrapped my arm around her waist and drew her near. "I was only saying how grateful I am to him for making me go back to Darlington, because if I hadn't, I wouldn't have experienced all the joy you've given me over the last few months."

Jody looked to Edmond for confirmation. "Joy wasn't exactly the word she used, but it was implied, and either way I'm happy to have played a part."

She smiled brightly at me and snuggled a little closer before turning back to Edmond. "In that case, what's the next step for getting Stevie's play produced on a wider scale? You know we're only in New York for a few more weeks."

"So I hear. Rory and Beth are giddy about having you two closer, but are you sure returning to Illinois is the right move?"

Jody turned, deferring to me on this topic as she had for the last month. She'd done well in New York, and I'd relished the freedom we'd shared, but seeing her work with the kids here reminded me of how much she had to offer the students in Darlington, especially now that she was out of the closet. "We have to go back."

"They haven't found a way to fire me yet," Jody added.

"Rory said she'll hire the best civil-rights lawyers in the state to represent you if the school brings suit."

"It won't happen that way." Jody sounded sad. "Illinois's laws are a lot more gay-friendly than they were when I started teaching, and even Drew Phillips realizes what a massive lawsuit he'd have on his hands if he fired me for no other reason than my sexual orientation."

I tightened my hold on her and clenched my teeth at the thought of her answering to that bigoted bully again. "What she's not saying is that he'll try to make her life as hard as possible until she quits."

"Then why go?" Edmond practically whined. "You've been a rousing success here. I can find you both plenty of work, and life would be so much easier without having to fight the small-mindedness every day."

I understood that impulse. It still woke me up many a night. I often lay awake watching her sleep and wishing for a way to keep her safe and happy. I wanted to find a smooth path for us both, but while my instinct to avoid conflict still pulsed through me, it was no longer my strongest impulse.

Jody lifted her chin until our eyes met, then gave me a little squeeze, seeming to sense my concern. "It won't be easy."

Did she worry I would run? Or did she know that I pulled all the strength I needed from her? I kissed her quickly and resolutely, calm flowing through me along with the sense of purpose she inspired. Looking into her deep-blue gaze, I replied with the truth only she could've made me see. "I know it won't be easy, but some things are worth fighting for."

About the Author

Rachel Spangler never set out to be an award-winning author. She was just so poor and easily bored during her college years that she had to come up with creative ways to entertain herself, and her first novel, *Learning Curve*, was born out of one such attempt. She was sincerely surprised when it was accepted for publication and even more shocked when it won the Golden Crown Literary Award for Debut Author. She also won a Goldie for her second novel, *Trails Merge*. Since writing is more fun than a real job and so much cheaper than therapy, Rachel continued to type away, leading to the publication of *The Long Way Home*, *LoveLife*, *Spanish Heart*, *Does She Love You*, and *Timeless*. She plans to continue writing as long as anyone anywhere will keep reading.

Rachel and her partner, Susan, are raising their young son in western New York, where during the winter they make the most of the lake effect snow on local ski slopes. In the summer, they love to travel and watch their beloved St. Louis Cardinals. Regardless of the season, she always makes time for a good romance, whether she's reading it, writing it, or living it.

Books Available from Bold Strokes Books

Timeless by Rachel Spangler. When Stevie Geller returns to her hometown, will she do things differently the second time around or will she be in such a hurry to leave her past that she misses out on a better future? (978-1-62639-050-8)

Second to None by L.T. Marie. Can a physical therapist and a custom motorcycle designer conquer their pasts and build a future with one another? (978-1-62639-051-5)

Seneca Falls by Jesse Thoma. Together, two women discover love truly can conquer all evil. (978-1-62639-052-2)

A Kingdom Lost by Barbara Ann Wright. Without knowing each other's fate, Princess Katya and her consort Starbride seek to reclaim their kingdom from the magic-wielding madman who seized the throne and is murdering their people. (978-1-62639-053-9)

Uncommon Romance by Jove Belle. Sometimes sex is just sex, and sometimes it's the only way to say "I love you." (978-1-62639-057-7)

The Heat of Angels by Lisa Girolami. Fires burn in more than one place in Los Angeles. (978-1-62639-042-3)

Season of the Wolf by Robin Summers. Two women running from their pasts are thrust together by an unimaginable evil. Can they overcome the horrors that haunt them in time to save each other? (978-1-62639-043-0)

Desperate Measures by P. J. Trebelhorn. Homicide detective Kay Griffith and contractor Brenda Jansen meet amidst turmoil neither of them is aware of until murder suspect Tommy Rayne makes his move to exact revenge on Kay. (978-1-62639-044-7)

The Magic Hunt by L.L. Raand. With her Pack being hunted by human extremists and beset by enemies masquerading as friends, can Sylvan protect them and her mate, or will she succumb to the feral rage that threatens to turn her rogue, destroying them all? A Midnight Hunters novel. (978-1-62639-045-4)

Waiting for the Violins by Justine Saracen. After surviving Dunkirk, a scarred and embittered British nurse returns to Nazi-occupied Brussels to join the Resistance, and finds that nothing is fair in love and war. (978-1-62639-046-1)

Because of Her by KE Payne. When Tabby Morton is forced to move to London, she's convinced her life will never be the same again. But the beautiful and intriguing Eden Palmer is about to show her that this time, change is most definitely for the better. (978-1-62639-049-2)

Wingspan by Karis Walsh. Wildlife biologist Bailey Chase is content to live at the wild bird sanctuary she has created on Washington's Olympic Peninsula until she is lured beyond the safety of isolation by architect Kendall Pearson. (978-1-60282-983-1)

Tumbledown by Cari Hunter. After surviving their ordeal in the North Cascades, Alex and Sarah have new identities and a new home, but a chance occurrence threatens everything: their freedom and their lives. (978-1-62639-085-0)

Night Bound by Winter Pennington. Kass struggles to keep her head, her heart, and her relationships in order. She's still having a difficult time accepting being an Alpha female. But her wolf is certain of what she wants and she's intent on securing her power. (978-1-60282-984-8)

Slash and Burn by Valerie Bronwen. The murder of a roundly despised author at an LGBT writer's conference in New Orleans turns Winter Lovelace's relaxing weekend hobnobbing with her peers into a nightmare of suspense—especially when her ex turns up. (978-1-60282-986-2)

The Blush Factor by Gun Brooke. Ice-cold business tycoon Eleanor Ashcroft only cares about the three P's—Power, Profit, and Prosperity—until young Addison Garr makes her doubt both that and the state of her frostbitten heart. (978-1-60282-985-5)

The Quickening: A Sisters of Spirits Novel by Yvonne Heidt. Ghosts, visions, and demons are all in a day's work for Tiffany. But when Kat asks for help on a serial killer case, life takes on another dimension altogether. (978-1-60282-975-6)

Windigo Thrall by Cate Culpepper. Six women trapped in a mountain cabin by a blizzard, stalked by an ancient cannibal demon bent on stealing their sanity—and their lives. (978-1-60282-950-3)

Smoke and Fire by Julie Cannon. Oil and water, passion and desire, a combustible combination. Can two women fight the fire that draws them together and threatens to keep them apart? (978-1-60282-977-0)

Asher's Fault by Elizabeth Wheeler. Fourteen-year-old Asher Price sees the world in black and white, much like the photos he takes, but when his little brother drowns at the same moment Asher experiences his first same-sex kiss, he can no longer hide behind the lens of his camera and eventually discovers he isn't the only one with a secret. (978-1-60282-982-4)

Love and Devotion by Jove Belle. KC Hall trips her way through life, stumbling into an affair with a married bombshell twice her age. Thankfully, her best friend, Emma Reynolds, is there to show her the true meaning of Love and Devotion. (978-1-60282-965-7)

Rush by Carsen Taite. Murder, secrets, and romance combine to create the ultimate rush. (978-1-60282-966-4)

The Shoal of Time by J.M. Redmann. It sounded too easy. Micky Knight is reluctant to take the case because the easy ones often turn into the hard ones, and the hard ones turn into the dangerous ones. In this one, easy turns hard without warning. (978-1-60282-967-1)

In Between by Jane Hoppen. At the age of 14, Sophie Schmidt discovers that she was born an intersexual baby and sets off on a journey to find her place in a world that denies her true existence. (978-1-60282-968-8)

Secret Lies by Amy Dunne. While fleeing from her abuser, Nicola Jackson bumps into Jenny O'Connor, and their unlikely friendship quickly develops into a blossoming romance—but when it comes down to a matter of life or death, are they both willing to face their fears? (978-1-60282-970-1)

Under Her Spell by Maggie Morton. The magic of love brought Terra and Athene together, but now a magical quest stands between them—a quest for Athene's hand in marriage. Will their passion keep them together, or will stronger magic tear them apart? (978-1-60282-973-2)

Homestead by Radclyffe. R. Clayton Sutter figures getting NorthAm Fuel's newest refinery operational on a rolling tract of land in Upstate New York should take a month or two, but then, she hadn't counted on local resistance in the form of vandalism, petitions, and one furious farmer named Tess Rogers. (978-1-60282-956-5)

Battle of Forces: Sera Toujours by Ali Vali. Kendal and Piper return to New Orleans to start the rest of eternity together, but the return of an old enemy makes their peaceful reunion short-lived, especially when they join forces with the new queen of the vampires. (978-1-60282-957-2)

How Sweet It Is by Melissa Brayden. Some things are better than chocolate. Molly O'Brien enjoys her quiet life running the bakeshop in a small town. When the beautiful Jordan Tuscana returns home, Molly can't deny the attraction—or the stirrings of something more. (978-1-60282-958-9)

The Missing Juliet: A Fisher Key Adventure by Sam Cameron. A teenage detective and her friends search for a kidnapped Hollywood star in the Florida Keys. (978-1-60282-959-6)

Amor and More: Love Everafter edited by Radclyffe and Stacia Seaman. Rediscover favorite couples as Bold Strokes Books authors reveal glimpses of life and love beyond the honeymoon in short stories featuring main characters from favorite BSB novels. (978-1-60282-963-3)

First Love by CJ Harte. Finding true love is hard enough, but for Jordan Thompson, daughter of a conservative president, it's challenging, especially when that love is a female rodeo cowgirl. (978-1-60282-949-7)

Pale Wings Protecting by Lesley Davis. Posing as a couple to investigate the abduction of infants, Special Agent Blythe Kent and Detective Daryl Chandler find themselves drawn into a battle over the innocents, with demons on one side and the unlikeliest of protectors on the other. (978-1-60282-964-0)

Mounting Danger by Karis Walsh. Sergeant Rachel Bryce, an outcast on the police force, is put in charge of the department's newly formed mounted division. Can she and polo champion Callan Lanford resist their growing attraction as they struggle to safeguard the disaster-prone unit? (978-1-60282-951-0)

Meeting Chance by Jennifer Lavoie. When man's best friend turns on Aaron Cassidy, the teen keeps his distance until fate puts Chance in his hands. (978-1-60282-952-7)

At Her Feet by Rebekah Weatherspoon. Digital marketing producer Suzanne Kim knows she has found the perfect love in her new mistress Pilar, but before they can make the ultimate commitment, Suzanne's professional life threatens to disrupt their perfectly balanced bliss. (978-1-60282-948-0)

Show of Force by AJ Quinn. A chance meeting between navy pilot Evan Kane and correspondent Tate McKenna takes them on a roller-coaster ride where the stakes are high, but the reward is higher: a chance at love. (978-1-60282-942-8)

Clean Slate by Andrea Bramhall. Can Erin and Morgan work through their individual demons to rediscover their love for each other, or are the unexplainable wounds too deep to heal? (978-1-60282-943-5)

Hold Me Forever by D. Jackson Leigh. An investigation into illegal cloning in the quarter horse racing industry threatens to destroy the growing attraction between Georgia debutante Mae St. John and Louisiana horse trainer Whit Casey. (978-1-60282-944-2)

Trusting Tomorrow by PJ Trebelhorn. Funeral director Logan Swift thinks she's perfectly happy with her solitary life devoted to helping others cope with loss until Brooke Collier moves in next door to care for her elderly grandparents. (978-1-60282-891-9)

Forsaking All Others by Kathleen Knowles. What if what you think you want is the opposite of what makes you happy? (978-1-60282-892-6)

Exit Wounds by VK Powell. When Officer Loane Landry falls in love with ATF informant Abigail Mancuso, she realizes that nothing is as it seems—not the case, not her lover, not even the dead. (978-1-60282-893-3)